Murder 20/20

A Speed City Crime Writers Anthology

Edited by MB Dabney, Lillie Evans, and Shari Held

Published by Speed City Press

ISBN: 978-0-9963092-4-0 – Ebook
ISBN: 978-0-9963092-5-7 – Paperback

Any references to historical events, real people, or real places are used fictitiously. Names, characters, and places are products of the author's imagination.

Front cover design by Hawthorn Mineart.

Book design by Hawthorn Mineart and Elizabeth San Miguel.

Edited by MB Dabney, Lillie Evans, and Shari Held.

First printing edition 2020.

www.speedcitysistersincrime.com

SPEED CITY

INDIANA CHAPTER

SISTERS IN CRIME

CONTENTS

Introduction

by Susan Furlong

The term 2020 can mean many things: the new year, perfect vision, and of course, the often regret-filled saying, "Hindsight is 20/20." So, when a handful of Indiana authors get together and plan a Hoosier-themed crime anthology titled *Murder 20/20*, readers will undoubtedly experience stories as diverse as the state in which they're set.

From flat plains to rolling hills, the Indiana landscape may find Hoosiers a bit contrarian by nature. For example, time itself has been debated in Indiana since 1961, when the state was divided between Eastern and Central time zones. No wonder this anthology offers stories from different eras. In Hart's piece, "Dingo Dan," readers experience a futuristic twist, while Carley's unique and sensate characters harken back to the 1970s in, "I See What You're Sayin.'" Time also plays a crucial role when a century-old murder comes to light in Williams' emotionally resonate story, "One Hundred Years a Widow." Likewise, in Catt's entrancing "The Hundred-Year Time Capsule," readers will wonder if time may (or may not) hold the key to a current crime.

At harvest time, however, Hoosiers come together in their love for puzzles and food. Can any state out-corn-maze Indiana? In keeping with tradition, several authors in *Murder 20/20* pair mystery with food. A perfect pairing is evident in Mineart's inspiring "MD 20/20," where a sweet feline named Orange Jubilee makes an appearance. Winters' dynamic new-age piece "Arcana 20/20" will make teetotalers think twice, whereas, coffee lovers might want to check out Reddick's evocative story, "One Dead Politico." And hold on to your tin caps because the foody twists in Held's "Deception at the Double D Convention" and Shore's "Tailor-Made for Murder," will leave you breathless.

Indiana isn't all fun and good food. There's an undercurrent of darkness here, too. Just south of Indianapolis, Blue Spring Cavern boasts the country's longest navigable underground river. A thread of darkness also winds through this collection of stories. Terrell's shocking "In the Deepest Darkness" will leave readers contemplating themes of family strife and redemption long after the last word. Be sure to keep the lights on when you read Burrough's shiver-inducing serial revenge piece titled "Mr. 20," and wait until daylight to check out Koontz's "The 20/20 Club," where darkness is the cold-blooded goal of a revenge-seeking killing club.

Prefer heart-racing action? Perhaps Indiana is most recognized for the Indianapolis 500, "The Greatest Spectacle in Racing," where cars whip around the 2.5-mile track at break-neck speeds. If pulse-pounding is your thing, you're sure to enjoy San Miguel's story, "Cipher," where life hangs in the balance of a cryptic puzzle. And no doubt about it, the deviant stalkers featured in Henderson's "The Release" and in Couts' "It's All Relative" will kick up your heartbeat a notch or two.

If you prefer your fast-paced stories coupled with justice, you'll love Smith's heartening story "Inheritance" where a gusty heroine takes justice to the street, and Elizabeth Perona's "The Ear Witness," an intelligently crafted whodunit in which justice definitely rings true.

Indiana is called the "Crossroads of America" because of the highways that crisscross the state, allowing folks to traverse The Heartland to their awaiting destinations. In much the same way, the stories in this anthology intersect the central 20/20 theme, taking the reader on a wonderful journey. I'm confident that after the final page is turned, you'll realize that the members of the Speed City Sisters in Crime Chapter have created a twisted turnpike of plots that have led you to the perfect destination.

So, fasten your seat belts for an adventurous ride of mystery and mayhem, Indiana style.

— Susan Furlong, bestselling author of the *Bone Gap Travellers* series

Inheritance

by Andrea Smith

This is for you, Mason.

T Zara Carter turned those five words over and over in her mind as she stood on the front line. Feet planted. One hand clenched in a fist at her side. The other hoisting her hand-painted JUSTICE FOR ALL sign. She felt the moisture on her scalp between her box braids. Felt a trickle down the side of her face. Her mouth felt as if she'd brushed her tongue with sandpaper. Indianapolis police faced them looking like a Star Wars army, lined up two-deep shielded in helmets, bullet-proof vests and gas masks. Caressing deadly batons, ready to crack activists' skulls.

"THIS IS AN UNLAWFUL ASSEMBLY! DISPERSE NOW OR YOU WILL BE ARRESTED!! I REPEAT. YOU WILL BE ARRESTED!"

The threat bellowed through the bullhorn cut through the thick August air, but it only served to stir up the crowd even more. Defiance rippled through the air.

"Justice for all!" one of the Equal Justice activists shouted.

That's all it took. The protesters started moving.

"DISPERSE NOW!" the cops warned again.

The activists advanced toward the police line that stood fast. Head on collision coming. More protesters started shouting, drowning out the voice on the bullhorn. Zara gripped her sign and pushed forward with the line, ready to take the blows that would surely come.

Whooooosh!!!!

Objects sailed over their heads into the crowd.

Clang!!!

A teargas canister landed at her feet and a greenish cloud rolled up from the pavement, billowing around her. Zara's eyes began to burn and water, her chest tightened, and her breath now came in short bursts. Around her, Equal Justice activists were coughing and wheezing from the gas. Zara reached in the pouch strapped around her waist. She'd come prepared this time and brought milk that would soothe irritated eyes. Just as she got the carton out of the pouch, a heavy hand gripped her arm.

***

Judith Carter waited for the police to bring Zara out. She said another silent prayer of thanks that her daughter hadn't been seriously injured – or worse – at this latest protest. Grateful she and her attorney could bail Zara out so she wouldn't have to spend the night in jail. Judith understood Zara's need to fight for change. Two of her friends had been killed by police and now she'd lost Mason. It was a lot for a 21-year-old to handle.

A uniformed policewoman brought Zara out. Her braids and clothes were coated with white residue of the teargas. But she held her head high. Proud even in the humiliation of being arrested. Judith never dreamed she'd have a chance at motherhood. She and Oliver married well into their 40s. When most couples their age were welcoming grandchildren, they'd been blessed with a miracle, a healthy daughter. It was like God was making up for the losses she'd endured.

The thought of her baby being teargassed sent shivers through her and transported her back to that awful night when she'd lost Ethan. Judith gave her head a shake as if the movement would send those thoughts back to the mental grave where she tried to keep them buried.

They didn't speak on the ride home, and when Judith pulled into the garage and turned off the car, neither she nor Zara moved to get out. Finally, Judith spoke, choosing her words carefully. "Maybe you should cut back on the protests for a while."

She could feel her daughter's anger at that suggestion.

Zara shifted in her seat. "I have to do what I believe in."

"No one's trying to make you abandon your beliefs."

"I get it. It makes you look bad," Zara said. "Lantech's executive vice president of communications can't have a daughter who gets arrested with a violent mob. Mason was murdered a week ago. Skull caved in and thrown in a dumpster like trash and no one cares. We're going to protest until his killer is found. Sorry if your rep takes a hit."

Judith swiveled her head to look at Zara. Her words and the scowl on her face were hurtful. "That's what you think this is about? Me protecting my job?"

"Isn't it?" Zara shot back. "You don't know what it's like. When you were coming up, the establishment was so spooked they swung the doors open. Now they slam the doors in our faces and snuff us out like Mason."

Zara pushed open the car door, got out and slammed it. She stalked up to the door leading to the house. Judith sat for a minute to gather her nerves before she dragged herself out of the car. She'd been in the house five minutes when the doorbell rang, and someone banged on the front door. Judith's stomach clenched. Who had the nerve to show up at her home unannounced at this hour? She flicked on the porch light and peeked through the curtain and saw two white men in suits, impatient looks on their faces. "Can I help you?" she called through the door.

"Indianapolis police," one called back. "Looking for Zara Carter."

Judith opened the door an inch. "At two in the morning? Your identification."

The one with bristly blond hair who'd spoken looked at her as if she had no right to ask. Judith waited. Finally, they held up IDs and bristly blond hair said, "Detective Hunt. This is Detective McConnell. Got a few questions for Zara Carter."

Judith narrowed her gaze at him. She knew exactly where "just a few questions" could lead and wasn't about to let them grill Zara without their attorney. "About what?"

The detective jutted out his chin in annoyance. "Mason Richards, who was found dead last week."

"You mean murdered," Judith corrected.

"Do you mind if we come in?" his partner asked. Wearing black-frame glasses that made him look more like he belonged in a classroom instead of in a detective unit, he seemed to have a more patient demeanor.

3

"Why not," Judith said, opening the door wider. At that moment Zara came bounding down the stairs, ruining Judith's plan to keep them from questioning her.

"What's going on?" Zara asked.

Judith sighed inwardly. "Police detectives. They have questions about Mason."

Zara frowned. "Oh? Are you finally going to pretend to look for his killer?"

The one named Hunt raised his blond eyebrows. "Where were you the night Mason Richards was killed?" His tone was unnecessarily aggressive.

Judith speared the detectives with an angry glare. The one named McConnell lowered his eyes as if he agreed with her sentiments. "Shouldn't you be questioning real suspects instead of wasting time harassing my daughter?"

Hunt ignored her and asked Zara, "How much did you know about Mason Richards' activities?"

"I have no idea what you mean," Zara said.

He folded his arms across his barrel chest. "I understand you and he were, eh, hooked up?"

Zara narrowed her eyes at him. "He wasn't a hook-up. He was my fiancé."

"He was also one of my informants," Detective Hunt said with a chuckle.

If the detective had expected this revelation to throw Zara, he'd miscalculated. She returned his smirk with one of her own and said, "That's a lie."

"Is it? How do you think we always knew what moves y'all were going to make? Where you'd be protesting? Somebody found out, most likely somebody he was close to, who he would confide in, and they decided he needed to be silenced. Some folks say you two had a big fight. What was that about?"

Zara stared at him. "That's my personal business."

"You can leave now," Judith ordered. "Or do I need to call my attorney?"

Detective Hunt's face flushed in anger. He took a step toward her. "Folks threaten to call a lawyer when they have something to hide," he said.

How many times had Judith faced cops like him? Intoxicated with power. Ready to fly into a rage when challenged?

"Or when they know their rights," Judith said.

Judith saw Detective Hunt's jaw clench so tight she thought she might hear him crack a tooth. His partner, the reasonable one, put a hand on his partner's arm. "You know, Mike, we got enough for now. We can follow up later."

Detective Hunt took a breath. "Yeah, maybe."

Detective McConnell held out a card to Zara. "Listen, we just want to do our job and find out who killed your friend. If you remember anything that can help us, call. Otherwise, we'll be in touch."

Zara nodded.

After Judith bolted the door behind their unwanted visitors, she turned, intent on getting some answers herself from Zara about what the police had said about Mason, but her daughter was already stomping up the stairs to her room.

Zara didn't even bother to get out of her dirty clothes or think about getting the gook out of her hair. She flung herself across her bed. She touched a playlist on her phone and cranked up the volume. Then she buried her face in her pillow so her mother couldn't hear the geyser of tears she couldn't hold back. When it felt like she couldn't squeeze out another tear, she turned off the music, propped herself up on her pillows and checked her messages. There were several from her dad who was in Arizona on business. She touched his number to call him back.

"Hey, firecracker! About time you called. Your mother said you were arrested."

"And teargassed."

"You okay?"

"My eyes are still a bit irritated, but otherwise I'm good. The cops were here questioning me like they think I had something to do with Mason's murder."

"That's crazy. I'm surprised your mom let them talk to you."

"She didn't really." Zara told him how the visit from the police went. "When will you be back because I really need you to talk to your wife. She wants me to quit Equal Justice. Says she's afraid for me."

"My wife has good reason to worry," her father said.

"Come on, all mama cares about is that corporate job."

"Baby girl, I won't have you talking about your mother that way," he said. "You have no idea what your mother went through to get where she is."

"I know, I know. She put herself through college after her parents died. Worked her way up the corporate ladder . . . "

"Really, now stop." Her father let out a huge sigh. "It's time for you to know your history. I'm texting you a photo."

"Of what?" Her phone dinged before he could answer. Zara put him on speaker so she could look at the photo and talk to him at the same time. It was a photo of a beautiful dark-skinned young woman slaying a huge Afro. A tall, proud warrior in black jeans, black leather jacket. Clenched fist punching the air. Rifle in her left hand.

"Who is this?"

Her father laughed. "You don't recognize your own mother?"

Zara sat up in the bed. "That's mom? With a gun? How come I've never seen this photo?"

"Because your mother wanted to leave that part of her past behind. I respected her wishes. She didn't want it to hurt my career or your future."

"Mom was an activist?"

"At only 16. One of the most courageous Peoples' Party members in Chicago. I didn't know her then, but I'm told she could really handle a gun. I'd say you have her same fighting spirit."

Zara stared at the photo in awe. Her by-the-book establishment mother was a gun-toting 60s resister.

"She's going to want to break my fingers for telling you this," her dad said with a chuckle. "But for years I've respected her wish to let the past just be a memory. It's time for you to know exactly who your mother is."

"How long was she a resister?" Zara asked.

"Oh no, I've said too much already," her dad said, chuckling. "Talk to your mother."

After he disconnected, Zara booted up her laptop and put Peoples' Party Chicago in the Internet browser search field. Whoa. The hits seemed endless. And there were plenty of video clips on the assassination of Peoples' Party Chairman Frank Howell. Zara spent the next hour reading about the group's food programs and housing and medical care outreach. And like activists today, they fought against police brutality and for equal justice under the law for all. She searched her mother's maiden name, Judith Wilson. A photo of a group of Black women popped up. Mesmerized, she stared at her mother who was standing with five other women with perfectly shaped Afros. Wearing sophisticated black dresses, as if dressed for the corporate world, they stood on a stage at a rally, fists raised in solidarity. The accompanied article described her mom as the girlfriend of Ethan Johnson. Johnson, along with the Peoples' Party Chicago Chairman Frank Howell, was killed by Chicago police and the FBI in a horrific predawn raid. Ethan was on Christmas break from Harvard. He was only seventeen.

Gifted like Mason, Zara thought and blinked as her eyes began to moisten. God, she was so tired of crying. Would the freakin' tears ever stop?

Judith lay on her back, eyes fixed on the ceiling, unable to get the sound of Zara crying out of her head. Her daughter thought the music was loud enough to drown out her sobs, but she'd been wrong. Every sob was like the body blows the Chicago police inflicted on them when they dragged them to the police station on some bogus charges after a protest. But Judith had heard every cry. And her mother's heart was shattered. She and Oliver had worked so hard all these years to shield Zara from what she herself had lived, only to have failed.

The pills she relied on for sleep finally kicked in, transporting Judith in her dreams back to the day after the chairman and her beloved Ethan were murdered and she got a look at the murder scene.

Judith and other members of the Peoples' Party got into the apartment where Frank and Ethan were murdered the next day. The front and back doors were riddled with bullet holes and the smell of gunfire that still permeated the place made Judith want to choke. Tears welled up in her eyes as she looked at the chair where Ethan had been sleeping when the police burst through the front door pummeling him with bullets. Police had splayed shots through all the bedrooms in the apartment, 100 in total. The walls of the bedroom where Frank slept with his pregnant fiancé looked like swiss cheese. The sight of the blood-soaked mattress made nausea rise in Judith's throat and made her flee the apartment of death.

***

The next morning Zara heard her mother moving about the kitchen. It was Wednesday, her heaviest day of IT classes, but she was skipping them today. She showered and dressed in jeans and an Equal Justice t-shirt and made her way downstairs. Judith, wearing her usual corporate uniform of a tailored pants suit and a silk blouse, was standing at the island fixing her coffee for her drive downtown to the office.

"How come you never told me you were in the Peoples' Party?" Zara asked. She immediately regretted making the question sound like an accusation.

Judith looked at her. "What?"

Zara stood across from her mother. She opened her phone to the photo her dad had sent and held it up to her mother. "This is you, right?"

Judith glanced at the photo and said calmly, "Your dad talks too much."

"How can you tell me to stop fighting for justice when you did the same thing? You were younger than I am. Doesn't that make you a hypocrite?"

Judith leaned on the island facing Zara. "It makes me a mother trying to protect her child. You saw how that detective suggested you knew about Mason. They don't really care who killed him. They don't care if you're innocent. They just want to clear a case. If you're hiding something about Mason — "

"Aww. Mom, when will you get it?" Zara, twirling around in frustration.

Judith sighed. "You mean when will I be as *woke* as you? Let me tell you what woke is. Woke is being sixteen and targeted by Chicago police for extinction. Woke is missing being assassinated because you were tired, so you went home instead of stopping by the apartment to see your boyfriend. Woke is being followed every day, everywhere. Woke is hiding in sleepy town Indianapolis, burying yourself in corporate hell and wondering if it was worth it. Woke is seeing the same thing happening to your child and feeling rage and helplessness at the same time."

Zara stared at her mother, lip quivering.

Judith grabbed her coffee and her bag. "I'm not the enemy."

Zara parked her Honda in front of the storefront Equal Justice used as its headquarters on the eastside and got out. A dark car pulled up behind her, and the window rolled down. It was the detectives from last night. Zara steeled her nerves.

"Remembered anything you want to share with us?" Hunt, the obnoxious one, asked.

"Said all I have to say." Zara adjusted the tote on her shoulder and started toward the building.

"Heard the department might add charges for you and your friends' little demonstration. That's gonna make for some stiff sentencing." Hunt said.

Now Zara stopped and glared at him. "You're threatening me?"

Hunt laughed. "It is a warning, so you can consider your options. Let me know if your memory comes back."

Zara watched the car drive off. Shaken, she hurried inside.

She'd come to the storefront to pick up materials she needed to pull together information for their next action. They would not let last night's horror stop them. But all she could think about was Mason. Finally, she gave up and opened her contacts to Tony's number. He'd joined EJ after the police killed his brother who was unarmed and getting into his own car. Mason trusted him. Maybe he'd clued Tony in on whatever he was doing with the cops. Maybe Tony had noticed something off about Mason.

"Yeah," Tony answered.

"Me. Did everybody arrested get released?"

"All but Nicky. He has some old traffic tickets and they used that as an excuse to hold him."

"Shoot," Zara said. "He's such a good guy."

"Yeah. We're collecting bail money for him."

"The police came to my house talking crazy about Mason. They said he was their informant. I know he was meeting you the day he was murdered. You have to tell me what you know no matter how bad it may be."

Tony didn't say anything. His silence was like a confirming kick in her gut.

"It's true? Mason was working with the cops against us?"

"We need to talk, but not on the phone," Tony said almost whispering. "Meet me at my shop in an hour."

Judith inhaled deeply to fortify herself. Just composing this text message was taxing. She'd kept in touch with Sylvia over the years enough to know how to reach her if she needed to. And right now she needed to talk to someone who'd lived what she had. Who could help her test her thinking. She typed her text message and hit send. Thirty minutes later her phone buzzed.

"Well, that was quick for a busy Chicago alderwoman," she teased.

"I thought I was dreaming when I got your text. How in the heck is our Amazon Queen?" Sylvia asked in that gravelly voice of hers, unchanged in the decades she'd known her. Amazon Queen was the nickname her Peoples' Party friends had given Judith because she was five-feet-eleven without heels.

A smile almost managed to push its way through the anxiousness that constantly engulfed her. Despite the heartache, there were some good memories of those years, especially the joy she and Sylvia felt when they helped people get food or an apartment. It was a time when the community, folks of all backgrounds came together for a common, righteous cause. It was a time when they'd learned to love themselves.

"What's going on in your life these days?" Sylvia asked.

Judith told her about Zara. "It's like traveling back in time when we were targets. The police are trying to frame my child for murder."

Saying those words made Judith's heart rate accelerate.

"What are they saying they have on her?" Sylvia asked.

"You know they don't need anything. They'll make it up," Judith said. She told her about Mason's murder. "It all has thoughts of Ethan barreling to the surface, you know. It haunts me that I didn't fight harder to get justice for him. That I went into hiding instead."

"Come on, what more could you have done?" Sylvia said. "I think about it, too. It makes me work hard for the neighborhood I represent. We thought our fighting would leave the next generations a fairer, more just world but all they inherited from us was the battle just to exist."

"The day the cops ran up on me when I was buying groceries, I realized I couldn't keep living under constant attack. I had to leave," Judith said. "What's the latest on the detective who led the raid?"

"Bitterman? Last I heard that viper is enjoying retirement in Florida."

The image of the blood-splattered mattress flashed in her mind. Judith blinked it away. "Got away with murder. Am I wrong for feeling Jeremy Watts got what he deserved?"

Watts had been the chapter's chief of security and Frank's personal bodyguard, trusted with Frank's life. It was Watts who had given the cops the layout of the apartment, so they'd know exactly which bedroom Frank slept in. It was Watts who was suspected of drugging Frank and then Ethan, so they'd be unable to react when the cops attacked.

"You're not the only member of that club. I never bought that he committed suicide by walking into traffic on the expressway. I could almost guarantee after 20 years of using him to betray the community, the FBI had no more use for old Watts and gave him a little help."

"It makes me think about Zara's friend, Mason, who was murdered," Judith said. "Police claim he was an informant."

"Isn't it better that she knows the truth?" Sylvia asked.

Judith wasn't so sure. "It's going to break her heart."

After promising to not let another decade go by before they spoke again, Judith disconnected. Her talk with Sylvia reassured her the key to saving Zara was finding out who Mason had met with the night he was killed.

***

Tony's car repair shop was a small one-story stucco building desperately in need of a paint job. Several old cars were parked in front on the gravel lot.

There was a front counter in a small waiting area that had a few worn chairs. An entrance behind it led to the shop area. There were no sounds of people working. Just the faint sound of music.

"Tony!" Zara called as she walked toward the door to the shop area. She made her way between a row of cars in various stages of being repaired. Her breath caught. Poor scrawny Tony was lying face down in a pool of blood. A bloody wrench was on the ground next to his head.

Judith was pulling together the press materials she needed to review and approve when her phone vibrated. It was Zara. Breathless. And hysterical.

"Mom, he's . . . he's dead!"

11

Judith's heart leapt. She dropped the folders she was holding, papers scattered at her feet. "Who?"

"T-T-Tony. Oh my God. I went to meet him at his shop. He was going to tell me about Mason working with the police. I found him . . . he was . . ."

"Did anyone see you?" Judith asked.

"I don't know. I don't think so."

"Get out of there. I'll meet you at home."

✳✳✳

When Judith made it home, she found a shaken Zara pacing in the kitchen. She shocked Judith by running to her and squeezing her into a hug like when she was a little girl. Judith stroked her braids. "It's going to be all right, baby. Did Tony tell you anything?"

Zara shook her head. "He was afraid to talk on the phone, but I sensed he was going to tell me Mason was an informant." Zara put her hands on her cheeks. "I didn't know Mason at all. How could he do that to us? To me?"

"People can be pressured, baby."

Zara was quiet for a time. Then she said, "Those detectives that were here were parked outside our headquarters. They said the police are going to increase the charges against us."

Judith shook her head. "Oh, no. We're not going to let that happen. We have to find out who Mason talked with before he was killed."

Zara's eyes lit up. She reached for her laptop in her tote. "Police never gave his things or his phone back to his mother. But I don't need it; we saved everything to the cloud. I don't know his password because we change them all the time to protect our accounts. But I can try to hack his account."

"You mean all this tuition your father and I are paying for your IT degree might reap an early dividend?" Judith said.

Judith anxiously watched as Zara tried various password combinations without success. Finally, a dejected Zara leaned back in the chair and blew out a frustrated breath. "I give up."

"You? Give up? That's not the daughter I raised," Judith said.

Zara tried again. After about ten minutes she lifted her arms and cried, "Bingo! Yes! I'm in. He used Mandela, his hero."

With Judith peering over her shoulder, Zara scrolled through Mason's text messages. "He hacked their email accounts and saved all the messages to the cloud."

Mason's message apologizing for their argument on his last day on earth made Zara tear up. But the messages on the day he was killed were the most telling.

Mason: I can meet at eight. I have to catch up with my lady.

317-555-1212: You better show this time with what we need. Be a shame if anyone found out about your little arrangement with us.

"Doesn't sound like the police were forcing Mason to work with them?" There was a hint of hope in Zara's voice. She opened another message thread Mason had copied.

Ready to crack a lot of heads tonight. Should be good for four hours of overtime pay. These idiots' marches gonna help repair my roof.

Yeah, bonus is getting to bust these losers' heads. Regs say no force unless necessary. For me it's always necessary.

Nothing like being able to let off steam by cracking these idiots' heads and earning money for the new AK47 I've had my eye on.

Thought you'd killed that one thug you hit him so hard, Pete.

Yeah, I beat that joker like he owed me money.

The messages went on, each one viler than the next. It made Judith sick. "Monsters. Bragging about hurting innocent, peaceful protesters. Call that number."

Zara touched in the number and put the call on speaker.

"Hunt."

Zara clasped a hand over her mouth to stifle her gasp at the sound of the

13

detective's voice who had been harassing her. "Zara Carter. If you can fix it so I don't have to go to jail, I'll pick up where Mason left off."

There was a pause, then a chuckle. "Here I thought you were one of the principled ones."

"I like to think I'm practical and that I face the reality of a situation. Are you interested or not?" Zara said.

"Be in front of the building where y'all meet in an hour. If I like what I hear, we'll see," Hunt said and disconnected.

Judith opened the contact lists in her phone to get the Walt Bradley's number at WQQX TV.

"Judith! How's my favorite corporate public relations exec?"

"Doing well," she lied. "How would you like an exclusive on the Mason Richards murder?" she asked.

"Heh? When did you add murder cases to your portfolio?" Walt asked.

"Don't ask. Let me just say you'll want to lead with what I'm going to send you."

After she ended the call, Judith stood and walked over to help Zara finish her hair. She tucked in a stray braid, her hands shaking at the thought of what her child was about to do. "I'm going to follow you. I can keep them from seeing me."

"No," Zara said. "If they suspect anything, it's over."

"I can't let you be alone with those murderers."

It was Zara's turn to take her mother by the shoulders. "Just keep that app open. I can do this. I can make them believe I'm turning on EJ. You're forgetting I'm the daughter of an original 60s radical. I got this."

***

Despite the bravado she'd shown her mother, Zara felt as if she was operating outside of her body. She tried not to flinch when the dark car pulled up and the window on the driver's side rolled down. Detective Hunt jerked his head, gesturing to the back. "Get in,"

Zara walked around to the passenger side. The door opened and Detective McConnell was in the back. Zara gave him a puzzled look.

"Problem?" McConnell asked. His tone and demeanor were not that of the fair and understanding detective he'd presented himself when he'd questioned her yesterday.

Zara got in and sat close to the door. Her heart was beating triple time, but she kept her voice calm. "You're in the wrong line of work. Acting is more your calling. You play good cop so well."

"So, I've been told." Detective McConnell held out his hand, waggled his fingers in a beckoning motion. "Your phone. We don't want this little meeting ending up on the internet, do we?"

McConnell took her phone put it on the car floor and stomped on it, smashing it to pieces. Smiling, he picked up the pieces and put them in the pocket of his suit jacket. "Have to search you, too. Make sure you don't have any other devices."

Zara frowned at him. "Whatever."

McConnell moved close and ran his hands over her. Zara shuddered and at the same time the heat of anger warmed her cheeks. Hunt started the car, drove a few blocks and pulled into an alley.

Zara summoned her bravado again. "Well? Can you make the charges disappear? Because that's the only way we have a deal."

McConnell laughed. "Amazing how easily you *warriors* can be swayed from your causes."

"We do what we have to," Zara said. "Like Mason."

"And like Mason, you won't be calling any shots. Little thug thought his going to some college made him smarter than us. Right, Hunt?"

Hunt laughed. "Made him stupid."

"You killed him because he was smart?" Zara asked matter-of-factly, masking the rage boiling inside her.

Detective McConnell laughed. "What the hell. Doesn't matter if you know. We own you now. We can have you locked up at any time. Your boyfriend pretended to turn on your organization so he could infiltrate us. Take us down. Hacked our email accounts and text messages and was going to give them to the media. Bad news in this climate. I tried reasoning with him, but he was willing to die for a lost cause. Hope you're smarter than he is because, trust me, nothing's going to change. We're the law. We'll always have the upper hand."

Zara swallowed hard to keep the contents of her stomach from coming up.

McConnell added, "You supply us info we need, we make all charges go away and you stay out of jail."

He didn't give Zara a chance to respond. "We're done, Hunt."

Detective Hunt pulled out of the alley and drove back toward EJ headquarters. He pulled up to the curb two blocks from the building. McConnell reached over and pushed open the door on the passenger side. "I expect the plans for your next protest, pronto," he said.

Zara scrambled out and walked fast to get inside the safety of their headquarters where Judith was waiting.

Judith sprang from where she was sitting at the table, almost knocking Zara's laptop to the floor. She hugged her daughter so tight she was sure she couldn't breathe. "You did it, baby. You got them."

Smiling, Zara reached into the one place they counted on her not being searched — her braids. She unwound the big bun and removed the minicam that had recorded everything, allowing Judith to see their every move.

"Better than okay. We got him, Mom."

That night, Judith and Zara watched as the WQQX anchor played the video Judith had texted to Walt showing McConnell confessing to killing Mason Richards. They'd agreed not to release any information on her involvement. They reported McConnell was also suspected of killing Tony Davis, whose body had been found by a customer who'd come to pick up his car. Mason had confided to Tony that he was pretending to be an informant to expose the cops' brutality. They watched the police superintendent choke as he tried to explain the text messages where the cops bragged about using excessive force and arresting innocent people. Watched him make the hollow promise that the officers and detectives involved would be held accountable and how the police department would do everything it could to help the community heal.

"Yeah, sure you will," Judith said.

***

Zara blinked in awe at the image staring back at them in the mirror. Her braids and Judith's straight bob were transformed into big, thick, round Afros like Judith wore in her activist days. The photo of her mom with the other

Peoples' Party women, now Zara's screen saver, flashed in her mind. "You really should have told me about your resister days," Zara said.

Judith paused from patting her round Afro. "I was doing what mothers do. But I should have made sure you knew your history."

Zara moved close to her mother and kissed her cheek. "This is going to be our biggest protest yet. Ready for this?"

Judith laughed. "Ready? I'm overdue."

She'd submitted her retirement papers two weeks after McConnell was formally charged with the murders, and charges against Zara and the Equal Justice crew were dropped. Judith was leaving the corporate jungle in December for a new mission. Advising Equal Justice. Zara needed her in this fight.

"We'll probably get arrested tonight," Zara said.

Judith chuckled. "Your dad is standing by with bail money."

Zara lifted a fist in the air. "For Mason and Tony."

Judith did the same. "And Ethan."

One Hundred Years a Widow

by Janet E. Williams

"Is it true she murdered her husband?"

I didn't recognize the low, hushed voice. I couldn't even tell if it was male or female. But what did it matter? I lie here, tethered to IVs pumping life into me, a tube down my throat to help me breathe and a machine beeping at a steady rhythm to let the doctors and nurses know I am alive.

Alive? If you can call this living. I listened for an answer to the million-dollar question, the one everyone has been asking for one hundred years. I heard a long, deep sigh and then the door swung open.

"And how's our patient doing today?" It was that nurse with the high-pitched sing-songy voice that made me want to rise from my deathbed and smack her.

You tell me. You read the numbers, poke and prod me while I lie here, unable to move, barely able to breathe. I'm trapped in a gray, shrunken version of the person I used to be. So tell me, how am I doing?

"Any change?" My little Sarah, my great-granddaughter who isn't so little anymore.

"Same. She's holding her own, but . . ." The voice trailed off and I missed the rest.

Same yesterday. Same today. Same tomorrow?

After she checked the IV in my arm and adjusted the tube in my throat she left and it was Sarah at my bedside with someone I didn't recognize.

19

I tried to force my eyes open but all they did was flutter a little.

"I think she's waking up." The voice, my mystery visitor. It was male.

Sarah didn't reply but instead leaned closer, brushed hair away from my face, and spoke softly, "Gran, this is a reporter with the *Daily News*. He's here to do a story. You know, oldest living person and all."

I love that girl but what the hell was she doing with a reporter? But then, she wouldn't know, couldn't possibly understand what it's like when some nosy reporter digs into every crevice of your life. Or what it's like for everyone to know who you are or think they know you. How they pretend they don't see you while they cast sideways, furtive glances when they think you're not looking.

For years I was the notorious Hannah Brumbaugh, with whispers and gossip trailing after me wherever I went. It took some time, but eventually the next scandal, some new and salacious piece of gossip, overtook my notoriety, and interest in me faded. I evolved into the Widow Brumbaugh, who, as the years passed, was the old lady who kept mostly to herself in a cottage at the edge of the woods. There was a cloud of mystery, of suspicion, but nobody could actually remember the details any more. They just knew it was something and it wasn't good.

Of course, that was before Google, Facebook, and all those things on the Internet that laid bare every single thing in my life I hoped had been long forgotten. And that was before I turned one hundred, then one hundred and ten and, to the world's astonishment as much as my own, one hundred and twenty. I turn one hundred twenty-five next month.

Suddenly, I was famous for something else — living longer than anyone else on the planet. Like I actually had something to do with that. There might be an older man in Tibet, but he doesn't have the birth records to prove it. I do. Hannah Brumbaugh, born to Johann and Lenore Wineland on December 21, 1896. I came into the world in a four-poster bed in our family's home south of Indianapolis.

Now, the reporters are back, and at least one of them is at my bedside, ushered into this room by a member of my own family. My only family.

"I told you that you could see her, but she probably wouldn't be able to talk," Sarah told him.

"She was in pretty good health, I mean for her age, until . . . ?"

"Until about a week ago," Sarah said. "She collapsed at home. I found her in the kitchen."

"Living alone? She really over a hundred and twenty?"

"You've got the records."

Everything in my life was in those records. Birth, marriage, birth of my own daughter, granddaughter, war, and death. A lot of death, except my own. Until now. Maybe.

"You never really answered my question. I have old newspaper stories, court records, but they don't tell me what I really want to know. Did your great-grandmother murder her husband? Did she kill Austin Brumbaugh?"

I hadn't heard that name spoken out loud for a very long time. But when that reporter repeated it, I felt myself transported from this aged body and back more than a century to the evening when I first laid eyes on him across a dance floor in the basement of my old church.

Damn, he was handsome. Tall, wavy blond hair that flopped onto his high forehead and a smile that made his deep blue eyes crinkle when he flashed it. He just about melted my heart. And when his eyes caught mine, he floated across the dance floor with a long, confident stride and straight to me.

"The next dance is mine," he said, taking my hand. They were rough with thick callouses, but his touch was so light and gentle I hardly noticed.

As he pulled me onto the dance floor, a voice behind me said, "Hannah, that's supposed to be our . . . "

"My turn, Francis," was all he said as he pulled me close and led me in a simple three-step waltz. I didn't have a chance to say a word before he leaned down and pressed his cheek against mine.

"Francis is all left feet," he said softly.

I pulled my face away from his and glanced across the room at Francis, who fumed as my new dance partner gave him a slight nod and continued to sweep me across the floor.

"You and Francis friends?"

"Brothers."

That startled me because he looked and acted nothing like the small, dapper man who had escorted me to the church dance.

"Fine way to treat your brother."

"He'll get over it." He smiled and tightened his grip around my waist as we spun across the room.

It wasn't until the waltz ended and the next piece, a ragtime, started playing, that I had a moment to catch my breath and learn that my overbearing, yet charming, dance partner was Austin Brumbaugh. The renegade son of the Crown Hill Brumbaughs and little brother to Francis. The church dance was my first and last date with Francis.

That was the spring of 1915 and I spent every weekend through that summer and fall with Austin. I saw my first movie with him, Charlie Chaplin in *The Tramp*, went to my first play, first canoe trip down the White River. He took me to clubs around the city, places that seemed a little scandalous, where I was exposed to all kinds of music and dancing. I should have been a little fearful because some of the people seemed rough and there would be an occasional fight. But I wasn't. I was with Austin and he moved about easily, laughing and joking, friendly with everyone.

I had grown up the daughter of a drunken coal miner who died in a cave-in when I was in my early teens. My mother, my older sister, and I worked cleaning the houses of families like Austin's to support my six younger brothers and sisters. Austin showed me a world that had existed only in my imagination. More than that, he made me laugh. And that made up for the times he had a few too many beers or blew his weekly paycheck gambling with the men at those bars.

I knew that some considered him the black sheep of his family. While his older brother went off to college and on to a respectable career as a lawyer, Austin flunked out of Indiana University. He needed a job, so his father used his connections to get him one as an apprentice to a local builder. To everyone's surprise, he proved himself to be a skilled carpenter. But he still had a wild streak and that was what I loved most about him.

We married on October 26, 1915, in a small ceremony in the Lutheran Church his family had attended since the Civil War. Neither his parents nor Francis were happy about me or the marriage because Austin remained the spoiled little brother of the family. Even so, they made sure it was announced to the whole town in one of the daily newspapers — Miss Hannah Wineland weds Mr. Austin Brumbaugh.

✳✳✳

"Did she do it? Do you even know?"

That reporter, like a vulture hovering over me, anxious for one last scrap of my dignity, my privacy, my peace, dragged me back to the present, this body, my prison.

Of course she doesn't know! How could she? Austin Brumbaugh died half a century before she was even born!

"I don't need to know because I know Gran," Sarah said. "I know the woman who raised me from the time I was six years old, who loved me, cared for me when I thought I was alone in the whole world. And now, all you want is scandal and gossip."

That's my girl!

Girl! My great-granddaughter is 50 and she has a grown daughter. Turned into a strong woman who knows her own mind. That's the way I raised her.

She was such a tiny thing when she came to me. Her mother, my granddaughter, and her husband had been killed in car crash when some drunk in one of those monster-sized trucks crossed into their lane on Meridian and slammed into their car head-on. Killed instantly. Sarah had been home with a babysitter.

I was in the garden pulling weeds when I heard the gate squeak. My first thought as I wobbled to my feet was how I needed to oil that gate.

"Mrs. Brumbaugh?" A short, stubby woman with long gray strands of hair blowing in the wind stood before me with a little girl clinging to a tattered Raggedy Ann. At first, I didn't recognize the child. She had big, dark eyes under a mass of curly hair and looked like she had been crying. *Is this little Sarah, my daughter's granddaughter?* I'd only seen her a few times in her young life, the last time more than two years ago.

I nodded at the woman and removed my gardening gloves as I rose to greet her.

"Mrs. Brumbaugh, there's been an accident and . . . " The woman sighed heavily and looked from the child to me and back to the child again. "Can we go inside? I need to talk to you."

Accident? I couldn't imagine what kind of accident would bring this woman and child to my home.

I showed the woman, who was carrying a small duffle bag, and Sarah into my house and she took a seat at the kitchen table. The woman told Sarah to go into the adjoining dining room for a few minutes while we talked.

I'm not sure whether the woman identified herself because the next few minutes seemed like a scene unreeling before me on a movie screen, distant and certainly not part of me. I looked from her to Sarah rocking silently on the floor in the next room as she told me about the accident that killed Sarah's parents.

"Oh, dear, God." I don't think I cried exactly, but I felt my eyes well up and a tear or two might have trickled down my cheek.

"And you are listed as next of kin," the woman said.

"Me?"

That was almost as shocking to me as the news of the accident because, over the years, I had so little contact with either my daughter, who passed away years ago, or my granddaughter.

"As far as we can figure, you're the only living relative. I'm surprised the police or coroner hasn't been in touch with you yet."

I shook my head to say no one had contacted me about the accident.

"And her?" My voice cracked as I nodded toward the dining room where Sarah had crawled under the table where she cradled her doll.

"As far as we can tell, her parents didn't have a will or make any provisions for a guardian in the event, well, you know."

"The poor child."

"She needs to stay somewhere, Mrs. Brumbaugh. We could keep her in a shelter for a couple of days while we figure out a place for her, but . . . "

"But she's my blood," I said firmly. "She'll stay here."

"Until we get everything sorted out."

Those first days were painfully difficult. I couldn't let the grief I felt for my granddaughter get in the way of caring for this child who understood little of

24

what was happening around her. The only thing she knew was Mommy and Daddy were never coming home.

Those first few weeks she would curl up in my bed, her arms wrapped around that doll, and lay beside me. I'd listened to her crying softly night after night until she fell asleep. Even as she grew up and settled into the bedroom that had once belonged to her grandmother, she would crawl into bed beside me when a bad storm scared her. I had forgotten what it felt like to let myself love another person as much as I came to love that little girl, my Sarah.

***

"You were, what, six when you went to live with her?"

That damned reporter again.

"I'm surprised the child welfare folks would let you stay with her. She had to be over 80, right?"

"They tried to take me away, but Gran said she wasn't going to let me go," Sarah said. "Not this time."

"Not this time?"

"They tried to place me with a foster family not long after the funeral. They said she was too old to raise a little girl."

"Then what happened?"

I'll tell you what happened. I got a good lawyer who showed them that I was healthy and could do a good job raising my great-granddaughter. Besides, I wasn't going to let them take away Sarah like Austin's parents took little Florence after he died. It was only supposed to be for a few months while I got myself back on my feet and the scandal faded. But they were rich and they never let anyone forget how they believed Austin died. They knew the right judge and got custody of my little girl. I never got her back.

"I don't remember a whole lot of it except that we all went to court one day and a judge said I could stay with Gran," Sarah said. "And I did."

She squeezed my hand as she spoke. I would have given anything to squeeze hers back.

"Did she ever talk about her early life? I mean, look at what she's lived through. Look at all the changes she's seen right here. She was born when McKinley was president?"

"Actually, it was Cleveland."

25

"Cleveland? Wow. Plus two world wars? She ever talk about that?"

"Not much. It was because she hates war, always thought it was a waste. Wouldn't even let me watch old war movies on TV. Said they showed nothing but lies . . ."

That's right. There's nothing good or glorious in grown men, and women now I guess, blasting the hell out of each other for what? For nothing.

"Because of what her husband went through?" he asked.

"I don't know." After a long pause Sarah added, "Maybe."

✳✳✳

The Great War. The war to end all wars. I kept the clipping from the local paper when Austin enlisted: *Austin Brumbaugh off to France.* There was a picture of him in his Doughboy uniform looking straight into the camera. The article described how Austin could have gotten a deferment because he had a wife and baby daughter, but he was quoted as saying it was his duty to serve and save democracy or some grand words like that.

As much as I didn't want him to go, I had to admit he looked dashing in his uniform. He was a private assigned to a medical unit that shipped out with the American Expeditionary Forces in October 1917. I spent our second wedding anniversary home alone with baby Florence while he was on a ship in the North Atlantic.

Communication was so much slower then and maybe that was a good thing. I wouldn't have known that Austin was up to his knees in mud dodging bullets and bombs as he staggered from the trenches onto the field ahead of him, his medic kit slung across his body. His job was to reach the wounded and drag them from the battlefield back to the trenches. Mere yards separated him from the enemy.

I also wouldn't have known how he'd crawl across the limbs of dead soldiers or helmets half-submerged in the muck, only to discover a head still attached. He told me once that he could still hear the cries of the wounded soldiers he tried in vain to reach as shells exploded around him.

I didn't even know he had been wounded and was in a French field hospital until his mother came to our home, the one I still live in, and delivered the news. The Army had notified her, not me. A mustard gas shell exploded, killing several soldiers and leaving him with blisters on his hands, face, and lungs.

The war ended a few weeks later. I was relieved. Florence and I would soon have Austin back with us and we could start again to build a life together in our little cottage.

But Austin didn't come home right away. The Army sent him to a hospital in Philadelphia to recover from the mustard gas attack and from there, to another one in Chicago. I didn't know until I traveled to see him that the damage from the gas was minor compared to the damage to his spirit from the bombs, bullets, and death he lived through in the trenches in France.

"Florence says she misses her Da-Da," I told him as we sat in the sunny visitors' room that early spring morning. A small lie. Florence didn't miss him because she barely remembered him. But the thought that she did made him smile as he rocked back and forth, whispering her name.

"The doctor said you're coming along just fine, that maybe in a few weeks you can come home."

I wasn't sure I believed that, but Austin nodded as he reached for my hand.

"Soon," Austin told me, gently pressing his lips to my cheek as I prepared to leave.

"Yes, my love." I hurried from the room because I didn't want him to see me cry.

***

"They called it shell shock back then, didn't they?" Once again, the reporter's question brought me back. I didn't mind this time.

"It was treated more as a character defect then," Sarah said.

"Your grandmother tell you that?"

"Great-grandmother, and no, she told me a few stories about him, about how afraid he was whenever there was a storm with thunder and lightning. Or how fireworks left him shaking with fear."

"Classic PTSD."

I didn't hear what Sarah said next. I know she was curious and did a lot of research on her own. I would find books around the house about the war, about the hospitals where soldiers with shell shock were treated, about how damaged young men were shunned when they came home, how families no longer recognized them.

I could have told her all that from my first-hand experience, but I couldn't. Some pain never heals; some wounds run too deep. How could I tell her that the man I once loved with every ounce of my being turned into someone who terrified me? How could I ever get her to understand why I did what I did?

Sarah learned plenty from books — that shell-shocked veterans were treated as less than whole men. Austin's own father told him he was soft and that he should quit dwelling on the war, that a lot of men went through the same experiences and they came home just fine. His mother believed it was my fault, that I wasn't the kind of loving and supportive wife he needed to get him back on his feet. The remnants of my own family had moved to Chicago not long after our marriage and I only ever heard from them when they needed money. None of them had a clue about the depth of Austin's pain or the toll his suffering took on Florence and me.

Thank God for Francis. He never served because he had a deformed hand and couldn't handle a weapon. He tried to understand and support Austin and me, especially when the memories and fears overwhelmed all of us. I could count on him to come to our place to help calm Austin when he was in the throes of night terrors or when the depression was so deep he would lock himself in our bedroom for hours or days. Usually, Francis could bring him back from the edge of despair, from the trenches and horrors of the battlefield. But not always.

Austin had been doing well for weeks. No night terrors. No bouts of deep depression. No wild mood swings. Until the Fourth of July 1920.

We'd had a lovely day of picnicking and boating on the White River with his family and had settled in for the evening when fireworks began exploding with bright and colorful lights in the distant sky. I could see Austin, who held Florence on his lap, begin to tremble as we sat on the porch watching the fireworks begin. I knew what might be coming so I quietly took our child from him and led both of them into the house. I took Florence to her room upstairs as Austin, shaking, withdrew into a corner in the kitchen, pressing against the wall as if he were trying to disappear. As I returned to check on him, he lunged at me and with those large, calloused hands he grabbed me by my throat and began choking me. Lights flashed before my eyes as Austin, teeth bared like a wolf, screamed something incomprehensible.

"Austin! Stop!"

Francis crashed through the door, arriving moments before I was about to black out. Austin flung Francis to the floor with a single swoop of one hand while he continued to choke me with the other. Francis was only able to get him off me by hitting him across his back with a kitchen chair. I knew it wasn't me he was fighting but some imaginary enemy. Still, I had never felt such terror nor did I ever feel at peace in our home again.

"You should go, get away from here," Francis said after he helped Austin upstairs to our bedroom and quieted him down. "I have a little money saved up and I can help you rent a place in Fountain Square."

"No, Francis. This never happened before and I know it wasn't him. Not really." My words were raspy from the injury to my throat.

"But you have to think of the baby . . . "

"He'd never hurt Florence."

"What about you? What would she do without a mother and a father in prison – or worse?"

"No." I couldn't abandon him. I was his wife. No matter what happened he needed me. And I wouldn't let his parents be proved right about Austin or me.

"I can't always get here in time to protect you," Francis said. "I won't always be here."

"I know, Francis. I know," I said as I fell sobbing into his arms.

I didn't realize how prescient his words were. Late that summer, Francis came down with what he thought was a simple cold. It wasn't. It quickly spread to his lungs and by the middle of September, Francis was dead of pneumonia. Grief plunged Austin into his deepest depression yet. As for me, I never felt more alone.

***

A gentle squeeze on my shoulder brought me back. I knew that touch. Sarah.

"She's so thin." Her voice cracked. "She was always so strong. It's, it's so hard seeing her like this."

"She was never sick?" The reporter again, still at my bedside.

"No, she hardly ever went to the doctor that I can remember except for a routine checkup. She walked every day. Three to five miles until Buddy was too old."

"Buddy?"

"Her dog. He died last month. They were inseparable." There was a long pause before she added, "You writing that down, too?"

"It's part of the story. Part of who Hannah Brumbaugh was."

"Is!" Sarah spoke with anger.

"Of course. Sorry."

"You should have plenty for your story."

"Sure, I have a lot from the official records, but I still don't know who Hannah Brumbaugh really is, the woman who lived through wars and death, who spent years estranged from her own daughter and granddaughter, who's an enigma to almost everyone except you, it seems."

No, that's not what you want. What you really want to know, what everyone for the last hundred years has wanted to know, is what happened the night Austin died and whether I got away with murder. You want a yes or no answer, but there isn't one. Nothing is that simple.

"She never talked to me about that night, if that's what you want to know," Sarah said. "She told me a lot of things about her life, her family, but never about that night."

"The news accounts from the time said she was found standing over him with a gun in her hand."

"I know what the newspapers reported. I read them. I read them all."

That's right. That's exactly what they said, that Helen Brumbaugh was outside her son's home when she heard a bang and rushed through the door to see her daughter-in-law standing over Austin's body, a pistol in her hand.

But that wasn't the whole story. Words on a page in a newspaper or in a police report never tell the whole story.

"It was a Luger that he brought back from the war, wasn't it?"

"I don't know. I only know what I read in the papers and in the old police reports," Sarah told him. "And nobody could say for sure how he ended up with that gun."

I never knew how he got that gun, either. He certainly didn't have it when he finally got home from that hospital in Chicago.

I've had a hundred years to think about that night. What I did. What I failed to do. How I failed you, Austin.

It was the second anniversary of the end of the Great War, a Thursday. You had been working for your war buddy's construction business at a house on Washington Street east of the city. The night before, you had shown me the horsehead carving you were doing for a bannister. It was beautiful, a work of art. I took that as a sign that you might be coming out of your depression and taking an interest in the things you did before the war.

I couldn't have been more wrong.

Austin worked late that night. I say worked because that's what he told me as he stumbled through the back door. I could smell liquor and stale cigarettes as he whipped off his coat and flung it onto a chair. This was becoming a habit with him, drinking, maybe some gambling, especially since Francis died. I was reluctant to call him on it, relieved that he wasn't barricading himself in our room or flying into a rage.

"Where's Flo?" he demanded.

"In bed. She had her supper hours ago."

"I wanna see my little girl, my sweet Flo." He slurred his words as he pushed me aside to head upstairs where our daughter slept.

"No, Austin. Not like that." I grabbed his arm.

"Like what?" He shook me off.

"You've had too much to drink." I removed his plate from the oven and set it on the table. "Pork chops, your favorite. I kept it warm for you. You'll feel better with a little food in you."

When he hesitated, I felt a ripple of fear run through me because I wasn't sure what he would do. After a moment, he sat and ate while I cleaned up the dishes. I believed we had avoided another blow up. But as I finished washing the dishes, I heard something clang as it hit the floor. I turned to see that

31

Austin had dropped his fork and just sat there, staring ahead at nothing. I didn't know what to say or do. I never did.

He buried his face in his hands and began crying, softly at first, and repeating, "Tommy. Tommy."

"Tommy?" The only Tommy I knew was Tommy DiLauria who served with Austin in France.

"Tommy, he died last night," he said between sobs. "Killed himself."

Dear God, poor Tommy. I felt sick. He seemed like he was getting along just fine. Not like Austin. Suicide? His poor family would have to live with that pain.

"I'm so sorry, Austin."

I wanted to throw my arms around him and tell him that everything would be okay. But I was afraid that the wrong touch or wrong word would set him off. So, I backed away and went upstairs to check on Florence.

I stayed upstairs until I figured Austin had regained some control. I listened in the stairwell for his sobs and when I didn't hear anything, I crept back into the kitchen. His chair was empty. His dinner plate sat on the table and a glass lay on its side, water dripping to the floor.

"Austin," I said softly.

There was no answer but I heard a rustling in the darkened living room. I went in to see him sitting in a chair, a silhouette against the window.

"I killed him, you know," Austin whispered.

"Tommy?"

"Not Tommy," he said, pausing before he continued. "He was out there. I could hear him crying, calling for help, for me. I was supposed to go out there and, and ..."

His voice cracked as he began crying. I could see he was shaking as he wrapped his arms around himself.

"I was supposed to save him! That was my job!" Austin's voice rose. "But the shells, the shells were exploding everywhere. And I was afraid! I was too afraid and he died." He broke down sobbing.

"Austin, it wasn't your fault." The words sounded hollow even as I said them. I turned on the light and began moving toward him but stopped cold when I saw the gun in his hand.

"What the…where did you get that gun?"

"Stay back." He waved it at me. "Tommy got it right. Let's see if I have the guts … "

"No, don't." That's the last thing I remember saying as I tore across the room. I wanted to stop him. At least that's what I told myself over the years. Later, in my statement to police, I said that Austin had pointed the gun at his head, but I'm not sure if that's what really happened. I only know that I lunged for the gun, and as I tried to wrestle it away it exploded with a pop. Austin dropped to the floor. I might have screamed, but that could have been his mother. She had walked in through the kitchen to see me with the German Luger standing over my husband, a bullet wound in his chest.

"You killed him!" she shrieked.

I don't remember exactly what happened next, except that I dropped the Luger and ran from the house to my neighbor, who called the police. When they arrived, Helen was kneeling beside the body, wailing about how her poor son was murdered by that bitch.

The weeks that followed were a blur. Police questioned me over and over again; at the funeral everyone, including the pastor, eyed me with suspicion. There were non-stop accusations from the Brumbaughs, who were pressuring the newly elected county prosecutor to charge me. I figured it was only a matter of time before I was arrested because the family had contributed heavily to William Evans' campaign.

The coroner eventually ruled his death an accident, but that didn't matter. I ended up in another kind of prison because the Brumbaughs got custody of Florence and filled her head with stories about how I killed her father. I lost her forever.

Oh Sarah, there's so much I should have explained long ago and I missed my chance. It doesn't matter now. I am at peace in the knowledge that you've always known the truth and that our love for each other is absolute.

I hear a distant voice cry, "Nurse, nurse." *Sarah, you sound so frantic.* Nurses tug at the tubes and wires that have kept my failing body alive this past week.

"Do something," you yell. But I have a DNR. Do not resuscitate.

I want to hold you and tell you everything will be all right like I did when you were that scared little girl. But my body is no longer my own. A high-pitched beep that has been playing steadily in the background turns into a monotone buzz. Your cries of "Gran, Gran, I love you" fade as I find myself floating above my bed, outside this room.

I love you, Sarah, and though it's hard to say goodbye, Austin is waiting.

Mister 20

by J. Paul Burroughs

The day began with a pair of hearts – one filled with cherry cordial chocolates, the second stabbed repeatedly.

IMPD Detective Carl Harewood examined heart-shaped boxes of chocolates to give his wife for Valentine's Day in five days, when a call came through. Lionel Ritchie's "All Night Long" sounded on his phone. He immediately recognized the caller.

"Harewood here. What's up, Captain?"

Captain Robert DeAngelo cleared his throat before answering. "There's been a homicide. Just like the one last month. Killer left a torn half of a twenty-dollar bill on the body."

Harewood gulped. He didn't want to use the term, "serial killer" in public, but that's what both were thinking.

"Where'd you find the body?"

"In a dumpster behind an elementary school over on Sugar Grove Avenue."

"Jeez! Don't tell me a kid found it?"

"No, a custodian. The victim was part of the evening cleaning staff at the school."

"I'll be right there." Carl wrote down the address, paid for the candy, and drove to the school. Several patrol cars were already there as well as the medical examiner's van. To Carl's irritation, he spotted a familiar vehicle that belonged to a Dan Gleason, a blogger who regularly wrote derogatory material about the department and criminal activity in Indianapolis.

35

Carl, at 41, had been on the force for 18 years. He had risen from being a street cop to one of the city's top detectives by the time he'd turned 31. At six-foot-three, witnesses found him an imposing figure when questioned. He spotted the medical examiner and a uniformed officer loading a man's body inside a van.

Feeling the chill of a winter morning, he pulled his coat collar up and approached the pair. "Morning, you two. What have we got on that guy?"

"Victim's name is Will Nicholson, age 26," replied the officer. "Worked here at the school."

"Died of multiple stab wounds to the chest," added Matt Greenaway, the ME. "I estimate time of death sometime between10:30 and just after midnight."

Carl moved his head from side to side. "That's awful late to be working at school, even for a janitor."

The officer checked his spiral note pad. "Guy's only been with the school a matter of months. Started when school opened for classes in August. Guess newbies get stuck with the night shift."

The officer pointed to a figure watching them through the school's door glass. "That's Myron Bingham, the head custodian. He says the guy was single. Kept to himself pretty much. And before you ask, we found the torn half of a twenty-dollar bill on the body."

"So I heard."

"You know what that means? Whoever killed this guy probably killed the Williams woman. We got ourselves a serial."

One month earlier, on January 20th, Alice Williams, the manager of an Indianapolis IT firm, was found stabbed to death in the parking lot. They'd found the torn half of a twenty-dollar bill sticking out her coat.

"Maybe," Carl said, "let's wait for the medical examiner to finish before we jump too fast."

He raised his eyes, inspecting the top of the school. "Don't suppose a security camera picked up our killer?"

"No, the place doesn't have one. Wasn't there one at the scene of the Williams murder?"

"Yeah, it picked up a man in a hoodie, wearing a ski mask. We figure he's five-ten, weighing between 230 and 250 pounds. I'd just hoped we'd get lucky this time and see his face."

"No such luck."

A rumble of thunder overhead was immediately followed by a downpour. The medical examiner hurried into his van for cover, shouting orders for the officer to throw a tarp over the crime scene. Carl gave a nod towards the school building. "Y'know, I think I'll go inside and talk to his co-workers, myself."

***

The first up was Lou Mitchell, a short, scrawny figure in his late 50s. "Yeah, I worked with him, but to be honest, I hardly knew the guy," Lou Mitchell explained. "I can count on both hands the number of conversations we've had."

"Just tell me what you know," Carl urged.

"Well, I know he was unemployed for a coupla months before being hired by the school system. Got the impression he was fired from his old job for some reason."

"Did he talk about anything else?"

"He went to Washington High School. Dropped out his senior year. Told me that after Washington won a ball game last month."

"Was he seeing anyone? Did he mention the names of any friends?"

A shrug. "Sorry, no. Like I said. The guy rarely said a word."

"Did he ever want to borrow money, say twenty dollars?"

"Yeah, once. He wanted to borrow that much for gas money. I turned him down."

***

After stopping at a convenience store for coffee, Carl drove to where Nicholson lived. It was a large two-story house on North Delaware that, unlike the others in the neighborhood, had not undergone renovation over the past decade. In the 1970s, it had been converted into a series of small apartments. He located the landlady who let him into Will's unit. To describe it as Spartan would have been an understatement. The furniture consisted of a bed, a small table and chair, a floor lamp, and an easy chair that looked as

37

though it dated back to the 1940s. The "kitchen" consisted of a sink, a hot plate, some unwashed dishes, and a trash can that had begun to smell. If the smell from the trash can was bad, the odor from the tiny bathroom was imminently worse.

There wasn't a single thing to indicate the man's personality. No family photos, no letters, no laptop.

"Interesting place you got here," Carl commented.

"Hey, what you expect for 175 a month?" fumed the landlady.

"What can you tell me about your tenant?"

"He paid his rent on time the five months he lived here."

"Anyone come to see him?"

She shook her head.

"Did he ever mention anyone who might have had a grudge against him?"

"No, but someone must have. A couple of weeks before Christmas I saw him leave his room looking like the crap had been beaten outta him. I asked him what had happened. He told me he'd gotten in a fight at some bar."

"Any idea what bar?"

She shook her head.

Left to search the room, Carl went through the trash can. In it, he found a bag with a half-eaten sandwich, a receipt for the sandwich and a beer. He read the name at the top of the receipt: Snake Eyes Bar.

"Yeah, I remember this guy," the bartender at the bar on North Sherman Drive, remarked. "Comes in here two or three times a week. Told somebody he used to live around here when he was a kid."

"Did he get into a fight with someone here recently?"

He nodded, "Yeah, with a young hothead who comes here once in a while."

"This hothead got a name?"

"Yeah. Tony Caldera. That's Tony short for Antonio."

"Know where I might find this Antonio?" Carl inquired.

"Don't know where he lives, but he works at the supermarket in Linwood Square. Heard him mention he'd just gotten off work there one afternoon."

Carl thanked the bartender and then drove the eight blocks to Linwood Square. He found Caldera, a Hispanic in his 20s, working in the supermarket's loading dock. His ice-cold blue eyes glared when Carl identified himself.

When he asked if the detective could wait to question him during his break in 20 minutes. Carl agreed.

***

"Yeah, I got in a fight with the jerk," Caldera answered when Carl questioned him about the fight. "He came into the place in a bad mood, just itching for a fight. He called me some names, so I hit him. We exchanged punches until the bartender threatened to call the cops. I cut out. Never seen the guy before or since. If he got killed last night, I have an alibi. I was with some buds until about two in the morning."

"I'll need their names and addresses to confirm that."

Caldera grumbled with impatience but wrote down the names of his friends and their phone numbers.

***

"Well?" Captain DeAngelo asked as Carl laid down his phone after the last call.

"Spoke to all three of the names Caldera gave me. Every single one confirms his story."

"And you've not found any connection between Nicholson and the Williams woman beside the half of a twenty spot?"

Carl shook his head. "Nothing I've found. They have nothing in common. He was single and living alone. Alice Williams was divorced with two grown sons. He lived in a rat hole on North Delaware. She lived in a nice place up in Lawrence. As far as anyone knows, those two never knew one another."

"You're saying this killer picks his victims at random?"

"No, there's got to be a connection. My gut feeling tells me so. I just don't see what."

"Go back to the first murder and try to work it from there," the captain suggested.

"I've already tried that. Originally, I suspected the ex-husband, but he had an airtight alibi. He'd been working the night shift at the factory at the time of the murder and had a dozen coworkers to support his story."

The captain took a sip of the coffee he'd been nursing. "Any chance the ex and Nicholson might have known one another?"

"Well, both work nights. Maybe they crossed paths somewhere after work – a diner, a convenience store. I'll check it out."

The captain massaged his chin with his thumb and forefinger. "This could be a copycat crime, and not a serial killing. You know the department didn't reveal the fact that half-a-twenty-dollar bill was left on Alice Williams."

"Well, that secret's out, Captain. I spotted that blog writer Gleason at the school talking to staff members. By now it's all over the Internet."

"Yeah," the captain replied. "Already read his blog. He's calling our killer 'Mister 20.'"

***

"You're home on time," Nina, Carl's wife, cheerfully commented giving him a peck on the lips. "I'll start supper. I heard about the second murder by this Mister 20 guy. I expected you'd be working late on the case."

"Nothing to go on at the moment," he admitted. "I feel like I'm banging my head against a brick wall."

"Well, don't bang for too long. I'll have supper ready soon."

He looked up the stairs. "What is Carmen listening to up there? Sounds like two alley cats spoiling for a fight."

"Some new rapper, I suppose."

"Whatever happened to good music? Lionel Ritchie, Diana Ross, Stevie Wonder? Theirs was good music."

"They got old. New generation, new types of music. Don't start to talk about the good old days as though you were an old man. We're still young."

"Sorry. It's this case. I feel like I'm getting nowhere."

"You'll solve it." She brought her hands to his shoulders. "Tell you what – suppose I give you a neck massage to help relieve the stress?"

"A neck massage would be great, but I don't think it will help with stress. I have a nasty feeling that very soon, our killer will strike again."

***

He turned out to be right. Weeks later on February 29th he was called to a crime scene at Garfield Park on the city's southeast side. A body had been found behind some trees a distance from the park drive. When he arrived, he spoke to the officer at the scene.

"What have you got on the victim, Ed?" he asked.

"Name's Keenan Greene. Fifty-three with a wife and three kids. He runs an insurance agency on South Madison. Body was found by an early morning jogger. Stabbed in the chest three times." The officer pointed to something green that had been stuffed in the dead man's pocket. "It's half a bill. Gotta be Mister 20."

Carl groaned. "Just great. Now *you're* calling our killer by that name."

"Hey, it's kinda catchy."

Carl spotted the ME and walked over to question him. "Got anything that Officer Abrahams hasn't told me?" he asked.

"For starters, our victim wasn't killed here. Like the others though, he was stabbed in the chest. Would have been plenty of blood loss, but not on the ground here in the park. The ground shows he was dragged here from a spot along the road."

"Might mean he knew his killer. The wounds – are they exactly like those from the other two murders?"

The ME drew the sheet back. "Can't say for sure, but likely. They were made with a short, serrated blade. My guess, a hunting knife – possibly a Kay-Bar Mule or a Spyderco Pacific Salt. You could check out all the stores in the city that sell those things, but I doubt you'd get very far. Knife could have been bought years ago, maybe not even in this area."

✳✳✳

"Officer Abrahams was right," Carl later relayed to the captain. "We found the victim's car about a mile from where the body was dumped. Behind it was a trail of brake fluid that ran back to Madison Avenue. Had our people look under the vehicle. The brake line looked as though it had been cut. I drove back to the area behind the insurance office where Greene usually parked. Found some drops of a liquid that I'm sure are brake fluid.

"My take is that the killer cut into the brake line shortly before Greene left for the day. Followed him until the brakes started acting up and he was forced to pull to the side of the road. Our killer pretended to be a Good Samaritan, offering him a ride. Then drove into the park, stopped for some reason – possibly suggesting car problems of his own. When Greene got out of the car and there was no one in sight, the killer stabbed him. Didn't want the body to be spotted right away, so he dragged him back out of sight. Found blood beside the drive about 50 feet from where we found the body."

"That's a lot of supposition," DeAngelo responded.

"This guy's smart. Definitely isn't killing at random. Probably stalks his future victims for days, studying their habits, places they go, and times."

"Any prints or DNA?"

"No, it's been cold. Killer probably wore gloves. No surveillance cameras at the place where Greene worked either. We checked what few cameras there are at the park, but came up with nothing. Something did hit me, though."

"What?"

"The dates of the murders. The first was on January 20th. The second on February 9th. This one was on the 29th. Each was 20 days apart from the previous one. Another connection."

"This latest victim, what do we know about him? Anything connecting him to that number or the other victims?"

"He lives on the southeast side, 10 miles from the park. I spoke to the wife. She says she knows nothing about him being connected to that number. I'm thinking it might be connected to his job. Been in insurance for 30 years. He opened his current office in 2012. I've made an appointment tomorrow to speak with those who work with him on a daily basis. One was out of town when I dropped by. The other was across town at the time. Hopefully, they'll help me come up with something. We have to find this guy and put him away. If I'm right, he'll strike again in 19 days."

***

"Thank you for the taking time to speak with me," Carl began the next day. Seated with him at the table were two of the victim's coworkers and the secretary.

"Keenan was more than just our boss," Ray Fuller said. "He was our friend."

"Both Ray and I have been with him since he opened the office eight years ago in 2012," Mark Ross added.

"Did he have any enemies? Any unhappy clients? Someone not satisfied with how a case was handled?"

"Keenan was well-liked," Mark commented.

June Crane, the secretary, raised a small hand. "There have been situations where a client was not pleased at some decisions that were made. I can count at least half-a-dozen just off the cuff. Several involved a threat made against Mr. Greene."

"May I go through your records?" Carl asked. "If you need a warrant, I can get one."

Fuller shook his head. "Sorry, no can do. Our files are confidential."

Carl set a card on the desk. "Well, if you think of something, that might help me, give me a ring."

Frustrated, he left the office. Getting a court order to review the files would be a long, drawn-out process. By the time he got a look at them, he feared a new murder might be committed.

A full day later, his phone at headquarters rang.

"Detective Harewood. What can I do for you?"

A female voice on the line spoke in a low voice. He recognized it as the Crane woman. "I have something for you. But you mustn't tell anyone. I'd lose my job if the others in the office found out."

He arranged to meet her in a quiet restaurant just off I-65. He spotted her at a far table and sat down across from her. She slid a folder across to him.

"I remembered a case from over a year ago. I pulled it up and made this copy."

He began to read. The case involved a health insurance policy for Ann Davidson. On December 20, 2018, she had been involved in a traffic accident that had occurred on I-465 just past the 56th Street exit during morning rush hour traffic. According to the police report, a woman had been driving in front of her when another driver recklessly cut over into her lane just in front.

The woman hit the brakes, but when she did so, one of her rear tires flew off the car into the path of Davidson's Volkswagen bug. Davidson lost control, crossed two lanes of traffic, and struck a retainer wall. She was rushed to a local hospital in critical condition with a brain injury. The hospital placed her on life support.

The problem with the agency occurred weeks later on January 9th, when the insurance company told the husband that it could no longer pay for life support.

"I remember the husband began screaming at Mr. Greene, calling him a murderer," Crane remembered. "Said he would sue the agency."

Carl stared at the name of the woman whose vehicle had lost the wheel and felt a chill rush down his back.

It was Alice Williams. He'd found the connection!

That still left Nicholson. What connection did he have to the accident? Carl gave his word not to reveal where he'd obtained the information on the accident and returned to the school to again question Nicholson's coworkers on the night shift.

"You told me he had only been with the school since August. Did he ever mention where he'd worked before that?" he asked.

Benny Lincoln, who'd been out sick when Carl had first questioned the custodial staff weeks before, spoke up. "He told me he used to work at some car place."

"A dealership?"

Benny shook his head, "No, one of those businesses that do lube jobs and repair work — one of them Speedy Lube places you see all over town."

"Any particular one he might have put down on his job application?"

"Sorry, no."

Carl thanked them for their time and returned to his office. He pulled up the addresses and phone numbers for Speedy Lubes around the Circle City and then began a series of phone calls to see if someone named Will Nicholson had ever worked there. There were 18 in the metropolitan area. He got lucky on the 17th.

"Yeah, we employed Billy for a couple of years," the man on the line replied.

"What can you tell me about him?"

"Sorry, call coming in. Let me put you on hold."

After two minutes listening to Motley Crue's "Shout at the Devil," Carl hung up and decided to speak to the manager in person. He drove to the Speedy Lube in Lawrence. The manager was in the middle of supervising an oil change but agreed to talk with him.

"On the phone you said that Mr. Nicholson worked for you, correct?"

"Sure thing. With us for three years. "

"Is there a reason why he quit the job?"

"Didn't quit. Had to fire him."

Carl felt a rush of excitement surge through him, already anticipating what the manager was about to tell him.

"Got careless while working on a car and caused an accident over on 465. He fixed a flat on some woman's car. However, when he put the tire back on, he didn't tighten the lug nuts. Out on the highway, the tire came off, hit another woman's car and caused an accident. Heard the other lady died. We all liked Billy, but after all that, I had to let him go."

⁎⁎

As he got into his car, Carl took out his notebook and read through the insurance report. The beneficiary was Ann's husband, Russell Davidson. Their address was North Bradley on the city's eastside.

The home was a '30s era, single-story cottage. Carl walked up to the door and rang the doorbell. When no one came, he knocked. After waiting several minutes, he returned to his car and looked up where Davidson was employed. He was an assistant manager at a buffet restaurant in the Irvington neighborhood. Carl drove to the place, parked in the lot, and went inside.

The restaurant could have doubled for the dining room of a retirement home. Not a single customer in the place looked under 60. When he inquired about Davidson he was directed to the assistant manager currently on duty.

"Russ isn't here today. He's taken some time off. His wife died a year ago, and he's had a hard time dealing with it. You might try his home."

"Already been there."

"Russ isn't in any trouble, is he? He's a nice guy. Took Ann's death pretty bad."

"I just need to speak with him. That's all."

Undaunted, Carl returned to the home on North Bradley. To his surprise, the light was now on inside. He again rang the bell. Moments later, an elderly woman stepped to the door. "May I help you?"

"Forgive me, but this *is* where Mr. Davidson lives, correct?"

"Yes, that's right."

"Are you related to Mr. Davidson?"

The woman tittered. "Good heavens no. I'm Mrs. Duncan. I live next door. I told Russell I'd come by and feed Leopold for him while he's at work."

Carl raised an eyebrow. "Leopold?"

The woman stepped back to allow him a look at a copper-colored tabby seated on the carpet, giving him an admonishing glare.

Carl identified himself and asked when she thought Davidson might be home.

"Really can't stay. The restaurant where he works keeps him all hours. Didn't used to be that way. Since Ann died — Ann was his wife — he's just thrown himself into his work. But it's cold. Come on inside. Russ won't mind. Such a nice man."

Carl felt awkward about entering but agreed to get out of the cold.

"Would you like some coffee, detective? There's a pot on the stove. Only take a minute to heat it up."

"No, thank you. I really shouldn't stay with Mr. Davidson not here. Tell me, has he spoken much about his wife's death?"

"Yes, poor man. He's a nice person, but he has so much anger inside. He blames Ann's death on everyone connected with the accident — the woman who drove the car, the man who worked on the tire, the insurance company, and the man who cut in front of the other driver that started it all."

Carl blinked. If Davidson were the killer, who would be the next victim? He thanked her for her time and returned to his office. He spoke with the officer who had done the accident report.

"Did you find out who cut in front of Alice Williams at the time of the accident?"

Officer Reid shook his head. "Haven't the foggiest. Probably was caught on the highway camera, but that was a year ago. No way of checking that now."

Feeling like he'd again run up against a stone wall, Carl thanked him. However, as Reid reached the door, he turned back.

"Y'know there's someone you should speak to. When the accident happened, there was a guy who wanted to look at the camera footage for that morning."

"The accident victim's husband?"

"No, one of those reporters who does blogs on things happening around the city."

"His last name wouldn't be Gleason, would it?"

"That's the one!"

A neuron fired up in Carl's brain. Gleason saw himself as the city's "crusader for justice," or so he claimed in numerous blogs. If no one was ever punished for the death of the Davidson woman, might Gleason have crossed the line and been hunting down those responsible for what had happened? In recent months, his blog had received severe criticism from some of the higher-ups in both the department and city government.

At home that evening, Carl sat down and began pulling up some of Gleason's blogs for the past year. The man had a tremendous ego and never minced words. Carl stopped when he found a blog dating back to early December of 2019. In it, Gleason had raged over a lack of justice when a police investigation failed to find enough proof to tie a teenager to the hit-and-run death of a woman, aged 71.

The police of this city are dull-witted oafs who couldn't find evidence to put this killer behind bars even if footage of the accident was filmed and shown to them on an IMAX screen. What this city needs is an avenging angel who isn't afraid to make these criminals accountable, to strike out when the law cannot.

Did Gleason see himself as the avenging angel he wrote about? Carl decided to ask Gleason in person.

✳✳✳

"What do you mean, *where was I* when those three murders occurred?" Gleason ranted. "Are the buffoons in your department so befuddled at failing to solve this case that you'll accuse anyone in the city? Or are you trying to pin these murders on someone you think is a pain in your side, because he writes the truth about the department's inefficiency?"

47

"You haven't answered my question, Mr. Gleason."

Gleason sat down at his computer. "I keep a record of what I do each day and how many hours I put into my blogs. Read me the dates, and I'll tell you where I was at the time of the murders."

Carl read off the dates, one at a time, for him.

"January 20th, the day Alice Williams died."

Gleason's hands moved over his keyboard. "My wife and I attended a concert up in Carmel with another couple. Not only can they vouch for me, but I still have the program and tickets."

"February 9th, the Nicholson murder."

Again, Gleason pulled up the date. "My wife's mother was being operated on in Cleveland. We flew up to be with her mother at the hospital. If you check with the hotel where we stayed, they'll verify my story."

"What about the early evening of the 29th? You shouldn't need to look that up. It was only a few days ago."

"Ah, there you have me, detective. I *was* on the south side of the city. Oh, wait, would having dinner with a city councilman and his family at a restaurant on South Madison count as an alibi?"

"You know I'll check your statements out, right?"

"By all means. Make yourself and the department look even more ridiculous and inefficient than you already appear. Now is there anything else, or should I purchase some rope so you can convince the public to lynch me?"

Carl remembered why Gleason's name had come up in the first place.

"You covered a story about a traffic accident on I-465 that claimed a woman's life a year ago, did you not?"

"Yeah, I covered the story. I paid off someone in INDOT to let me see the footage of what happened. Saw the whole thing, read the idiot's license plate, and looked him up. Funny you should mention it. Although I didn't name the guy in my blog, I did say I knew who he was. Then a month ago, the woman's husband came to me. Said he wanted to sue the man and wanted his name."

"And you gave it to him?"

"Sure, the jerk caused the accident. I figured the husband deserved a chance to get back at him. Sue his ass off."

"Could I have the man's name?"

"Only if you give me first crack at reporting on the Mister 20 case when you solve it."

"It's a deal."

"Aaron Atkins. He works in securities."

✳✳✳

Half-an-hour later, Carl turned off 82nd Street in Castleton into a drive that led to a series of office buildings. As he drove back to the second building on the left, he spotted a man sitting in a Grand Am, car engine running, eyes fixed on a second-floor window. Carl glanced at the BMV photo of Davidson he'd taped to the dashboard. As he drove past the parked car, he looked at the driver and then back at the face on his tablet. They were one and the same.

He called in for backup and waited. Davidson remained in the car. Carl had figured that the killer spent some time getting to know his victim before each attack. Was he stalking Atkins in preparation for the next attack? That would be some 17 days away. Davidson dropped his hand over the gearshift. Was he about to pull away?

Carl decided he couldn't let that happen, even if backup had not yet arrived. He nonchalantly got out of the car and approached Davidson's Pontiac Grand Am. The driver was so fixed on the second-floor window, that he didn't notice Carl until he was standing beside the passenger side's door. Carl tapped the window.

Davidson glanced over with surprise.

Carl flashed his badge. "Mr. Davidson?"

Davidson's eyes went wide. He shifted gears and tore off, nearly hitting the detective in an effort to get away. Carl rushed back to his car and turned on his siren. He wanted to kick himself for approaching Davidson before backup arrived. By now, the killer had a head start.

Davidson cut around cars, stopped for the traffic light, shot in front of a car pulling onto 82nd, and went on the ramp for the highway. Carl followed siren blaring. He radioed in quickly, detailing the route of pursuit. The Grand Am raced through traffic nearly colliding with other cars as he tried to distance himself from his pursuer.

Davidson started to leave the highway at the first exit. When he heard the shrill of a siren ahead of him, he whipped left to try and return to I-465 and nearly collided with an SUV. A firetruck raced above on 56th headed for an emergency. He lost control and crashed against the underpass before the car came to a stop. Carl pulled up behind the wreck and approached the wreckage. Davidson's head was slumped against the driver's side window, blood smeared against the glass. The detective opened the door and felt for a pulse. There was none.

Lying on the passenger seat was the one piece of evidence that left no doubt in Carl's mind that Davidson was the killer.

It was the torn half of a twenty-dollar bill. Carl was certain it would match up with the half left on Greene's body.

In the distance was the sound of approaching sirens — this time the backup he'd called for. Carl looked past the cement barrier along the access way back to I-465 and shook his head in disbelief.

He'd carefully read the accident report from the previous year where the exact location was listed. Carl leaned against the barrier and estimated distance. Ironically, this crash was only a matter of some 20 feet from where Ann Davidson's fatal accident had taken place that morning.

Twenty feet. Exactly.

I See What You're Sayin'

by Ross Carley

I was just moseying along living my life when my brother Jeb up and died. His real name's Jebediah, but his friends call him Jeb. Called.

We was like peas in a pod growing up, but we moved a ways apart, so I didn't get to see him much. I'm real sorry he ain't around to talk to no more.

My name's Benjamin, by the way. Friends call me Benny.

Jeb lived just a hop, skip, and jump south of Nashville, in Beauregard. State of Tennessee.

So I had to take off work to go to his funeral. I don't like noise, and I had to ride a noisy bus with a bunch of jabbering people.

Actually, I don't like hardly any kinds of sounds. The reason being that I have something called synesthesia.

According to my doc, there's a bunch of different kinds of synesthesia, but they all got one thing alike. One of your senses, say vision, gets activated, and another sense, say taste, gets going at the same time. That's right, you taste what you see.

Some other folks with it feel what they smell. Certain odors cause 'em to feel particular shapes or textures. One smell might feel like smooth grapes, another one like burlap.

I ain't kidding you. And I ain't crazy. My doc says that around two out of every 100 of all people in the U S of A have some kind of synesthesia. Our brains are just wired different than most folks. Nothing wrong with us. Not a thing!

51

I got the kind called chromesthesia. I see colors whenever I hear something. At exactly the same time.

I can't control it. It's completely automatic. And it means that I only listen to a few kinds of music. The kinds that look nice to me.

My ma, God rest her soul, had something kind of similar. She saw colors anytime she read writing. Like numbers and words, especially days of the week. For instance, the number two and Wednesday both looked red to her.

My doc says that lots of times, synesthesia is passed on from parents to kids. Inherited.

That's probably why my sis Mandy has it, too. Sort of like mine except she sees shapes with sounds. Jagged lines, stars, squares and like that. She likes to joke that me and her have 20/20 hearing.

You'll see me walking down the street wearing earbuds plugged into the little AM-FM transistor radio in my shirt pocket. It's mostly off and I'm not listening to anything, just trying to make everything quiet. I hate listening to talk, especially politicians yakking about that Nixon Watergate mess.

I have a job where I don't *have* to listen to anything. Well – except my boss the mortician, who calls himself funeral director. I'm an embalmer. It's quiet work. Suits me.

Don't have to listen to the corpses. Except once in a great while one of 'em belches gas. The sound usually looks green to me.

Well, anyway, at least I didn't have to embalm Jeb.

But I got this rush job just before I had to catch my bus. I tried to clean up, but I was in a hurry and guess I must've still smelled like my work – people didn't want to sit next to me. Embalming fluid stinks to high heaven. Main reason is the formaldehyde. It's got a strong odor like pickles, but worse. Burns my nose and makes me dizzy if I'm not right careful.

Got to Beauregard. Cheapest motel I could find was the SnorZ Inn, a couple of steps down from Motel 6. Not down the block, down in fancy.

It was fine with me. First thing I done was take a shower so's I wouldn't smell bad. There was a packet of soap and little bottle of shampoo. Just for me. Free.

Only thing was, the walls was thin. Real thin. I could hear every dad-gummed word anybody said either side of me. They was so thin, I figured the folks on my right could hear them what was on my left.

Jeb's funeral was the next morning and I'd told my sis Mandy that I'd be a pallbearer. And once Jeb was in the ground, she wanted help with the pot luck dinner, making sure folks' sweet tea was filled up and such. Then cleaning up afterwards.

I pretty much go to bed and get up with the sun, so I put my earbuds in and was pulling the sheet over me about eight or a tad after when the gawldangdest ruckus you ever heard lit off right outside my room. I peeked out the curtain. It was too dark to see much.

About all I could make out was that there was three of 'em. My earbuds kept me from seeing much color. Mainly dark blobs here and there.

I was hoping they'd take their arguing somewhere else, and they did. Right into the room next to me.

I took out my earbuds. Might as well hear and see the show. Noise and colors.

There was generally at least two of 'em, sometimes all three, talking or yelling at the same time. I saw clouds and strips of colors, and black and brown shapes. Stuff all mixed up, boiling like. When just one of 'em was jabbering I could see the colors that went with his voice.

They was squabbling about money. Two of 'em said the third one owed 'em money. Something about a lottery ticket.

Third one says there was no damn way he owed 'em anything because *he'd* picked the winning numbers himself and he'd only *borrowed* the hundred bucks. First two claiming it wasn't no damn loan and they was equal partners.

It went on like that for a while, then one of 'em got mad and stomped out the door, slamming it so hard the picture on my wall got knocked cattywampus.

When only two of 'em was left, things simmered down a tad, but the third guy wasn't giving in none.

That's when I heard it. Sounded like one of them M80 giant firecrackers, except it had a sharper sound. Bursts of color with it. I figured it was a gunshot, and I must've been right, because I heard the second guy beat it out of the room and it got real quiet.

I snuck outside and peeked in their door since it was open. A guy was laying on the floor, looked dead as a doornail, blood all over.

I figured that as thin as them walls was, everyone in the whole doggone place must've heard the shot, but, being the upstanding citizen I am, I skedaddled to the office and reported it to the man in charge, who called the police.

The police siren was a jumble of oranges and reds, with yellow flashes jumping everywhere. Two policemen was in the car. Well, one man policeman and one woman policeman. The man policeman started stringing yellow tape.

The woman policeman was real nice and all interested in who I was and why I was in town. I told her about Jeb and how I had important stuff I had to do at his funeral and the dinner after.

I was glad I'd took a shower.

She wanted to know did I recognize any of 'em that was arguing, and I said nope, never had the pleasure of being introduced. Didn't never see their faces except for the dead guy.

The nice woman policeman asked did they call each other by their names, and I said nope, they just called each other bad names. Then she asked was there anything else I heard that might help the police.

I thought about it for a minute, then told her about the argument over the lottery ticket. And that one of 'em had stomped out before the other one shot the third one.

Now we're getting somewhere, she said, and that they could probably get a good idea who the guys was from lottery ticket payments hereabouts.

I told you she was nice. Well, she was right smart, too. And her voice was pretty, all yellow and dark pink, with just a tad of light green on the edges.

I said that if she needed help figuring who done it, I might could help. She looked at me weird and asked me again whether I'd seen the guys' faces. I said nope, just their backs in the dark. So you wouldn't recognize 'em. I said not by looking at 'em. If not by looking then how she wanted to know. By looking at the sound of their voices I said.

She looked at me like I was nutty as a fruitcake, got up, and started backing slow-like toward the door. I tried to explain about my synesthesia, but I could tell she still thought I was looney tunes.

Finally, I scribbled my doc's name and phone number on a pad beside the phone. I pushed the paper into her hand and told her, just call him. He'll explain it all.

She shook her head like she had water in her ears and slid out the door sideways.

I figured that'd be the last I'd see of her.

I was wrong.

Next thing I know, there's a banging on my door. In comes the man policeman holding handcuffs, the woman policeman following right behind.

He says that I have to come to the station with them. Either I come peaceful like or he'll put the cuffs on me. His voice was greens and oranges with black spikes. I didn't like it none.

The woman policeman says now, now, Billy Bob, he don't look like no criminal. So he puts the cuffs away and grabs me by the arm. Next thing I know he's pushing my head down while he shoves me into their patrol car. I was shaking and sweating, afraid that something bad was going to happen to me. Maybe they thought I killed the guy.

In a little tiny room that smelled like sweat and pee they asked me questions. The same ones over and over. After a while, they went away. Told me to stay put. I was really scared that I was gonna be locked up overnight. I was real glad I'd had a shower at the SnorZ Inn.

About a half-hour later that seemed like a whole lot longer they come back in with a piece of paper they call a statement that they wanted me to sign. They even brought me a cup of coffee. It smelled like burned toast and tasted like it too, so I just put it down after one sip.

The statement was a list of their questions and my answers. No big problem. I signed it. Then the man policeman said I was free to go. Go where? I wanted to know.

The woman policeman said she'd take me back to the motel. But the one called Billy Bob says that I can't leave town until they give me permission. I ask how I'm supposed to work. They just look at me and don't say anything. Maybe they still thought I could've killed him.

The woman policeman dropped me at my room. Said she'd call my doc in the morning, but I could tell she didn't believe me about my synesthesia.

This time I was *real* sure I'd never see her again.

I was dead wrong.

***

Come morning, I splashed on Old Spice, dressed up in my Sunday-go-to-meetin' duds and carried my suitcase to the little church where Jeb's funeral was at. I was planning to catch a bus after the potluck meal. I had to change buses in Nashville, but I'd still get home by seven, and could take food along so I wouldn't worry none about eating supper.

Darned if that nice woman policeman didn't come in and set herself in the back row just before the start of the service. She was respectful and all, and stood up when we all stood, and sat down when we all sat. Even knew the words to the Lord's Prayer.

I couldn't rightly see her voice, pinks and all, because it was all mixed up with the others. Truth be told, I wanted out of there. The voice sounds muddled together appeared awful, and the organ music was a mishmash of purples and reds, with white flashes all around. Part of the time, it reminded me a little of the police car siren. I wished I didn't have to look at it, but there wasn't nothing I could do.

After us pallbearers wheeled Jeb's coffin to the hearse, I felt this hand on my shoulder. It was the woman policeman. She wanted to know if she could talk with me after the dinner.

I'd never had a woman say she wanted to talk with me before. So of course I said yep, just please don't bother me if I'm doing something for my sis Mandy. She nodded all solemn like and said she'd watch out and not do that. I was glad I smelled good.

Mandy walked up wiping her hands on her apron and invited the woman policeman to eat with us. Said there was plenty of food. The woman policeman smiled and said that was real nice and maybe she'd have just a little.

The dinner was something to see. And better to eat. Fried chicken, yams, cornpone, and squash, and green beans out of someone's garden. And sweet tater pie for dessert.

After we was done cleaning up, the woman policeman got me and my sis over in a corner. She thanked Mandy real nice for the food. Said her name was

Coreen. That's a pretty name. Goes with the colors I see when she talks.

Then she surprised us. Told us she'd talked with my doc, and that he'd explained my synesthesia. Mandy's, too.

Coreen said could I come to the police station. I said sure.

Mandy looked at Coreen and asked if it was OK if she come along. Coreen said it was just me had witnessed stuff they was interested in, but you betcha Mandy, long as you keep quiet you can watch.

Coreen asked me to tell her a few things I'd heard 'em say, over there in the next room at the motel. I told her I weren't sure of the exact words, but I remembered a few things they shouted at each other. Some of it was them bad words and bad names they called each other that I'd told her before.

Then I remembered that I was supposed to catch a bus. Coreen says don't worry. They'd pay for me to stay over another night, and put me up at the Motel 6, a darn sight fancier than the SnorZ Inn. Mandy had driven her own self from where she lived about a half-hour away, so she'd make it home after the meeting with the police by bedtime.

In a room at the station with a big mirror on one wall, Coreen explained why they wanted to see if I could help. The policeman she'd called Billy Bob wasn't there, and I was glad of that, but another nice man policeman was. He even shook my hand.

They'd nabbed both guys that had been in the room with the feller that got killed. Each one of them was saying that the other one done shot the guy. So they was gonna do a special kind of lineup.

I said I seen them lineups on TV, but since I never seen neither of 'em, I couldn't recognize which one killed the fella.

Coreen says not that kind of lineup. We're gonna have six guys in a line all right but they'll be behind a tarp, so's we can't see 'em. We can only hear 'em.

Well. It dawns on me. Of course, I can tell the difference. My synesthesia can help the police solve a murder.

While we was waiting for the lineup to start, Coreen asks me if my synesthesia was always there, and if it'd ever changed. I tell her yep and nope. It's always there and hasn't changed since I first remember having it as a little kid. But I pay attention to it more sometimes.

I tell her it's sorta like standing in front of Dooley's Bakery looking in the window at the items for sale. I see the cakes and cookies behind the glass and at the same time see my reflection in the window. The baked goods and my reflection are always there together, and I always can see both, but sometimes I notice one more than the other. And I can switch my attention between them any time I like.

So they get these six guys behind a tarp, and have 'em say the same kind of words I heard the two fellers shout. Bad words and all.

Heck darn, it was easy for me to tell which one was in the room when the feller was shot. I picked him out right fast.

But Coreen was cagey. I told you she was smart. She mixed them guys up in a different order behind the tarp, and we done it all again. Trying to bumfuzzle me.

Still weren't no problem. Easy as pie, I picked out the guy again.

After doing this three more times she was satisfied. Said I'd ID'd the same fella every single time.

Then she asked me what she called the 64-buck question, which was how I done it. "Easy", I said. "The killer was the only one with indigo in his voice."

Mandy nodded. She said that she didn't know who the killer was, but the guy showing indigo to me was the only one with five points on the shape of his voice.

Coreen nodded. Must've made sense to her. She thanked me and had me sign a paper saying what I done.

About a week later, a newspaper reporter from Beauregard calls the mortuary and asks for me. I don't have a phone over at my place. Never hardly needed one, and if I did I just used the one upstairs in the hall.

Anyway, the paper guy says that the killer had gone and confessed so he wouldn't get executed, and that everyone is talking about me in Beauregard, and could he come talk to me and take my picture.

I says sure, so next day, there he is. And there's a guy from a TV station with him.

Next thing I know, I'm in Beauregard getting a reward for what I done. Mandy met me there. Said she was right proud.

The town was paying for another hotel night, so I asked Coreen if she'd have dinner with me. She said yep. We talked about police business mainly. Her voice looked real pretty.

Maybe she'll be my girlfriend and come visit me sometime. If she does, I'm gonna make sure I smell good.

The Ear Witness

by Elizabeth Perona

S ometimes I work a murder case in the dark.
  Don't dismiss that statement when you learn I work nights. It wasn't meant to be a joke. Sometimes you just have to close your eyes and *listen* to the evidence. Justice is not the only thing that's blind. Sometimes it's the witness.

On this particular night I was responding to a run with two victims, both dead. Sergeant Bryan Ingram had discovered the bodies on patrol. He'd requested two things: help in locking down the scene and for Homicide — that's me — to come investigate.

I pulled up and got a wave from Officer Kylie Evans who moved the crime scene tape aside to let me in. I don't kid myself that she recognized me personally as Don Talbot, 15-year homicide detective for the Indianapolis Metropolitan Police Department. What she recognized was the old Crown Vic I was driving. Patrol officers get new Chargers. We detectives get the hand-me-downs. Admin says we'll get new Ford Interceptors soon. Not holding my breath.

The bodies lay just under the old railroad bridge that ran above Capitol Avenue between Louisiana and South Streets. The bridge was built in the early 1900s so it has an historic feel. Capitol Avenue, the one-way four-lane street which runs under it, has wide sidewalks on either side and concrete supports that run down the center, dividing the four lanes into two.

The night was rainy. I parked under the bridge where it was dry. I pulled my rain jacket out and shrugged it on before I closed the door. I figured I'd be out in the weather eventually.

"What's going on?" I asked Evans. She didn't answer but pointed me toward Ingram, who was hustling toward the Crown Vic. As I said, they all know who drives this kind of car.

"Two drug dealers apparently killed each other," he said. "Chef Gillespie and Nervy Highsmith. I would have recognized their faces even if I hadn't found identification on them. They've been at each other for months."

"Any eyewitnesses?"

"No *eye*witnesses," he answered smugly, "but we have a witness." He pointed toward the center of the east sidewalk where a person sat up against a door at the top of a semi-circle of bricked steps. "His name is George Ferrand," Ingram continued, "and he's blind."

The thought that it was George made me smile. "I know him," I said, which seemed to unsettle Ingram. "I'll take it from here."

The passageway under the bridge is one of the best lit in the downtown area. You wouldn't think this would be the place someone would choose to commit a murder, but murders tend to be crimes of passion, not planned. Or sometimes murderers are too cocky for their own good.

Ferrand was a musician who parked himself regularly on downtown sidewalks to play his guitar and busk for tips. I knew him from nights my wife and I passed him on Washington Street where he set up. We usually crossed his path as we headed for the symphony on Monument Circle after dinner at one of the restaurants around the Circle Center mall. We never failed to stop and appreciate his music and throw money into his hat. He was a very talented guy.

As I strode up to George, I passed close enough to the bodies to smell urine, reminding me that the dead have no control over bladders. I sighed, disgusted that the acrid smell had become so familiar it's almost expected. Beyond the crime scene tape I could hear the chatter of news media sending reports back to their home stations. No one was talking to the press until our Public Information Officer arrived, and I guessed she was not in a hurry to get there.

"George, I'm Detective Talbot from Homicide. You're a bit out of the way from your regular spot, aren't you?"

"Mr. Talbot," he said with a smile, his white teeth resplendent against his ebony skin. "I recognize your voice. Always appreciate your patronage."

"Any particular reason you're here?"

"The rain," he said. "I was gettin' back home but got tired a bein' wet, so I stopped here. The rain never let up."

I didn't know much about George other than his talent, but it heartened me to hear him say he was headed home. I hadn't been sure he had one, since you never know about street musicians. "So you just plopped down here? How long ago was that?"

"Captain!" Ingram called to me. "We have the lights set up now."

"I'll be back, George."

"Not goin' anywhere," he replied. "Sergeant Ingram'd pin this on me if he could. He was surprised to find me here and must've asked a million questions. I think if I wasn't blind he'd of handcuffed me and hauled me in."

I gave a non-committal response and made my way over to where the light truck Ingram had ordered now lit up the scene. The bodies lay about 10 feet from each other, stiff, lifeless hands gripping handguns pointed toward each other. I knew Ingram was adept at managing crime scenes. We'd had far too many of them this year. Though it was only early May, we were already on pace for a record number of murder cases.

"Tell me what you found when you got here," I said, knowing he was a talker and I wouldn't have to pull any details out of him.

"I was driving through on patrol when I saw two people down on the sidewalk here," he said. "Thought at first they might be homeless people settled down for the night. We discourage that, of course, but it was rainy. I wouldn't have thought much about it except they weren't up against the wall where most choose to sleep. I was already past them before I thought of it, though, so I drove around the block and came back to check it out. From the blood, I was pretty sure they were dead, but I pulled on gloves to determine there was no pulse whatsoever. I called in the 10-0, asked for Homicide, and then checked for ID, which I found in their wallets."

Another cop might have called for an ambulance, given the same circumstances, but Ingram was always sure of himself. He celebrated his self-assurance like Donald Trump celebrated the spotlight.

I nodded. "Chef Gillespie and Nervy Highsmith, you said earlier." Both were minor stars in the drug world. I recognized their names. "Do I recall correctly that the chef was famous for cooking his own meth?"

"Yes," Ingram said, clearly unhappy I'd interrupted. Before he could start again, I said, "And that Highsmith was diversifying into opioids?"

"We don't know that for sure, but we've heard it on the street." He eyed me. "Rumors had them poaching each other's clients. Can I continue?"

There was a tinge of sarcasm in that remark, but not so much that I felt a huge obligation to respond in kind. I simply nodded my head, and he continued rambling as I examined the scene before me.

Ingram went on to review every detail of what he'd found and done. His limbs moved constantly while he talked. I listened for the critical details when he got around to them. Mostly I watched him dance. *Maybe he drinks too much coffee*, I thought.

I knelt down to see how many casings were on the ground. Three. When he paused to take a breath, I asked, "So, do we know what they were doing here?"

"No indication," he said.

"What about George Ferrand? Do you think he's a suspect?"

"Not a suspect, but it doesn't sound like he'll be able to confirm much about what went down since he's blind. He didn't indicate he'd heard much of anything during my initial questioning."

He sounded dismissive of George because of his eyesight. Just because he didn't have 20/20 vision didn't mean he wasn't a credible witness.

I got up from my crouched position and felt the rain slow to a drizzle. Crime Lab arrived and one of their specialists began bagging what he could find. One of my fellow detectives also arrived to assist. I put him to work taking photos and video. I was just about to get back to George when the specialist growled. "Someone's been going through these pockets." We both looked at Ingram.

"Only to find the wallet so I could make an ID," he said, at once defiant. "Are you accusing me of something?"

"Only in being overly zealous in searching the victim. Did you turn this front pocket inside out?" His gloved hand pointed to Gillespie's front jeans pocket. It didn't look fully turned inside out to me, just partially. Still, I could understand the tech's irritation.

But Ingram was even more irritated. "No, of course not. The wallet was in the back pocket. Why would I do that?"

The tech didn't answer but continued to work. "And the vic doesn't have a cell phone either. In fact, neither do. That's unusual."

Evans, who was listening in, nodded. "Especially for drug dealers."

Ingram was taken aback. "What do you mean there aren't any cell phones?"

The evidence tech shrugged. "Just what I said."

"I'm sure there were cell phones when I found their wallets."

"Was one of them in the front pocket? Cause I don't see it in there now."

Ingram glared at him for a moment as though deciding what to say. In the end, he sputtered and stomped off.

I wondered about all that. A front pocket would have been a good guess for a cell phone, especially if the wallet was in the back pocket. But so far as we knew, Ingram was the only other person to touch the vic. Pondering that, I returned to the steps where I'd left Ferrand.

"So George," I said, sitting down next to his guitar case and red-tipped cane. "As a witness, I'll need to take you downtown for an interview. Want to make sure we have your testimony recorded properly. You have nothing to worry about. If you let us know who in your family to contact, we'll advise them as well."

"I'm not under arrest? You don't suspect me of shootin' anybody, right?"

"No."

"Then okay."

"Before we leave the crime scene, though, can you tell me a little about what happened?" I asked. "Start with when you got here."

"I was on Washington Street doing my gig when the rain started. It was slow at first, but so were the tips. Not too many people downtown with nothing happenin' at Lucas Oil or the Convention Center. So I called it a night and packed up. I hurried to Capitol, then came this way home."

"What time was that?"

"I didn't check the time till I got under cover here. It was maybe ten. The rain was coming down like needles, so I planned to wait it out."

"In this particular spot, or were you somewhere else and then moved here?"

"Not on the steps, but to the left here close to the wall. I laid down and pretended to be asleep. Most people won't bother you. They think you're homeless and don't have any money on you."

"How long had you been here before you realized something going on?"

"A long time. Over an hour. I have a watch that talks to me, but I wasn't checkin' it in case someone else was here."

"Please continue."

"There was shufflin', definitely footsteps. Someone came in from the north but didn't get too close to where I was. I guessed it was someone like me tryin' to get out of the rain. Then I heard a second set of footsteps. They stopped quick. Then there were two shots, one right after the other. You better believe I kept real still after that. A short time later, maybe a couple of minutes after my ears recovered from the gunshots, I heard moaning."

"One voice or two?"

"One."

"And then?"

"Then I heard another set of footsteps coming from the same direction," he said, pointing toward the entrance. "There was a third shot, and my ears rang like crazy. I might have heard footsteps going away, but I couldn't swear to it. After maybe a minute I noticed the rain slowed, so I knew my ears recovered. A few cars came and went. One of them slowed way down, but it passed out of the tunnel without stopping. I was glad because you never know. Anyway, just after that I heard more feet shuffling from that direction again. Whoever it was seemed to be in a hurry. I hugged the wall, hoping to make myself as small as I could. The shuffling stopped, and there was a pause. And that was when I heard a cell phone buzz. An A flat, in fact."

"What?"

"It was A flat, like in the musical note. I have perfect pitch. I can hear that sort of thing."

"Okay. Then what?"

"Then I heard running footsteps heading out. Later, a car pulled up. Must've been Sergeant Ingram's squad car because I heard him call in the report."

"Had you called in the shots?"

"No. When you're blind, you want to make sure you're safe before you give yourself away. I was pretty sure no one knew I was on this side of the steps."

"But you have a cell phone?"

"Uh-huh. It buzzes in F."

I couldn't decide if he intended it to be funny or not, but I suppressed a laugh.

Before I could ask another question, Evans appeared again. Kylie was a young, recent recruit who'd trained under Ingram. I didn't know her well, but she was five-foot-five, a solid 150 pounds, and carried herself like she would kick ass first and ask questions later. I'd think twice before I'd take her on, and I'm six-foot and 180 pounds. She had dark hair, a long sharp nose, and eyes that were darker than brown but not quite black. They were inquisitive eyes, and I could tell she had some questions.

"Yes?" I asked.

"We found one of the vic's cars. Highsmith's. It was parked on Meridian." Meridian was two streets to the east. "Do you think you'll be able to get a search warrant? We've looked inside and all we can tell is that he was a fan of White Castle. Tons of crumpled bags in the back seat."

"Sure. Hopefully the Crime Lab'll find the cell phone in there." I stopped because she was giving me a look my wife often does, like I'm dense.

"Why didn't *either* of them have a cell phone on them?" she asked. "Seems weird to me that both the vics were running around in the dark on a rainy night and neither one had his cell phone."

George interrupted. "If neither had their cell phones, then whose buzzed in A flat?"

Evans looked puzzled. "A flat?"

"A bit of a story," I told her. I turned to George. "You're absolutely certain that was something you heard?"

"I'm blind, not deaf," he snapped.

"We need to get you to the station so we can record your testimony. I'll find someone to take you there and get you comfortable. I should be along in a little while."

***

Back at the station George gave essentially the same testimony. I sent him home in a squad car along with the breakfast I'd brought from home. He might have been naturally skinny, but I interpreted it as being malnourished. I figured I could get breakfast later. Maxine's Chicken and Waffles sounded good.

I ran the search warrant for the car by the screening prosecutor and he signed off on it. Then we caught a lucky break on the search warrant. One of the judges was at a late-night party and still awake. He okayed it immediately, and we were in business. I took the crime lab tech with me to preserve the chain-of-custody for handling evidence. We found nothing of value. I called Ingram and Evans into my office to discuss the results because I wanted to see their reactions.

"The car was clean," I said.

Ingram twitched. "Clean?" The irritation in his voice was palpable.

"As far as evidence was concerned," I said. "It was far from clean otherwise. What kind of mold grows on week-old White Castle sliders?"

No one even chuckled. So much for my jokes.

Ingram glowered at me. "So no cell phone?"

I shook my head. "No cell phone."

Evans, by contrast, seemed undeterred. "We're still scouring the area around the crime scene, but so far nothing. We're hoping daylight will help."

I glanced outside my office window. Dawn was going to be a fiery event. Red-tinged clouds from last night's rain hung over the horizon. The yellow glow of the unseen sun was building under them. "Should be daylight soon," I said. "Any luck finding Gillespie's car?"

Ingram answered. "Gillespie's car was in his driveway at home. He didn't live that far from the crime scene. Presumably he walked. With the car being on private property, it's taking longer to get a warrant."

I nodded. "Keep at it," I said. So far, I hadn't told anyone about the mysterious cell phone that George claimed to have heard. Although Evans had been around when George referenced the A flat vibration of the phone, I believed that she didn't understand his reference. Nor had I explained it to her.

Ingram and Evans left and I took a phone call from the coroner's office. The coroner was getting ready to autopsy the two bodies and asked if I could get away. It's never my favorite thing, but it's my duty. Plus, our coroner is a riot.

This is true: Pat Thorndike is a coroner when he's on duty but does stand-up comedy when he's not. Most people have this vision of coroners as dour sorts with personality defects who prefer the dead to the living and keep solitary lives. Pat lives with his girlfriend, a concierge at the JW Marriott downtown, and the only solitary thing I know he does is write jokes. While he can cut open the dead, he's even better at skewering the living.

When I got to the coroner's office, he was already gowned and gloved. "Ready to go, amigo?" he said, holding a scalpel. "We're going to do Gillespie first. His girlfriend de jour was in an hour ago identifying the body. Know what she said? "That's him. The Chef." She wasn't a bit sorry. "When you cut him open, if you find any ephedrine stuffed up his ass, it's mine. I know he was hiding it from me. I could never figure out where. I got asthma, you know."

Pat was really good at voices and I couldn't help but laugh.

"I've got to find a way to work this into my routine," he said.

He went to work on the body. "Got any ideas who shot who first?" I asked him after a while. I'd seen the three casings and had my own ideas, but it's the prosecutor who makes the presumptive observations on what kills our victims.

"From what I saw at the crime scene, Highsmith either got the jump on Gillespie or was a bad shot or maybe both. I'm guessing from the thick glasses that Highsmith had really bad eyesight, probably from drug use. So, if he shot first and Gillespie was able to shoot back, then Gillespie made a darn good shot for being so critically wounded. His single shot killed Highsmith. Not right away, apparently, because Highsmith got in a second shot."

But a little later he was frowning at the bodies. His frown intensified as he ran a couple of scenarios through his head. I could tell he was acting it out by the way he twisted his body.

"The angle of the bodies, at least one of them, doesn't make sense."

"How so?" I asked.

He waved me toward the body. I wasn't fond of seeing human flesh laid out like a spatchcocked chicken, but I wasn't squeamish about it either. At least not after so many years as a detective. Using his scalpel as a pointer, he went through his analysis.

"This bullet here, the one that only wounded Gillespie, went in at an angle like this perpendicular to his stance. But this second one, which went through his heart and killed him, went in at a different, higher angle. You might think, well, Gillespie was on the ground by then, which is likely, but at this angle Highsmith would been standing nearly over him when the second shot went into his heart."

"Couldn't Highsmith have staggered over to where Gillespie was to make that shot?"

"I haven't opened up Highsmith yet, but the sketch of the scene shows the two bodies several yards apart. I don't think Highsmith could have staggered back, and more importantly, why would he?"

"Then you're saying someone else made the kill shot instead of Highsmith?"

"I'm not saying anything, you know that. I'm just saying there's a discrepancy between the way it looks like it went down versus the way it likely went down. I'll know more when I get to Highsmith."

Highsmith's autopsy was no more enlightening. Thorndike confirmed the angle of the first two bullets was consistent with the distances of the bodies and the presumption that Highsmith caught Gillespie unaware and so both had been standing at the time. Highsmith's wound, however, was clearly enough to kill him and even if not right away, it would have put him on the ground. The angle of the kill shot, in our coroner's opinion, should have been very different. I thanked Thorndike for his time.

Back in my office, I received a second visit from Officer Evans. This time she had a man with her who vaguely resembled Highsmith. He was maybe an inch or two taller than she was. "This is Mr. Derek Highsmith, the brother of the deceased Mr. Highsmith," she said. "When I went out to notify him of his brother's death, he told me some things I thought you should hear. I asked him if he would come with me to meet with the investigating detective and he agreed."

He was wiry and very nervous. The way he danced as he talked reminded me of Sergeant Ingram. Highsmith had a squeaky voice and bad grammar. I couldn't decide which one irritated me most.

"So we ain't gone to sleep that night cause we was up partyin' with some hoes he hired and my brother gets a call. He says he ain't goin' out in the rain for nobody, but then he shuts up and hears somethin' he likes. He smiles, seems okay. Thanks the guy. Nate grabs his pistol, throws some bucks at the bitches, says he'll be back once he fries the Chef. On the way out he's mutterin' out loud, says if someone ain't comin' through this time he's goin' let some freakin' cop know Ingram's dirty. It ain't the first time I hear him say the name Ingram. He complains so often I think maybe Ingram's the name of some new kind of dope he's dealin'. Anyway, he shoves the blower in his pocket and leaves."

He stopped talking so I guessed he was done but he couldn't stop the dancing. I wondered if he were on speed.

"You're sure he said Ingram?"

"As sure as my brother hires hoes with big tits." He gave a smile revealing teeth that needed a dentist like my teenage son's room needed a housekeeper.

"And you say he had his cell phone in his back pocket?" I asked him, looking for confirmation. "What does it look like?"

"Yeah," Highsmith said, "back pocket. It's an iPhone X with a putrid green case and cracked screen. But what about, ya know, the dirty cop? You gonna do somethin'?"

It's not unusual for a member of the drug dealing community to accuse the police of having dirty cops on the payroll, so I took that part of his testimony with a grain of salt.

We recorded Mr. Highsmith's brief comments. Before Evans took him back home, she asked him to wait outside my office and closed the door. "Did you think Sergeant Ingram was acting a little hinky last night at the crime scene?"

"He was pretty animated, but he's always that way."

"You only see him when there's a homicide. He's only that way sometimes. Like he can turn it on and off. Like," she paused before she spat out the last part, "like maybe he's taking meth."

"You know this for sure or you're speculating? You understand either one carries serious consequences for him if you're right and you if you're wrong?"

She hesitated again but nodded. "I've seen it."

Now it was my turn to pause. I took a deep breath. Ingram was ambitious. Meth turns brain functions up. His jitteriness and his constant talking could be symptoms. "Why haven't you come forward before?"

"It's only been recently I discovered it. And I still may not have, but now we have Derek Highsmith on record that his brother said a cop named Ingram is dirty. Let me toss a question at you. Where would be the safest place in a search area to hide two cell phones you don't want anyone to find until you had a chance to dispose of them?"

I hated to go there, that Ingram was definitely dirty. But Evans had been his partner, if only for training purposes. For the moment I played along. "A place no one would search," I said.

"Like his car." she said.

I didn't say any more and neither did she. She spun on her heels and left my office. I could swear she was hurrying out before she smiled smugly, which I detected anyway. Maybe she was confident I would check it out. If so, she was right.

*＊＊

I contacted Internal Affairs and they agreed to investigate. Like me, they didn't like where this was going but between Derek Highsmith's testimony and Evans's accusation there was sufficient cause to check it out.

I called Ingram's supervisor and asked a few questions about Ingram and Evans. She asked why. I said I noticed tension between the two and wanted to be sure it wasn't getting in the way of my investigation. "Do they get along?" I asked.

"It's an uneasy relationship. Evans is self-righteous. She's so by-the-book that she won't accept free coffee at McDonald's even when we have "Coffee with a Cop" neighborhood meetings where it's free for everyone. I think that clashed with Ingram's more cavalier attitude. He took advantage of anything that came his way."

Internal Affairs found the cell phones in the car. One of them matched the description we'd been given by Highsmith's brother, so we were off and running. After a number of steps and some nice work by the Cyber Crimes unit, we had the information we needed.

So how had this played out? I listened to George Ferrand's testimony a couple of times before trying to piece it together. I closed my eyes and tried to hear it like George had.

The two dealers had met, possibly arranged by Ingram, and possibly one, Highsmith, was given some information so he could get the drop on Gillespie. But he only wounded Gillespie, who was able to shoot back. That accounted for the first two bullets. George heard a moan, so one of them must've still been alive. But was it Highsmith, who was then somehow able to stagger over to Gillespie and fire a second shot into his heart? And then stagger away to die with his gun pointing at Gillespie? Our coroner didn't think so.

George had reported a significant time lapse before Ingram arrived to call in the 10-0. He'd also reported hearing footsteps and the A flat phone buzzing. It was possible that Ingram, having arranged this, left his car parked and department-issued phone in it, walked over to the scene, removed the dead men's cell phones, stored them in his car, and then drove back. That would account for the actions we had on record for his car and cell phone that night. And the cell phone George had heard could have been Ingram's personal phone. But why would Ingram have said he thought the dead men had cell phones on them? If Ingram had removed the cell phones because they had his personal phone number on them, wouldn't he have been clever enough to replace them with burner cell phones purchased with cash? Maybe he hadn't thought to buy burner cell phones. Or maybe his statement was meant to throw off any suspicion. Or maybe it was something altogether different.

Later that afternoon I had a meeting. I invited Evans, Ingram, Thorndike, a Crime Lab specialist, and our witness George Ferrand. My office wasn't big enough to hold everyone, so I'd reserved the conference room. It had a table we could all sit at, a white board we could draw on, and was soundproof. I didn't want anything getting out in the event I was wrong on all counts. We filed in and sat down. Evans, Ingram, and Thorndike were on one side of the table; me, Crime Lab, and George on the other. I don't think George had a clue why I'd insisted he come.

"I wanted to review the details of the case," I said by way of introduction. "I think we may be close to a solution. First, I'd like to ask Pat to present his findings."

Thorndike was serious this time, which I'd expected him to be. He knew he was presenting a situation that had negative repercussions. He drew a diagram on the white board showing the approximate positions of the vics and how he would have expected the weapons to be fired, and what that would have meant as far as trajectories of the bullets were concerned. Then he drew a separate schematic of Gillespie's body and where the bullets had entered. He showed the discrepancy.

"Given the angle of the second bullet," I said, "where do you think Highsmith's gun was fired from?"

Thorndike wiped the back of his hand across his brow like he was wiping away sweat. I don't know if he was that nervous to be sweating like that, but I guess I would understand if he did. He drew an 'x' right next to Gillespie's body, up in the air. "It was angled down into the heart. The shooter had to be right above him."

The room fell silent. It was that way for maybe fifteen seconds before Ingram spoke. "Highsmith must've staggered back," he said, shrugging as though that were the obvious solution.

"But wouldn't there have been a blood trail?" Evans asked. She directed the question toward Thorndike, but I was pretty sure it was aimed at Ingram.

"Absolutely," Thorndike said. "But that was if he even could have made it back that far. I'm not sure he could have. And Highsmith's wound is consistent with the original distances of the two bodies."

Silence again.

"And then we have the testimony of our witness, George Ferrand," I said. "George advises us that shortly after the third shot was fired, he heard a cell phone buzz. In A flat."

Ingram snorted. "A flat?"

I nodded. "George has perfect pitch. He can determine the note at which a cell phone buzzes."

"So, if we had the vics' cell phones, we would know which one buzzed?" Ingram asked. He didn't wait for confirmation from me. "But we don't have the cell phones. None were found on the bodies."

"We found them," I said.

Ingram got indignant. "Where?"

"Let's hold off on that for right now."

I directed the specialist to slip on a pair of gloves and pull the cell phones out of the bag. "I'm going to ask Crime Lab to call the cell phones now," I said. "George, if you please, I'd like to you tell me what note you hear."

Gillespie's was the first. I directed the specialist to let it buzz several times before hanging up. "George?" I asked.

"F," he said. "Same as mine."

"Interesting," I said. Highsmith's phone was next. "C sharp," George said.

Again, there was silence. I gave it a few seconds, but since no one rose to the occasion, I continued. "So, even if the phones were found on the scene, George would have heard a different buzz tone. Now I'm going to call a number we found on both phones."

Ingram's personal phone buzzed. "A flat," George said.

"That doesn't prove anything," Ingram said, way too fast. "You yourself said that other cell phones can produce that sound."

"I did. And it doesn't conclusively prove my point. But nonetheless, your number was found on those phones. Is it possible you called these two dealers who hated each other, arranged for them to unknowingly meet under the bridge that night, knowing they would try to kill each other?"

"Why would I do that?"

"Because you're addicted to meth," Evans snorted. "I've known about it since you trained me. And one of them was threatening to turn you in if you didn't stop squeezing him for meth."

Ingram became nearly hysterical. He pointed to the specialist. "Your buddy on the scene lied then. He said there were no phones on the bodies, and there were. But those couldn't have been their real phones."

"Why not?" I asked.

He realized at that moment we were doing a criminal investigation on him and he shut up immediately.

Ingram's supervisor, whom I'd stationed outside the door, led him down to the interview room where he would be questioned and likely read his rights. "Thank you, everyone," I said, standing up. "George, if you'll wait outside, I'll make sure you get home okay. Officer Evans, could you stay for a moment or two?"

She seemed surprised and remained standing as they left. I closed the door behind them. "How did you know the cell phones were in his car?"

"It seemed logical. He would have wanted them to be gone. His number would be found in both phones. He couldn't afford that happening."

"But I believe him when he accused the Crime Lab specialist of lying about cell phones not being on the drug dealers. Ingram knew something was wrong at the crime scene. He was puzzled because he had planted burner cell phones on the victims when he took their real phones. That's why he was angry about the front pocket being turned inside out, which he was accused of. That's where he'd placed one of the 'other' cell phones he just mentioned. Plus, George's testimony has the cell phone buzzing at the time Ingram would have been scurrying back to his car after shooting Gillespie, clutching the cell phones he'd taken off the dealers. If that's true, then who removed the burners he planted?

"Here's what I think. You figured out Ingram's plan, but you didn't actually see him kill Gillespie, or you could have testified to it. You came in too late for that. So you had to do something else. By getting rid of the burner cells — and confident he'd stashed the real ones in his car — you could lead us to find enough evidence to convict him. But justice hasn't been served, because you tampered with the evidence."

She didn't say anything. She just turned and walked out. I guess she thought I couldn't back up my accusation. I followed her until we were both in George's presence.

"Hold up, Evans," I said. She stopped. I called a number on my phone. Her personal phone. It buzzed. "George?" I said.

"A flat," he responded.

One Dead Politico

by D.B. Reddick

"Come in, Charley," Jerry Zimmerman said as he stood up and walked around the corner of his humongous oak desk to shake my hand. He had a firm handshake.

"Have a seat," he said, turning and pointing at the two seats in front of his desk. "Make yourself at home."

Jerry Zimmerman, or the Z-man as he prefers to be called, owns WZMN-AM, News Talk Radio 790. The station occupies a four-story building on Monument Circle in downtown Indianapolis. For the past two years, I've hosted the station's all-night talk show. It airs Sunday through Friday from midnight to 5 a.m.

"Your assistant called an hour ago and said you needed to see me right away," I said, settling into one of Z-man's plush leather chairs. "She woke me up out of a sound sleep."

"Oh, that girl," Z-man said, with a lecherous grin on his face. "Jenny's definitely not the sharpest knife in the drawer, but, oh my, she has the longest, most shapely legs I've ever seen. I can't bring myself to fire her. Besides, her daddy's company is one of our biggest advertisers."

"So, what do you want to talk about?" I said, wringing my hands.

I hope Z-man isn't planning to fire me. It's a common occurrence in radio.

"Oh, yeah," said the Z-man, returning from his brief visit to Fantasyland. "I wanted to tell you about Willie."

I figured Z-man was referring to Wild Willie Wilson, the station's early morning guy for the past 40 forty years. I listened to him on my way to school in the eighties. Willie was already a successful shock jock when Howard Stern was still in diapers.

"Willie walked in yesterday. Told me he was quitting on Friday. Something about meeting a senorita from El Paso on an Internet dating site. I can't believe it. Willie's close to eighty and yet he still chases women half his age. He's my hero."

"Have you found his replacement?" I asked.

"As a matter of fact," Z-man said, sitting straight up in his chair. "I'm looking at him. Charley, you're an experienced broadcaster. You can handle any callers that come your way. Look at all those crazy insomniacs who call you each night."

"What about Zach?" I asked. He produces my overnight show.

"No problem," Z-man replied. "I've already promised my sister, Peggy, that Zach can produce your morning show. She's ecstatic. Zach's been dating a girl he met at IUPUI. My sister can't wait for him to graduate this year, get married, and make her some grandbabies."

"What will happen in my time slot?"

"I'm replacing you with a syndicated paranormal talk show. The show's host sounds like a real kook, but the trade press says he has decent ratings in other markets around the country. So, what do you say, Charley?"

I smiled. "Meet your new morning guy."

***

Two weeks into my new gig, the Z-man dropped by our main, street-level studio one morning to see how things were going.

"I'm still adjusting to working mornings and the people who gawk at us through the large studio window," I said. "It's a little weird after doing my all-night show from the second-floor studio. Aside from that, too many callers still want to talk about Willie instead of what's happening in the world."

"I'm not surprised," the Z-man replied. "When I bought the station five years ago, I wanted to fire Willie, but the consultants I hired said I couldn't.

They claimed Willie was a local legend. Our listeners would revolt. Thank goodness, he's run off to Texas to find the latest love of his life. You're already doing a better job than he did. You'll bring us better ratings."

"Thanks for the vote of confidence, Z-man."

"No problem, but that's not why I dropped by," he said. "Everyone is already excited about the upcoming 2020 elections. We'll need to grab our share of campaign advertising dollars. I want you to begin interviewing candidates on your show. Zach can set up the interviews and prepare background information on each candidate. What do you think?"

"Sounds like a plan," I replied.

"I'll also have Zach accidentally drop any more calls from the Willie worshippers."

***

The next day, Zach stopped by after our show ended.

"Charley, I've set up a candidate interview for tomorrow."

"With whom?"

"His name is William Jackson. So far, he's the only announced Democratic candidate for governor."

"Never heard of him."

"Me neither. He's a lawyer and the mayor of Tell City, a small community along the Ohio River. When I called him yesterday, he jumped at the chance to be interviewed. He said Indianapolis voters needed to learn more about him."

"He sounds a little too eager."

"I agree," Zach replied. "One of my political science professors recently told me that Jackson might be the only Democrat to run against our incumbent Republican governor."

"Okay, I guess. What could go wrong?"

***

William Jackson showed up Tuesday at 5:45 a.m. but Sam Parker, our overly vigilant security guard, wouldn't allow him inside the station until Zach vouched for him.

Zach introduced me to Jackson after they wandered into the main studio. He didn't look like your typical politico. He wasn't middle-aged or overweight. Instead, he reminded me of that South Bend mayor running for president. They could be twins. Unfortunately, I had to excuse myself to read the six o'clock news.

The Z-man instituted some new procedures after Willie's departure. My show now starts at six instead of five, but I must read the news at six and seven, plus update local traffic and weather conditions every 15 minutes. Fred Jones, our long-time news director, doesn't report to work now until seven-thirty. Go figure.

Most folks call during the first two hours of my show when they're either already at work or on their way. One caller said he'd received a tweet that Wild Willie tied the knot in Texas for the fifth time.

"I just want everyone to know about Willie's nuptials," the caller said. "I seen a picture of the bride. She's a real hottie."

Enough about Willie, already!

Once Fred Jones finished reading the News At Eight, I turned to Jackson and introduced him to my listeners. He'd been sitting patiently at our studio table for nearly two hours, sipping his coffee.

"Good morning, Mr. Jackson," I said. "Let's start by having you tell us something about yourself."

I love to start interviews with that softball question. Most guests will spend several minutes describing their backgrounds and accomplishments. He wasn't any different. That gave me time to read his background information.

When he finished talking about himself, he said he had a big announcement to make for improving public schools.

"Hold on, sir," I said. "I need to update the traffic and weather conditions so my listeners can get to work on time."

As I finished my updates, I looked up and noticed that Jackson was struggling to catch his breath. I quickly motioned to Zach in the adjoining control room to run a commercial.

"Are you okay?" I asked.

He glanced at me with panic in his eyes before he fell forward and struck his head on the studio table.

80

"Zach, call 911," I shouted. "And run some more commercials."

Within five minutes, two paramedics had arrived to check on Jackson.

While they examined him, I ran next door to the control room and used the microphone there to update the traffic and weather reports once again.

What should I tell my listeners about what happened?

I wasn't sure what to say next, but one of my callers came to my rescue. He'd found Willie's Facebook page and wanted to tell everyone how to send their best wishes to him.

It took the paramedics less than three minutes to place Jackson on a gurney and wheel him out of the main studio.

"How is he?" I asked as I held the studio door open for the paramedics.

"His pulse is faint," one of them replied.

***

It was approaching 9:30 a.m. when I parked my '94 Cadillac Deville in front of my Queen Anne cottage on East Vermont Street. As I walked to my front door, my next-door neighbor, Matthew Malone, bounded out of his two-story Italianate home and blocked my path.

"What happened to William Jackson?" he demanded to know. "I could tell from the tone of your voice that something was terribly wrong with him."

"I was hoping my listeners believed me when I said he left early for another appointment."

"Now, Charley," Matthew said, looking at me with his hands on his hips. "You can't fool me. Remember, I've been in the theater for years. I can detect the slightest change in a person's voice. Especially if that person is lying."

"You got me then," I said before telling him how Jackson passed out at the studio table.

"I hope he's okay," Matthew said when I finished. "Listen, I'd love to stay and chat, but I'm starting a new job today."

"Where are you working this week?"

"I'm a volunteer with the LGBTQ campaign committee for Pete Buttigieg."

***

81

"Mornin', Charley," Sam Parker said as I approached his security desk at five-thirty on Wednesday morning. "A couple of guys are waiting for you in the main studio."

"Who are they?" I asked.

"Cops."

Why would two cops be waiting for me? Unless, they're here to arrest me for not paying my outstanding parking tickets. I thought I'd done that last month.

"Good morning, gentlemen," I said, entering the studio a minute later.

"Are you, Charley O'Brien?" the taller of the two officers asked. "I'm Detective Thomas Murphy and this is my partner, Marty Smithers. We'd like to ask you a few questions about William Jackson."

I motioned for the detectives to sit down at the studio table while I checked to see if the news staff had left me some stories to read at six o'clock.

"Guys, I'm on the air in fifteen minutes," I said, looking at my watch. "What do you want to know about him?"

"We understand he passed out while you interviewed him yesterday," Murphy said.

"That's correct," I said before explaining how he showed up early on Tuesday and waited patiently in the studio until I began the interview after the eight o'clock news. "My first question was about his background. He then fell headfirst on the studio table while explaining one of his policy proposals. I have everything on tape."

"Was Jackson acting unusual in any way before he collapsed?"

"No, he seemed perfectly normal to me."

"Did you offer him any coffee or food before you interviewed him?"

"No, he brought his own cup of coffee with him," I said. "Listen, detectives, I really need to end this interview. Can you come back later? I'm on the air in a few minutes."

"Okay, Mr. O'Brien," Murphy said, handing me a business card. "If we have more questions, we'll be in touch."

"How is Jackson doing?" I asked.

"Haven't you heard?" Murphy replied. "He died at Westside Hospital last night."

***

I was still gathering my notes after the show ended when my cell phone started vibrating. Caller ID said it was Matthew.

"Charley, did you hear about Jackson?" he asked, then added, "Of course, you did. Silly me. I heard your news director read a story about him at eight o'clock."

"Yeah, a couple of detectives stopped by before my show began this morning. I had the feeling they thought I had something to do with him falling over in the studio. That was before they told me he died."

"Someone from the Buttigieg campaign headquarters called around 10 last night to tell me about Jackson dying. I didn't want to wake you with the news," Matthew said. "I know you go to bed so early."

"I appreciate that, but why are you calling?"

"Charley, we need to talk more about Jackson," Matthew said. "I'm worried that the cops may be looking at you as a suspect in his death. You can't let that happen, or you're liable to lose your job. Why don't you drop by on your way home and I'll fix breakfast for you? I have a quiche cooking in the oven."

Quiche? I'm not really a quiche kind of guy.

***

I'll admit that Matthew's quiche was very tasty. But I'm not ready for a steady diet of sharp cheddar cheese and spinach with my eggs in the morning. And, where was the bacon?

"So, what more do we need to know about Jackson?" I asked, leaning back on a kitchen chair, sipping my second cup of coffee.

"Let me tell you what I've found out about him so far," Matthew said, picking up my dirty dishes. "I've been calling folks all morning. He checked into the Downtowner Hotel on West Ohio on Monday night and ordered room service. A double cheeseburger, medium well, and fries."

"How do you know all that?"

"My friend, Deion, is the night desk clerk."

83

"Anything else?"

"Jackson checked out at 5:30 a.m. but not before buying a vanilla mocha venti at the coffee stand in the hotel lobby. Then he walked to WZMN a block away."

"Deion, again?"

"No, Cindy. She's the day desk clerk. I really don't know her, but I'm good friends with her life partner, Cheryl."

"Is that it?"

"Of course not, Charley," Matthew said, a big smile on his face. "I called Raymond. He's a certified nursing assistant at Westside Hospital. We dated a few times in high school. He was reluctant at first to help me. Something about HIPPA rules and regulations. After I promised to take him to dinner next Tuesday, he talked hypothetically about how a patient could arrive at the emergency room and never regain consciousness. Raymond also said it was possible that Jackson could have been poisoned. In cases like this, Raymond said, a toxicology test will be ordered, but the results won't be known for a few days."

"What should we do in the meantime?" I asked. "Z-man will be furious when he returns today from his business meeting in New York. He's liable to think I had something to do with his death. Z-man hates controversies involving the radio station."

"Don't worry, Charley, I have a plan."

Turns out Matthew's plan was to meet Deion for lunch at the Potbelly Sandwich Shop on Monument Circle near WZMN. Before we left, I rushed home to feed Bruce. He's the 20-pound Maine Coon cat I inherited along with my house after my uncle died two years ago. Bruce likes to rip up things if he isn't fed on time.

Deion was already waiting for us at the Potbelly. He was the tall, skinny guy wearing an expensive pair of diamond earrings. He gave Matthew a huge hug. I shook his hand.

"Heard anything more about the guy that stayed with us on Monday night?" Deion asked after we ordered. A roast beef sandwich for me. Turkey clubs for Matthew and Deion.

As we sat enjoying our sandwiches, Matthew told Deion how his friend at Westside Hospital thought Jackson may have been poisoned, although he didn't know for sure.

"Notice anything unusual about him when he checked in?" I asked Deion.

"No, he told me that he would be interviewed on WZMN Tuesday morning. He ordered room service and asked for a four-thirty wake-up call."

"Did you see him the next morning?" I asked.

"No, my shift was over. It ends at five. Cindy would have checked him out," Deion said.

"Matthew, maybe we should go see Cindy."

***

Cindy was standing behind the front desk at the Downtowner when Matthew and I approached her fifteen minutes later. She was a petite woman with purple hair and a nose ring.

"Hi, Cindy," Matthew said, introducing us. "Remember checking out a guy on Tuesday morning named William Jackson?"

"Is he the guy who collapsed and died while being interviewed on WZMN?" she asked. "I read all about it in the *Indianapolis Star* this morning."

"They didn't get it exactly right," I said. "He collapsed during my show, but he died later at the hospital."

Z-man will go crazy once he reads the Star's story.

Matthew asked Cindy if she noticed anything unusual about Jackson when he checked out.

"No, the guy was in a terrific mood," she said. "Said he was looking forward to his interview on WZMN. Told me I should listen. He then took a swig of the vanilla mocha venti he bought from the coffee stand before he left the hotel."

Matthew and I looked at each other. "Of course, the coffee stand."

We walked over to it and asked to speak with the manager.

A minute later, a guy named Joe Sloan approached us.

"Hi there. What can I do for you?" he asked.

"Anything unusual happen at your coffee stand on Tuesday morning?" I asked.

85

"Are you talking about my confrontation with Carlos Ruiz? I suppose he's hired the two of you and wants to sue me for firing him."

"Oh, no sir, we're not attorneys," Matthew said. "However, I happen to live with an attorney and I once played Atticus Finch in a high school production of To Kill A Mockingbird."

"What happened with Ruiz?" I asked, reassuring Sloan again that we weren't attorneys.

"I showed up at five on Tuesday to talk to Carlos again," Sloan began. "I'd received several complaints that he was taking too long to fill orders and causing our hotel guests to miss their shuttle to the airport. I told Carlos that he needed to shape up or I'd have to let him go.'

"How did he react?" Matthew asked.

"He told me I didn't have the balls to fire him."

"What did you say?" I asked.

"Watch me. I then walked into my office and called another employee to come into work as soon as possible."

"What happened next?" Matthew said.

"When I came out of my office, I spotted a strange plastic container on the floor behind our counter. I picked it up and saw that it was a container of antifreeze."

"Omigod, Charley," Matthew screeched. "I watched something like this recently on a true crime show. This guy killed his wife by pouring antifreeze into her coffee mug."

I reached into my wallet and pulled out Detective Thomas Wilson's business card and called him. A half-hour later, he and his partner, Marty Smithers, showed up at the Downtowner. The coffee stand manager repeated his story about confronting Carlos Ruiz.

When Sloan finished, Wilson turned and thanked us for our help. "We can take it from here," he said. "You don't need to interfere in this crime anymore."

The detectives turned and followed Sloan to his office to obtain a home address for Ruiz.

"That was rude," Matthew said.

"I agree," I replied. "The cops wouldn't have known about Ruiz if it wasn't for us. Sloan certainly didn't bother to call them."

"What should we do now?" Matthew asked.

I looked at my watch. "Z-man should be back from his business trip. He'll be looking for me. Let's go tell him what happened to William Jackson."

***

When the Z-man's assistant saw us walk in, she said, "Oh, Charley, I'm so glad you showed up. Mr. Zimmerman has been looking for you."

"I'm here," I replied.

"Want me to stay out here?" Matthew asked.

"No, come with me," I said. "I'll introduce you to Z-man. Besides, there's safety in numbers."

A minute later, Matthew and I walked into Z-man's office. I introduced him to Matthew before we sat down.

"What the hell is going on?" Z-man shouted, waving a copy of the *Indianapolis Star* in the air.

"As usual, the *Star* didn't get it entirely right," I said. "Thanks to Matthew and his friends, we tracked down Jackson's whereabouts from the time he showed up in Indy on Monday night until he passed out on my show Tuesday morning. Today, we learned he may have been poisoned by a disgruntled coffee stand employee who apparently poured antifreeze into a coffee container."

"That's horrible," Z-man said. "Did anyone besides Jackson drink the coffee?"

"No, the manager quickly realized what may have happened. He fired the employee on the spot and emptied the contents in the container before anyone else could drink it. To his knowledge, nobody else has turned up sick or dead."

"That's quite a story," Z-man said when I finished. "And, that was some enterprising work on your part Matthew. Ever thought of a career in radio?"

"You mean like being a deejay?" Matthew asked. "I love spinning records at my house parties."

As he spoke, Matthew's cell phone rang. He looked at the screen before saying, "Sorry, but I really need to take this call."

After Matthew left, the Z-man leaned forward in his chair and told me he'd received a call of his own a few minutes before we showed up.

"Who was it?" I asked.

"Wild Willie Wilson."

"Let me guess," I said. "Willie wants his old job back."

"Yeah, his little senorita dumped him once Willie showed up in person and he wasn't the guy in the photo he had emailed her."

"But a caller told me the other day that Willie got married."

"Fake news."

"So, what did you tell Willie?"

"Told him you were my new morning guy. If he wanted a job, he could apply for a part-time position on weekends."

"What did he say?"

"Even I'm too embarrassed to repeat his response."

Just then, Matthew returned to Z-man's office.

"Now, Z-man, what were you saying about a career in radio?" he asked.

Before Z-man could respond, I asked Matthew what was so important about his call that he had to leave. "That was unprofessional on your part."

"Sorry, Charley, but it was Raymond. He wanted to know if we could have dinner on Tuesday night. I swear he still has a crush on me. This is awful. What if Daniel finds out and thinks I'm carrying on with Raymond again? Have I made a huge mistake? This could ruin my life."

"Matthew, stop it," I said. "Daniel will understand. Now, did Raymond say anything more?

"No, silly. He can't talk about him. Remember, HIPPA rules and regulations?"

Z-man chimed in.

"Like I tried to say before, Matthew showed some real enterprise in tracking down what happened to Jackson. He could be a good addition to our news staff. Go introduce him to Fred, tell him about your adventures and have Fred write a story for the five o'clock newscast."

As we rode the elevator to the second-floor newsroom, Matthew suddenly broke into his best broadcast voice. "What do you think, Charley? This is

Matthew Malone reporting for News Talk Radio 790. Or, this is Matthew John Malone for News Talk Radio 790. Or, better yet, how about this is M.J. Malone reporting."

And, Z-man thought his problems ended when Wild Willie left the station.

In the Deepest Darkness

by Stephen Terrell

*Whoever curses his father or mother,
his lamp will be extinguished in the deepest darkness.*
– Proverbs 20:20

Six Weeks After the Darkness

The priest's words echoed off the high ceilings and cavernous emptiness of the church. The first sunlight streaming through stained glass images of the Stations of the Cross dimly lit pale statues of the saints. A dozen worshipers for morning mass were scattered in the first few pews, but Hanna Carmichael sat in the back row, an observer rather than a participant.

Without moving his head, the priest subtly slid a small scrap of paper resting on the pulpit to where he could see it. He recited the words familiar to the faithful, which he had long ago memorized. "Remember our brother . . . " The priest looked at the slip of paper. "David Edward Carmichael, who has fallen asleep in the peace of your Christ, and all the dead, whose faith you alone have known. Admit them to rejoice in the light of your face."

A few moments later, as Hanna unlocked her car, she heard footsteps hurrying behind her. She turned to see the priest scurrying toward her. "Wait please," he said, through quick breaths that showed exertion.

Hanna stood, keys still in hand, but did not say anything.

The priest, his graying black hair and paunch showing the onset of middle age, stopped just beyond an arm's length away. "I need to get more exercise," he said breathlessly. After a few seconds he continued. "I'm Father Glenn. I saw you in the back of the sanctuary. Did you know the person we remembered in the service?"

"He was my son," Hanna said in a matter-of-fact tone. "My cousin Ellen attends your church and requested you say the mass for David."

"Ellen McQueen?"

"Yes."

"Oh, I know Ellen well. She's such a wonderful woman."

"She is. She made the request. Today would have been David's seventeenth birthday."

Father Glen dropped his eyes and shook his head somberly. "I am truly sorry for your loss. A loss at such a tender age is always an unspeakable tragedy. I hope the service today provided you with some comfort."

"I know you mean well, Father. I know it helped Ellen. She's very strong in her faith. She believed she was doing something for David . . . something for me. I'm grateful for that. But when you lose a son, it's all pretty hollow."

"The loss of a young person is always a challenge to our faith. But we must find comfort in the Lord's promises of comfort and life everlasting. What happened to your son, if you don't mind me asking?"

"David was killed in a school shooting."

Father Glenn's hand covered his mouth which was open in shock. "That's just, well, just horrific. When did this happen?"

Hanna's eyes shifted and stared off into the distance. After a long silence, she said, "Six weeks ago."

***

Three Years Before the Darkness

Alan Carmichael slammed his cup on the breakfast nook, coffee sloshing over the edge of his cup. "You coddle that boy too much. He needs a firm hand."

Hanna's eyes flashed with rage. "Taking your belt to him is not being firm. Why don't you take out your handcuffs and put them on David like one of the thugs you're arresting?"

" I've never hit that boy with a belt," Alan said, ratcheting his voice down several decibels. "I know I said I'd take a belt to him. That's what my mom did to me. But I've never done it."

"You just can't yell and threaten him. He's your son." Hanna walked to the toaster and put two slices of bread in the slot. She turned back toward her husband, taking a deep breath. "I know he's difficult. But he's a good kid at heart. You just have to be patient."

"I try, but it's frustrating. I spend time with him. I take him out to the shooting range with me. He likes that well enough, but I think only because it's like those damned video games he's always playing. He just spends so damned much time up in his room playing those video games. I tried to take him bowling or to a football game, but he's not interested. He doesn't have any friends. I just don't know what's wrong with him."

✲

Three Weeks Before the Darkness

David banged hard into his school locker, then lost his balance. As he fell, his books and papers flew from his hands and scattered across the hallway.

"Better watch where you're going, David," the tallest boy said, his voice in a sing-song taunt. "You have trouble walking?"

The three boys who crashed into him laughed uncontrollably as they walked on down the hall.

David clenched his jaw tight, grinding his teeth to fight back tears and rage. He leaned to begin gathering his things.

"Assholes." It was a soft voice behind him. David turned and saw Constance Griffith standing behind him. Even with a look of disgust on her face, Constance was gorgeous. She kneeled next to David and picked up his scattered papers as David retrieved his books. "Those guys are such immature dicks," she said. Constance handed the papers to David. "Hope you're not late to your next class." With that, she headed down the hallway in the same direction the boys had gone.

✳✳✳

Eight Days Before the Darkness

David sat by himself at a table for four in the school cafeteria. His daily routine of two sloppy joes, fries, and a Snickers Bar he brought from home were nearly gone. Sounds and laughter of lunchtime conversations reverberated around the room, but David was oblivious. He had been planning this moment for the past two weeks. He kept his eyes fixed across the room where Constance Griffith sat with three other girls. They were carrying on an animated conversation punctuated by fits of laughter.

David looked at the scrawled note he had pulled from his pocket. "Do this now!" David took a deep breath, then stood. In tentative steps he walked across the room to where Constance and her friends were sitting.

"Hi Constance," he said, his voice barely croaking out the words. No one turned to notice him. He tried again. This time the words boomed out as if he were yelling across the entire cafeteria.

Constance jumped a bit, then turned. Her faced showed puzzlement and perhaps a little concern. But she recognized David and gave a polite smile. "Why hi, David. I didn't see you there. Can I do something for you?"

David had rehearsed his lines for hours in his bedroom with the door closed. He had tried different words – cute, clever, romantic. They all worked perfectly. But now as he stood here, he couldn't recall any of them. And his courage deserted him.

Looking down at his hands that were folded in front of him, David talked in a voice barely above a whisper. "I, uh, well, I, uh, just wanted to thank you for the other day. When those guys knocked me into the locker and you helped pick up my books, that was very nice."

Constance smiled broadly. Her cheeks flushed with a hint of pink and puffed out so that her smile covered not just her mouth, but her entire face. "There's no need to thank me. Lots of people would have helped. I just happened to be there."

Constance started to turn back around, but David started speaking again.

"I'd like to do something to thank you. If you're not doing anything Saturday, maybe I could take you to a movie."

The smile dropped off Constance's face, her mouth forming an open "O." In an instant, David knew he made a horrible miscalculation.

"I, uh, don't think so, David. I already have plans for the weekend."

David knew that it didn't matter whether she had plans or not. He hung his head even further and turned to walk away.

"But thank you for asking," Constance said.

As he walked away, David heard the words behind him.

"Did that perv just ask you for a date? Oh my God. He really did, didn't he."

"Be nice," Constance said.

"Did he really think you'd go out with someone like him. Oh my God. Can you imagine kissing him?"

Then he heard a sucking sound, followed by all of the girls laughing.

***

Seven Days Before the Darkness

The morning after being turned down by Constance, David walked through the school in a fog. Somehow, he made it from one class to the next, but at the end of each class, he could not recall a single thing that happened the previous hour. Through the edges of the fog, it seemed that everyone was looking at him, pointing, laughing. He knew it was his imagination, that no one in the entire school even knew he existed. Not even his teachers. So often he wished he could just disappear. And if by some miracle it happened, no one in the school would even notice.

Lunch period came. As always, David went through the line by himself, ordered the same food he did every day, then carried his tray to a table against the wall where he sat eating by himself. As he ate, he sensed eyes on him. He looked up and saw several people quickly look the other way. At one table, a girl looked at him, then laughed and shared what was on her phone with the girl sitting next to her. At another table, two boys were laughing and one pointed directly at him.

It wasn't David's imagination.

David lowered his head and concentrated on his sloppy joes. When his tray was empty, he reached into his backpack for his Snickers bar.

Curt Marcum, a boy who had been in David's classes since elementary school, took a seat across the table from David. Freckle-faced and lacking social graces, Curt was an outsider, too. But his easy-going nature and willingness to help those who didn't have his unfathomable ability in math and science left him free from being the target of taunts and bullying.

"Hey, David."

David looked up surprised. No one had sat with him at lunch since he started high school. "Hi, Curt. What's up?"

Curt leaned in and lowered his voice. "David, I just don't think it's right what's going on. I want you to know I have nothing to do with it."

David's mind was blank. "What do you mean? What's going on?"

"The stuff Angie Blankenship started about you on social media. There's just no excuse for it. And I told her so."

"What stuff?"

"You haven't seen it?"

"No. What are you talking about."

"Oh, Jesus, David. I don't want to be the one to tell you."

David's voice rose. "Tell me what?"

Curt looked away, his mouth tight. After a long moment, he turned back to face David and pulled out his phone. "You sure you want to see this?"

"Show it to me," David demanded.

Curt punched his phone to life and scrolled until he found what he was looking for. He handed his phone to David. The social media post showed more than 200 "Likes" and "Laughing" responses, and a long list of replies.

David glared at the screen, then read:

"That perv David Carmichael asked Constance Griffith for a date. Can U imagine. Can you imagine kissing that pimple faced freak? Ewwwwwwwwwwww!"

The first reply was even worse:

"Deformed David Carbuncle?" Attached to the post was a photo showing David's school yearbook photo superimposed with a boil oozing puss. There were so many laughing face emojis that David couldn't count them all.

Post after post followed. "I wouldn't kiss Carbuncle with your mouth." "Hey Constance, I'll give you $20 if you stick your tongue in Carbuncle's mouth." "I've seen his pecker in gym. Maybe it should be TW Carbuncle – for Teeny Weeny."

David fought the urge to throw the phone. He slid it back across the table to Curt. He looked across the cafeteria and it seemed that every eye was on him.

David swiped his tray, sending it flying across the room. He stood without saying anything and walked out of the cafeteria and out of the school.

***

Two Hours Before the Darkness

Alan Carmichael sat at his desk in the detective squad reviewing incident reports from the previous night. As he sipped on his third cup of coffee of the morning, he made notes about the follow-up investigation, and filled out the assignment sheet on which detective would handle the matter. He always kept the most interesting cases for himself.

The phone on Alan's desk buzzed. "Detectives. Carmichael speaking."

"Alan, we've got a shooting on the west side." It was the familiar voice of Assistant Chief Ben Truman. "One of our young patrolmen, Gary Storey, answered a call to a domestic. When he got there, he found a woman dead on the front porch, her husband still standing over her, swearing at her."

"Is the guy in custody."

"Yeah. Pretty open and shut. But I think this is Storey's first murder scene. He seems pretty shook up. Can you take it?"

"I'm on my way. Be there in 15."

***

Thirty Minutes Before the Darkness

"Get up, David," Hanna shouted as she pounded three times on the door to David's room. "You haven't gone to school all week. You have to go today.

Otherwise they're going to kick you out."

There was no sound. Hanna tried the door, but it was locked. She cursed under her breath about allowing David to have a lock on his door. She hit the door again. "Get up!"

This time there was a response, but only the series of F-bombs were understandable, then something hit the door from the inside.

"I'm not going to tolerate this. You can't say those things in this house."

"Whatcha gonna do, mommy?" The sarcasm dripped from each word. "You going to call daddy at work and tell him to bring the handcuffs home and arrest me?"

"Just stop it. I don't know what's wrong, but you have to go to school."

Hannah heard moving and thrashing around inside David's room. The commotion lasted for minutes without a single word being spoken. Finally, the door flew open. David, wearing a wrinkled t-shirt and the same jeans he had worn all week, barged out of the room. "

"Get out of my way, bitch," he yelled. As he passed, David's backpack crashed into Hanna, knocking her into the wall.

Hanna stood in the upstairs hall, rubbing the place where her shoulder banged into the wall. She could hear the sounds from downstairs as David thrashed around. The refrigerator opened and closed with a slam. So, too, did the cabinet doors. There was a rattling of dishes and silverware.

Hanna's heart pounded in her throat and her breathing was hurried and short. She walked into her bedroom and sat down hard on the edge of the bed, trying to remember the techniques Dr. Oz had taught on his show to reduce stress.

From below, Hanna heard the sounds of David rooting around like an angry bear. Doors opened and shut, furniture scraping across the floor, muttered curses.

"Bye, bitch!" she heard, and the front door slammed.

Dreading what she would find, Hanna got up and walked downstairs. She looked out the window in the door and saw David getting into her car, her spare car keys in his hand. She started to open the door, then paused. She just could not face the confrontation.

The engine started up and the tires squealed.

Hanna opened the door and looked out. David had backed out of the drive. As she watched, he accelerated away toward the school. In the morning sunlight shining through the car windows, she saw a glint off black metal leaning against the passenger window. As her car disappeared around the corner, a shiver ran down Hanna's back. "Oh God, no."

***

Eight Minutes Before the Darkness

Alan Carmichael took one last look at the blood-splattered front porch and the lifeless body of Mary Henderson, then slipped his notebook into his shirt pocket and walked toward where Gary Storey was standing under a small maple tree smoking a cigarette.

"You know you're not supposed to smoke in uniform."

The patrolman turned sharply. He pulled the cigarette from his mouth. "Sorry, Lieutenant."

"Your first murder scene?"

"Yes, sir. I've not seen anything like that before. Her face was just gone." The young patrolman started to drop the cigarette.

"Finish your cigarette," Alan said. "The first one is always tough. At least you didn't lose your breakfast. That's what I did on my first death scene."

Storey nodded and gave a sheepish smile.

"I'm done here," Alan said. "Crime scene boys will be working here for the next couple of hours. Stick around for crowd control until they're done. That will give you a chance to catch your breath. If your commander says anything, tell him I didn't want any nosey neighbor screwing with the scene until the techs are done."

"Yes, sir."

"I don't care if you sneak a cigarette. You probably need it. But don't let anybody see you."

The radio on Storey's shoulder crackled.

"All units. All units. 911 call reports possible school shooting underway at St. Benedict High School. Repeat, possible school shooting underway at St. Benedict's. All nearby units respond. SWAT is being called."

"That's my son's school." Alan said. "We're five minutes away. Tell them we're responding. And don't forget your vest."

Alan ran to his unmarked car. He grabbed his Kevlar vest from the back seat and threw it on over his dress shirt. Sliding in behind the wheel, he started the car, put it in drive, and pushed the accelerator to the floor.

***

Deepest Darkness

David pulled his mom's sedan into the St. Benedict High School parking lot. There were a few spaces open in the back row, but David saw that handicap spaces closest to the school entrance were open. "Screw it," he said aloud, and whipped the Toyota around the aisle and into the handicap spot.

David stepped out of the car and grabbed for his dad's 9 mm Glock that he had taken from the cabinet where he knew it was kept. The gun slipped through his sweat-drenched fingers and nearly fell to the pavement, but David finally got it in his grasp. He wiped his hands on his jeans, racked a round into the chamber, and slid the gun behind his back into his belt. Then he pulled the shotgun from where it was propped against the passenger seat. He took a deep breath and walked toward the school entrance.

David heard the first sirens in the distance. There were two from different directions. Then more. It became a wailing symphony growing louder with each second.

Pulling the shotgun to his shoulder, David hastened his pace to the glass double-door entrance. Inside, a woman was locking the door. It was Mrs. Smithson, the principal. As the first police cars squealed to a stop, David took aim and let go with a blast.

One glass door shattered, sending shards and fragments exploding like crystal snow into the morning light. Mrs. Smithson was blown to the floor by the blast. As she scrambled to get away, David took aim and fired again. The second shot blew out the bottom half of the door, but Mrs. Smithson was now on her feet, running around a corner and out of view.

David heard more cars stopping. The sound of the sirens was all around.

Then came an amplified voice. "Stop! Put your gun down and get on the ground!"

David stood still but did not turn or lower his gun. Everything went still. Then David heard his dad yelling behind him.

"It's my son. It's my son. I'll handle this."

David turned to see his dad standing on the sidewalk about 50 feet away. Behind him was an array of police and emergency vehicles. More than 20 armed officers wearing bullet-proof vests pointed their weapons directly at David.

Alan and David stood unmoving, frozen like statutes. Slowly Alan holstered his service handgun and held open palms toward his son. Cautiously Alan moved his hands to his jacket and undid the straps on his Kevlar vest, then dropped it to the sidewalk. With deliberate motions, Alan began walking forward.

"David, let's all take a deep breath and calm down." Alan's voice was calm but firm. "All you've done so far is a little bit of vandalism. That's no big deal. We can handle that. You don't want to do something that can't be undone. Come on, son, put the gun down and let's talk this out."

David hesitated, then dipped the barrel of the shotgun ever so slightly. Alan continued to walk. When he was only two steps away, he reached his hand out for the shotgun. David moved the weapon a few inches, paused, then held out the gun. In a single, sharp movement, Alan grabbed the barrel. David shook his head. "No," he shouted and snatched the Glock from its resting place in his belt. David fired three fast shots into Alan's chest.

A barrage of gunfire exploded from the officers perched behind their cars. David staggered backwards, then fell into the blanket of glass shards covering the sidewalk, blood pouring from every part of his body.

***

Six Weeks After the Darkness

Realization dawned on Father Glenn's face. "That was your son? The one at St. Benedict's? I heard about that. Your son was the shooter?"

"Don't worry, Father. The only person he killed was his dad."

"He shot his dad?"

"He was a detective; one of the first cops at the scene. He tried to talk David down, but David shot him."

The priest stood motionless. Silent.

"You want to take back your prayers?"

Father Glenn placed a hand on Hanna's shoulder. "Of course not. Those who are troubled, who are tormented, deserve our prayers, too. Only God is to judge."

"That's not the way most people think. That's why Ellen requested the mass for him here. None of the churches in our area would say anything for David. She thought maybe people around here wouldn't know his name. I'm sorry if she caused you any trouble."

"He's your son. No matter what he did, that doesn't change. I will keep him and your husband in my prayers."

Hanna's stoic expression remained unchanged, but a solitary tear rolled down one cheek. "I appreciate your prayers for my son. My husband, too. But if there is a god, if he is so good, then why didn't he help my boy before he died? David was deeply troubled. We tried everything, but there was no help for him when he was alive. If there is a god, why didn't he give David a chance to find peace in his life?"

"We can't know God's plans. All we can do is have faith and pray for His mercy and love. I'll pray for you, too."

"Mercy? What mercy? There was no mercy for David. As for your prayers, you can save them. I'm past that."

"No one is past the reach of prayer. If we open ourselves to Him, God will grant forgiveness and peace, even to those who suffer more than they think they can tolerate."

Anger flashed in Hanna's eyes. "You know the Bible, don't you?"

Father Glenn nodded. "Of course."

"You know Proverbs 20:20? A son that curses his parents will be extinguished in the darkest pit. Something like that. That's what the priest at our local church told me when I asked about a service for David."

Father Glenn shook his head. "That is awful. He should not have done that.

I believe in a loving, forgiving and merciful God, not a vengeful God who turns his back on those in need."

"There are some things beyond prayer, beyond forgiveness." Hanna wiped away her tears and her face hardened. "You see, I made the calls."

Father Glenn looked at her, not understanding. "Calls?"

"When David drove away, I saw the shotgun in the car. I was afraid of what he might do, so I called the school. Then I called 911."

They stood motionless, looking at each other. In a nearby chokeberry bush, a mockingbird trilled its vibrant morning songs, changing cadence every few seconds. The song went on undisturbed for minutes, with no other sound. In a world of such momentary beauty, it was difficult to imagine the horror of that morning at St. Benedict's.

Finally, Father Glenn spoke, his voice so soft it could barely be heard above the songbird. "But if you hadn't called, so many other children may have died. It took someone brave, someone who cared about others, to make that call."

"It took someone scared. I was so damned scared that I couldn't think straight. You think I would have sacrificed my son for any of them?"

The priest lowered his eyes as if in prayer. "My child, that is exactly what God did."

"I'm not God!" Hanna shouted. "My son and my husband are dead, and I'm responsible. So, go say your prayers for someone who wants them, and leave me in my own darkness."

Hanna got in her car and sped away, leaving the silent priest in her wake.

Deception at the Double D Convention

by Shari Held

January 3, 2020

The pale blue envelope addressed in fancy script stood out amid all the bills and advertisements in Boone Moretti's daily mail. He tossed the rest aside, grabbed an ornate paper knife from his desk, and opened the blue envelope first. As he unfolded the letter, a subtle floral scent flirted with his nostrils. It reminded him of someone, but he couldn't remember who.

He grabbed a glass from the bar and plunked a few cubes in it. Then he eased his six-foot frame into a generous-sized, chocolate brown leather armchair with nail-head accents. He poured a glass of bourbon from a cut-glass container on the adjacent table and settled in to savor the letter's contents.

The salutation — Hey There, Lover Boy — was promising. A quick glance at the bottom of the page didn't reveal a signature. But there was no doubt the sender was female. His favorite sex. He wondered which one of the many women he'd been with recently was reaching out to him. Perhaps the letter was from one of the Daring Divas. Now there was a group of sexy, uninhibited 30-something women on the rise. And, fortunately for him, on the make. He'd sampled about five of them since a chance meeting at the Get Lucky Lounge one night a few months ago. The girls were having cocktails after their bi-monthly get-together and invited him to join them. He'd been enjoying their company ever since.

Could he help it if women lusted after his movie-star good looks — thick, dark hair, warm brown eyes, and a gym-enhanced physique? No. And he made it a point to never deny any of his admirers.

"If there were a *Guinness Book of World Records* listing for sexual prowess, your name would be at the top of that list, Boone, boy," he said to himself. Modesty was not a trait he admired, whether in his business deals or with the women he bedded.

"Let's see what we have here," he said, tossing back his drink, then putting the empty glass aside.

Hey There, Lover Boy,

It's been a while since we've gotten together. Too long. I've thought about you often since our last tryst. You really know how to treat a woman, Boone. You took me to sexual heights I'd never scaled before. Now it's your turn. Your time to be treated like the sex god you are.

Have I aroused your attention? If so, here's what you need to do. On Friday, January 17, 2020, come to the Maxim Hotel at 11 p.m. promptly. At the desk, identify yourself and request the key card for Room 502. The room has been prepaid by yours truly. When you get there, you'll find another set of instructions. Once you've done as you're told, the fun will begin. I will fulfill fantasies you never knew you had. If you're the male stud I think you are, a man who craves and needs sexual adventure as much as you need air to breathe, you'll be there.

Until then,

Lusty Lady

***

4:00 p.m. January 17, 2020

"Heidi, I wish you'd accompany me to the club for dinner once in a while," Jim Harrelson said. "It won't kill you to show up and play nice once a month. People are beginning to talk."

His wife snorted. Then she gave him a cold stare that made her look more reptilian than human. "Like I care. I presume you mean the Mortons. That bloody Al you think is utterly fascinating is so boring I want to super glue his nostrils and mouth shut just for fun. And his wife Karen, when's the last time she hauled her 200-pound ass to the beauty salon? She's so dowdy she makes Mrs. Doubtfire look like an Indy 500 Princess!" Heidi poured a glass of Pinot, then smoothed her ebony hair and inspected her porcelain complexion in the floor-length mirror. Satisfied, she sat down on the white leather sofa and started flipping through the pages of the latest *Vogue*.

Jim counted to 10 backwards under his breath. He'd seen this behavior more times than he'd like to remember. It wasn't a good sign. "All I'm saying is everyone would like to see you. And I'd really enjoy being with you, as a couple, like we used to do. Remember when we'd go to the club and have dinner and drinks, then play cards with the Mortons for hours. We had fun, then, didn't we?" He hated that his voice sounded so weak and whiny.

"Jesus, Jim. You call that fun? No wonder I have to go elsewhere to entertain myself. Yes, Jim. I'm sure you suspected it, but let's make it official. I've gone out on you. And not just once or twice. There've been so many men I don't remember all their names. Most weren't from around here, if that makes you feel better." She laughed at the pained expression on his face before continuing her barrage.

"And you want to know why? Because you're a spineless, yellow-bellied little chickenshit. You don't even have the guts to tell me to stop, you putz. You just put up with it. Is it because you love me so much, pookie? Or because you don't want to share all that glorious green cash you have from your family trust. Until you grow a spine, you're just going to have to live with whatever I dish out."

Thank goodness he wouldn't have to listen to her vitriol much longer. Soon she'd be leaving for the Daring Diva convention. "I'm not the putz you think I am, Heidi. You'll see!" He turned and escaped to the safety of his study.

***

9:00 p.m. January 17, 2020

Jim checked the clock in his study for the umpteenth time. Finally, he headed for the bedroom to get dressed. Heidi had left hours ago to join her fellow sisters at the hotel for the Daring Divas 2020 National Convention. The convention was the last place Jim would ordinarily want to be, but tonight he was on a mission. A mission to get revenge. And he didn't want to be late.

He rummaged through Heidi's lingerie chest until he found an unopened package of pantyhose. He pulled them out and held them up.

How in the world do women wear these things? I hope these things stretch. Okay. Let's see. One leg in and one — Damn!

Jim's big toe poked clear through the sheer hose. He found another pair that looked like they'd been broken in and managed to pull them on with no mishaps.

Next up was the bra. Fortunately, he had dressed in drag for the Governor's Halloween Ball last year. He already had the bra, sequined dress, heels, and blond wig.

Jim held the bra and inserted his arms in the straps. He stood in front of a mirror and tried to fasten it by grabbing both ends behind him. No success.

How did I get this thing on last year? Oh, yeah. Heidi helped me. Damn!

Fastening it first, then slipping it on was a no-go, too. He practically pulled his arm out of joint. Finally, he hit upon the winning solution: Fasten the band in front, then tug the thing until the boob holders were in front where they were supposed to be. Then he stuffed them with socks.

He plopped down on the bed. How had he sunk so low? Although he came from a wealthy family, he was a successful businessman in his own right. He used to be confident and carefree.

Now, look at me. I'm happy I found a way to get my bra on. How pathetic is that? About as pathetic as the rest of my life. What went wrong? Heidi. It all came down to Heidi.

He sighed. If only he'd married Penny, his childhood sweetheart. By now he'd probably have three kids and a dog. And they'd all be living happily together in an English Tudor decorated in chintz, with a lovely rose garden in the backyard.

Instead, he had no kids, no pets, no yard. Just a sterile, ultra-modern penthouse that was about as inviting as head lice. And Heidi. Heidi, a prima donna with no regard for others. A loose cannon who thought rules didn't apply to her. A hedonist who went after whomever and whatever she wanted with the single-mindedness of a tomcat stalking a feline in heat.

Heidi's latest lover, at least the latest one he knew about, was Boone Moretti.

Boone? For Christ's sake, what kind of name is that for an adult man in his 30s?

Despite the ridiculous name and his penchant for other people's wives, Moretti was a successful technology salesman. A mover and shaker who looked like a Greek god. Jim had met Moretti once at a business function, and the prick had the gall to ask if Jim would nominate him for induction in the country club.

Jim snorted just thinking about it.

Like that would ever happen. I might not have a say when it comes to sharing my wife with him, but I'll be damned if I'm going to share the one place I truly belong.

Jim inspected himself in the mirror. At age 38 he'd still retained his boyish good looks. He was average height, with a slight build, blondish hair, and blue eyes. Not an exotic bone in his body. Plain vanilla. The story of his life.

What had Heidi — Heidi of the model-like perfection — ever seen in him five years ago? He laughed a thin, bitter little laugh.

I must have had dollar signs floating above my head the night we met. Or a sign that said 'SUCKER' on my back. Probably both.

He pulled on the black sequined dress and stuck his feet in the black heels.

Better get used to walking in these things so I don't fall on my ass.

If he were being totally honest, his time with Heidi hadn't been all bad. In the beginning, when she still faked feelings for him, being with her was exciting. She was his adrenaline and he was her willing junkie. She forced him out of his comfort zone and gave him a taste of life he'd never experienced. Introducing him to people he would never have met without her. Getting him to travel to places he'd only ever read about.

But that soon changed when he couldn't live up to her standards. Couldn't keep up with the lifestyle. That's when Heidi's affairs and her involvement with the Daring Divas began.

When their marriage began to break down, so did he. For Jim, divorce was out of the question. Even though no social stigma was attached to divorce these days, it would be undeniable proof to himself that he was a failure. Besides, he didn't relish having to give Heidi any part of his estate. The trollop didn't deserve a thing from him. With or without money, Heidi had the chutzpah to reinvent herself and get on with her life. He wasn't so sure he could.

But she doesn't have to rub my face in it. Speaking of face, I need to put mine on. I just hope I don't glue my eyelids together with that damned eyelash glue.

He hobbled into Heidi's dressing room and sat at the vanity. With false eyelashes, makeup, rouge, lipstick, and the blond wig, Jim's transition was nearly complete. He raided her jewelry box for some earrings and found a black hat with a veil in her walk-in closet. As the finishing touch, he sprayed himself with the floral perfume he'd used on the letter he'd sent to Moretti.

Jim had been impatiently waiting for tonight, opening night at the Daring Divas 2020 National Convention. Months earlier, at Heidi's request, he'd reserved a block of rooms for Heidi's Indy chapter. A couple weeks before Christmas two of the women cancelled. That's when he got the brilliant idea that would give him his revenge and prove to Heidi that he wasn't a spineless coward, her favorite term of endearment for him.

He'd kept one of the reservations. Then he sent a provocative invitation to Moretti that he knew the bastard wouldn't refuse.

And tonight, he'd get his revenge. He'd take Moretti down a notch. Make him a laughing stock. And Heidi would know that he, weak-kneed, baby-faced Jim Harrelson, was responsible. Who knows? Maybe his unexpected action would earn him her respect. And because of that newfound respect, maybe things would go back to the way they were before she started going out on him. Even if it were an act. He'd settle for that.

He grabbed a bottle of wine, a corkscrew, a box of chocolates, and some paraphernalia he'd found online and stashed them in a black patent tote. He checked the bedside clock.

Showtime!

***

Boone Moretti arrived at the hotel promptly at 11 p.m. to retrieve the key. His thoughts were focused on what a fun romp he'd soon have. A sexual adventure initiated by one of his ladies. It didn't much matter which one. That was part of the fun.

The sign in the lobby announced the hotel was hosting the national convention for the Daring Divas. That narrowed the list of his potential lovers to members of the Double Ds, as they called themselves. He thought about each of them in turn and felt himself beginning to get turned on.

Whoa, boy. Better save yourself for the festivities awaiting you in Room 502.

Moretti opened the door and looked around for his Lusty Lady. No one was there. The room, suite really, was elegant and understated. The sitting room featured a crystal chandelier, an elaborate floral bouquet, and plush carpeting he'd enjoy sinking his toes into.

He stepped inside the bedroom. In the center was a king-size brass bed. No one here, either. But a pale blue envelope addressed to him was propped against the base of the lamp. He picked it up and smelled the same floral perfume that had scented the other one. Well, the first letter had said he'd receive instructions.

Bring it on! Let the fun begin!

He opened the envelope.

Hey There, Lover Boy,

If you're reading this you've taken me up on my offer. I'm so happy you did. I've been thinking about this, anticipating this, too long. Let's get started, shall we?

For our first adventure, I want you to strip down to your birthday suit. Open the drawer of the bedside table where you found this note. You'll find a set of royal blue, tasseled nipple pasties, and a mankini. Hope you like them. I think blue's your color, don't you? Put them on. You'll also find a satin mask. Turn out the lights, place the mask over your eyes and lie down. Then, get ready for a mind-blowing experience. I'll join you soon. No peeking!

Until then,

Your Soon-to-Be Sated Lady

Moretti picked up the pasties and matching satin mankini. Not his style, but he'd play along.

They do say a tease is more of a turn-on than the full Monty.

✳✳✳

11:30 p.m. January 17, 2020

Jim made his way past the bar and through the lobby to the elevators without catching anyone's attention. The place was filled with boisterous women. Most, dressed to the nines. It had been a real pain to dress in drag, but he blended right in. It was worth it.

He paused when he reached Room 502. Would Moretti be there? More importantly, did he follow instructions and use the blindfold? Jim hoped so. He didn't have a Plan B.

He opened the door. All was dark, illuminated only by the artificial glow of various technologies. He peered into the bedroom. Sure enough, Moretti was there, all gussied up in the get-up as directed.

God. He looks like a Thanksgiving turkey!

"I'm here, lover boy," Jim whispered in what he hoped was a throaty, sexy voice reminiscent of Kathleen Turner in *Body Heat*. "Stay where you are. I'm going to turn on the light to arrange the finishing touches so we'll be all ready to play.

"What about you?"

"Oh, I'm ready. Just looking at you does it for me," Jim said, trying not to gag. Now came the risky part. He'd already attached the wrist and ankle restraints to the bed during an earlier visit. Would Moretti go along with it? Only one way to tell. He fastened one of the restraints around Moretti's wrist.

112

"Hey, what the heck?" Moretti started to object as Jim quickly restrained his other wrist and then worked his way down to Moretti's ankles. Fortunately, he settled back down. "Well, I guess there's a first time for everything."

"I'll be right back," Jim whispered. He plucked a rose from the bouquet in the sitting room, then pulled off the petals and dropped each one on Moretti's torso. Next, he opened the bottle of wine, placed it and a couple glasses on the bedside table, and tossed a handful of his favorite ganaches around them.

"So, are you going to keep me in suspense all night?" Moretti asked, moving his head to try to follow Jim's movement. "When's the fun going to begin?"

"Soon, lover boy, soon," Jim said as he placed the glow-in-the-dark silicone ball gag in Moretti's mouth.

One quick check to make sure he hadn't left anything, and Jim walked out the door, leaving it ajar. As the final touch, he taped a sign on the door that read:

Adult Entertainment Room

All Double Ds Welcome

***

"Whoo hoo!" yelped the first person off the elevator, a tall blonde from Idaho in a sequined, skin-tight sheath and ruby stilettos. "It's not quite midnight and I'm still up for fun. I've got a bottle in the room for anyone who doesn't want to call it a night."

"Now you're talking, Betsy," said a petite brunette bringing up the rear.

"Whoa, divas." Betsy stopped so fast she almost stepped out of her heels. "Let's put a hold on that. Do you see what I see?" In case they didn't, she read the sign. "Adult Entertainment Room. Double Ds Welcome." She turned to face the group. "Well, I don't need an engraved invitation. How 'bout the rest of you?"

"Adult entertainment? Hell, yes! Let's go!"

They walked into Room 502.

"Hey, it's dark in here," one woman said, reaching toward the light switch.

"No way, Doreen," her companion said, stopping her. "It's called atmosphere. I may not have much experience with this kind of thing, mind you, but even I know it's best to view an adult show in a dimly lit room."

"Shhh. There's someone in there."

"There'd better be," Betsy said. "Otherwise, where's the entertainment?"

Like a gaggle of geese, they followed one another into the bedroom.

"OMG," Doreen said. "When the board of directors said they were going whole hog on entertainment for our 2020 convention, they weren't kidding!"

"Now, this is more like it," Betsy said. "I don't know where they got him, but this guy's built like an Adonis." She stopped talking to admire the view.

"Are we supposed to tuck dollar bills in his . . . his briefs?" Doreen whispered. "I'll need to get some cash — and a lot of dollar bills!"

***

Who are these women? And what in the hell are they talking about — tucking dollar bills? Damn. I've been set up!

Boone Moretti began fighting against his restraints. There was no way he was going to be the butt of someone's joke.

As soon as I find out who's behind this, they're dead meat.

More women joined the original group. Moretti heard their cat calls and the sounds the women made milling around the room. He also heard the clicks as they took turns taking pictures of him on their smartphones. He started struggling harder at that point, but the restraints wouldn't budge.

Then one of the women sat down on the bed and patted his chest. "Calm down, hon. We're not going to hurt you. Just having some fun. That's what us Daring Divas are known for." She put her arm around him. "Hey, Maddie, take my picture with him, will you?"

She was soon followed by the others.

"Come on, Doreen," Maddie said. "You want to tuck some bills? Here's a few for you. Give me your phone and I'll take your picture doing it."

Oh, god. I hope these don't make it to Facebook or Instagram. If anyone at works sees these — or my clients. If only I could get this gag out . . .

The women parted to let a shapely redhead through. "Hey, what's going on

114

here?" she asked. "And who's he?"

Betsy responded to the president of Daring Divas national. "He's our adult entertainment, like it says on the door. Didn't national arrange this?"

"Hell, no!"

Thank god, finally someone who'll get me out of here and stop this sick joke.

"I'm taking that sign off the door before we get reported to hotel management. And keep the noise down!" She pivoted on one heel and stomped out.

Don't go. Don't go. Tell them to let me out of here.

"Does this mean we have to go?"

"No, Doreen," Betsy said. "We just have to keep it quiet."

"Well, how do you think he got here if national didn't set it up?"

Betsy shrugged. "Who knows. But we might as well enjoy the show."

∗∗∗

At that point Heidi Harrelson, dressed in a floor-length, low-cut gown and long gloves burst into the room with her gal pals from the local chapter. They pushed their way up front.

"OMG! Is that Boone Moretti?" one exclaimed.

"Sure is. And he's never looked better."

"You *know* him?" Doreen asked.

"Oh, yeah — and make that in the biblical sense!"

"You, too?" several Indy Double Ds clamored in unison.

"Keep it down a bit, ladies," Betsy said. "Looks like someone's making this tom pay for all his catting around."

Heidi's eyes narrowed as she surveyed her lover — make that ex-lover — lying on the bed dressed like an exotic male dancer.

How disgusting. This Lothario once made me feel like a million bucks. But he's played me. Now, I feel like a fool. Heidi clenched her fists at her side. "You'll pay for this, Boone Moretti," she said under her breath.

"Wonder if it was a jealous husband or — say, you don't suppose the cheating jerk was married, do you?" Heidi's friend asked no one in particular.

"If I were his wife and I found out he'd been servicing women all over town, I'd do more than this," another one remarked. "I'd cut the bastard's balls

115

off!"

"Do you think it was one of us?" Heidi's friend Judy whispered.

"I don't know what to think," Heidi said. She started to pour a glass of wine. It was a bottle of Russian Valley Chateau Eldridge Cabernet Sauvignon. *One of Jim's favorites.* She thought he was the only person around who still had bottles left from that winery. It went kaput five years ago or so. Then, she saw the candy. She'd recognize those beautifully decorated ganaches anywhere. Again, Jim's favorite. He ordered them online from some fancy French confiserie.

"What are the odds?" Heidi asked herself.

"Did you say something?" Josie, one of Heidi's buddies, asked.

"No, just thinking out loud," Heidi responded. *So, Jim was the mastermind behind this. Ever polite and politically correct Jim. I didn't think the little putz had it in him. He must really love me.*

"This isn't the time to think, girl! This is the time to enjoy." Josie promptly poured a glass of wine, sat on the bed, and began stroking Boone's chest as she murmured something in his ear. Then she smacked him on the side of his head and got up, saying, "You may be quite the stud, Boone, but this time you went too far and pissed somebody off big-time. You dirty, rotten, two-timing scumbag!"

Heidi smiled, savoring the knowledge that she was the reason Boone was in this predicament. That Jim had done this for her. Then another thought hit her. This was an opportune setup. She could get rid of her cheating lover and exit her boring marriage without giving up any of Jim's money. All she'd have to do is set things in motion and sit back and enjoy the show. And, if her plan didn't work, well, que sera, sera, as the corny old song said. Her life with Jim would remain status quo and she'd soon find a replacement for Boone.

Without hesitating for a moment, Heidi reached into her purse and pulled out several pieces of foil-wrapped peanut butter fudge. She never left home without them. Jim had his little foibles when it came to confectionery delicacies, and so did she. She scattered them in with the others while pretending to look for a chocolate she liked. Then she helped herself to a ganache. She'd leave all the peanut butter fudge for Moretti.

A few women started running their fingers down Moretti's body and he began struggling again. While the women were focused on him, Heidi pocketed the EpiPen from his jacket, which was hanging on a chair.

Now for a little Russian roulette, Boone. And I'd say the odds aren't leaning in your favor. Sooner or later someone's likely to feed you a piece of peanut butter fudge. And then, payback time!

***

God, what have I done? Jim Harrelson placed the empty glass, that minutes ago had held two fingers of Scotch, on the bar along with a twenty-dollar bill. The drink was meant to relax him before he left the hotel. Instead, it magnified his awareness of what he'd done. *I'm no better than Heidi if I let this revenge vignette play out. What a fool I've been.*

He hoped he could get back to Room 502 to minimize the damage. And if Moretti found out he was the person behind it, so be it. He'd probably have to pay for this ill-fated prank by recommending Moretti for membership in his club.

He took the elevator back up to the fifth floor. The sign was no longer on the door. Jim breathed a sigh of relief.

Good! Maybe someone let Moretti go and that will be the end of it. He'll never know it was me!

Jim realized that wasn't the case when he walked into the suite and saw the women surrounding the bedroom door.

How in the world am I going to get them all out of here? Maybe if I push the fire alarm —

"Hey, hon, you haven't had a turn," Doreen said. "Give me your phone and I'll take a picture of you with him."

Jim was trying to turn her down so he could set off the fire alarm when he heard a familiar voice.

"Here, let me. I'll be glad to take her photo with this hunk of beefcake." Heidi whipped her own phone out of her bag and captured Jim standing by the bed.

"Give me your email and I'll send you a keepsake of the evening," she said pulling a shell-shocked Jim to the side of the room. "I can guarantee this will be an evening you won't ever forget."

"Hey, let's give the guy a sweet treat," Doreen said. "Who knows how long he's been here. Hey, Maddie, take a picture of this." She removed the foil from a piece of peanut butter fudge, pulled his gag up, then popped the entire piece into Moretti's mouth. Before Moretti could spit the peanut butter fudge out, she laid one on him. Then she snapped the gag back in place. "Did you get that?"

Thatta girl, Doreen! Take that, Boone!

Heidi smiled and turned toward Jim, slipping the EpiPen into his black patent tote as she did. "In the next few minutes it's going to get real interesting in here, Jim. You see, I know you're responsible for this. The police will soon know, too."

"The police?" Jim asked in alarm. "Can't you help me get these women out of here so I can make amends and let Moretti go? There's no need to bring the police into this."

"Oh, but there is. I just saw someone give him a piece of peanut butter fudge. And Boone is deathly allergic to peanuts."

Moretti began struggling for air. Doreen screamed. "Oh my god, he's choking! You don't think my kiss did that to him, do you?" She froze and the room became deadly silent. Then, several women stampeded out of the room. Finally, someone called the front desk while another woman removed his restraints.

Heidi checked her watch. "By the time the front desk responds and gets a doctor up here, it will be too late for Boone.

"But . . . but I didn't put the peanut butter fudge there," Jim said. "And I had no idea he was allergic to peanuts."

"No, but you're the one who reserved the room and brought the Chateau Eldridge, a wine I'd be surprised if anyone else has in all of Indy. Then, there's your French chocolates. And I bet you purchased the sexy get-up and restraints online, like everything else you buy. Even the peanut butter fudge I special order from the Trappist Monks is in the pantry at home. You don't think they won't trace all that back to you?"

A bead of sweat slowly trickled from Jim's temple down to his jaw.

"Then there's the little matter that he was screwing me. I'd say that clenches the motivation part."

The medics arrived and started working on Moretti, whose face had turned blue in contrast to the ugly red welts cropping up over his body. One of them shook his head and they all stepped away from the body. Within seconds, the police arrived and requested everyone move to the sitting room for questioning.

Jim felt the blood rush from his face and his legs nearly gave way.

"And have you thought about how you're going to explain why you're here? Not to mention your attire." Heidi took one last look at her dead lover and then back to her soon to be ex-husband. "Better enjoy the next few hours, sweetie. I'll wager it's a slam dunk you'll be arraigned and in the clinker before the weekend's over."

Arcana 20/20

by T.C. Winters

Downtown Nashville, Indiana, had changed since my hasty departure following graduation. Designed as an art colony, the area had transformed into a quaint tourist village with a bustling center of commerce — clothing, leather and woodworking shops in addition to the obligatory fudgery. Surrounded by tree-covered hills, Brown County State Park was a haven for leaf watchers when the green colors changed to a cornucopia of browns, reds, oranges, and yellows. As I expected, Nashville swelled with out-of-town guests during this colorful fall season.

The situation at Trina's Trinkets, located along a garden path in the center of town, was *not* what I expected. I'd expected to find Trina, surrounded by her homemade jewelry, ready to dish about our latest boy-versus-girl drama.

What I found was Trina's corpse slumped face down on a card table, a pool of saliva under her chin, her body resting on a metal folding chair. At her left elbow was a purse, the contents sprinkled across the intricately crocheted tablecloth, including an explosion of Sephora products and essential oils from her cosmetic bag. Fingers accented with blood-red nails wrapped around a piece of paper rolled like a cigarette.

The pine floor squeaked as I tiptoed over to check for a pulse. Finding none, I backed away and called 911. Anyone with Netflix knew to not leave prints at the scene of a death investigation.

Paramedics arrived in minutes, followed by Austin Schonfeld, a deputy with the Brown County Sheriffs department. I was relieved Austin had shown up instead of Nashville Police Chief Ben Seastrom, who was a prior headliner in a dish session between Trina and me. My relief was short-lived because Ben showed up just as the crime scene techs finished whatever it was that they did.

We ignored each other as the paramedics loaded Trina's body onto a gurney. Her soft brown hair hung limply around a face that had turned a light shade of blue. As they lifted her, the rolled-up paper slipped from her hand and fell underneath the card table. Apparently, no one else noticed — or cared. I pushed away from the wall I'd been holding up but stopped when Chief High-and-Mighty sent me a laser-like glare that nearly dissolved the unwanted hairs on my chin.

The deputy and the chief were fine-looking men, albeit polar opposites. Austin was a few years younger than me. By a few, I meant five — or 10-ish. His sun-kissed hair and lean, tall physique lent him a surfer-dude air. Catnip to a cougar like myself.

Ben was about my age, dark-headed, with a calm demeanor, nocturnal tendencies that left him with permanent raccoon eyes, and an unnaturally curious temperament. In the six months since I'd relocated to Nashville, I'd fallen into an easy routine. An early dinner with Austin and late-night drinks with Ben, but Ben's inquisitive spirit had derailed my party train when he'd questioned my lack of free time during the daylight hours. I liked keeping my options open since I had concerns about inviting any unnecessary nuptials.

Ben felt differently.

Austin slipped between us as if to diffuse the tension.

He didn't have a problem with my distaste for monogamy.

The overpowering scent of rosewater from a spilled essential oil bottle gagged me, and I longed to open the shop's front door for fresh air, but a low buzz of excited voices and shuffling feet indicated a crowd had gathered, drawn by the flashing lights.

"Why aren't her hands bagged?" Chief Ben spoke to the older of the two paramedics who was tucking Trina's hands across her stomach. "Need to make sure this isn't the same kinda thing that happened out at the park."

The man straightened. "Overdose?" He lifted a shoulder. "The techs said there was no evidence of foul play. Did *you* find anything, Chief?"

Ben scanned the shop and shook his head. "Not at first glance, but we need to follow proper protocol. Could be an overdose. Maybe a stroke or a heart attack."

I stifled a gasp. Trina and I were close in age. Way too young for our bodies to give up the ghost. She was health conscious. I knew she'd never do drugs. I opened my mouth to ask about the pool of saliva but decided any interference would not be well-received.

Austin pulled what looked like baggies from some sort of a kit, slid them around Trina's hands, then wrapped tape around her wrists. When finished, he nodded at the paramedics, who unlocked the brakes on the gurney.

As her corpse was rolled out the front door, I turned my back to avoid reliving the scene in my dreams.

"Deputy Schonfeld, please escort Miss Blaine from the building. Use the door to the back alley." Ben stood with his legs spread and his arms crossed, as if daring me to question his authority.

From an amateur's point of view, finding the cause of Trina's death should've been the priority, not the proper way of extracting me from Trina's Trinkets without giving the fine folk of Nashville cause to gossip. *I* didn't particularly care if they talked. I'd reinvented myself as a real estate broker in my hometown, and for those of us in sales, any talk was good talk.

Austin stepped forward and put a hand on my back, skimming his fingers down my spine. "Let's go."

Trina had called me early that morning, asking if I'd come to the shop because she had a "situation" she wanted to discuss. She'd lured me with the promise of a tarot card reading, something she'd been studying since Crystal had opened a New Age store in town a few weeks ago.

Trina had been divorced twice. As a 30-something, newly divorced, blonde female who loved men, my attitude was wine 'em, dine 'em, do 'em, and dump 'em. We were kindred spirits.

The call was all I could think about as Austin led me outside to the narrow brick alley behind Trina's shop.

"Willow." He tipped my chin upward. "I need to go with the body. Will you be all right?"

I managed a nod. When he left, I replayed Trina's call in my head. She hadn't sounded worried, but she'd sniffled a little about her breakup with Chet, the man she was going to marry in two weeks. Juicy stuff. She'd told me yesterday about the breakup, and I'd been excited to get the details, but here I stood, alone, in a grimy alley while Trina was headed for the morgue.

Remembering the slip of paper under the table, I tried the back door, but someone had turned the lock. Stumbling to the front of the building, I found that one unlocked. The crowd had dispersed, probably to the coffeehouse to dissect the scuttlebutt on Trina's death. Tossing a quick glance over my shoulder, I pushed inside.

Trina's shop was eerily still as I crawled under the table and snagged the paper. Backing out on all fours, I encountered the shiny black shoes of Chief Ben Seastrom.

"What the hell?" His voice boomed in the deathly quiet.

Belatedly, I realized my error. Chief Ben never half-assed anything, so a cursory glance at the scene of a death investigation wasn't adequate.

Struggling to a sitting position, I bumped into the uniformed legs of Deputy Austin Schonfeld.

Austin glanced down, his gaze tracking mine. "Put that down before you damage evidence." The warmth in his voice tempered the stern warning.

Ben caught sight of the paper, and both men bent to retrieve it from my hand, bumping heads — something I assumed happened figuratively more often than literally. Ben recovered the quickest and snatched the scrap with his gloved hand.

Ben turned before smoothing the note on the flat surface of the table. "She indicate any problems?" At my shrug, he pinched two corners of the note and held it to the light.

I strained to read over his shoulder. Written in uneven brown lettering was the word Arcana followed by the number 2020.

"Trina wrote that with her eyeliner." I didn't have a clue what Arcana 2020 meant, but I recognized Trina's looped handwriting.

Ben turned, narrowing his eyes. "How'd you know? You see her write it?"

I pointed at the table were Trina's purse had overturned. "The techs took everything, but eyeliner was among the scattered makeup and the cap was off. The color is the same shade as the lettering."

Ben didn't seem impressed by my attention to detail. "You know anyone named Arcana?" He shifted, moving his feet shoulder-width apart.

"No. I've been gone 10 . . . uh, 20-ish years." His aggressive posture made me uncomfortable. I swallowed hard, too intimidated to continue with the fabrication regarding the number of years I'd been gone, and by extension, my age.

"Trina ever share an address beginning with 2020? Maybe a lockbox?"

A loud crash prevented me from answering. Austin had bumped into a display case and knocked over a shelf of earrings.

"Damn it, Schonfeld, you're trampling the evidence. Get the hell out." Pointing a finger, he said, "Stop moving, Willow. You don't want your footprints mixed up in this mess. If she didn't die from natural causes, you're a suspect since you're the one who found her body, and you sneaked back in here without authorization."

Adrenaline flooded my veins, kicking my temperature up a notch. A *suspect*? My expression must have reflected my dismay because Austin took my elbow and ushered me out the front door and onto the sidewalk along Main Street.

"What do you think the note meant?" He leaned in close when he spoke.

"There's a quandary for you and Ben." Picturing poor Trina grasping for anything to write her last words sent my pulse galloping. I blurted out, "She told Chet she wouldn't marry him next weekend." Austin and I had planned to attend the ceremony together — our first social event as a couple.

Sun glinted against the window, forcing Austin to squint. "You think Chet was angry enough to kill her?"

"I don't think he gave a rat's patootie, but his family may have. They were on the hook for an extravagant reception."

"Did she tell you why she called off the wedding?" Austin moved out of the death ray bouncing off the window. Using a hand to shield his eyes from the residual glare, he focused his blue eyes on me.

I stepped back and whispered, "She said she hadn't intended to get engaged. He surprised her at the July 4th picnic by proposing in front of a crowd.

The diamond was so big she plucked it out of his hand to get a closer look. Everyone assumed the answer was yes, and she was in love with the size of that rock." My heart constricted and my thoughts drifted to the day she'd shown me the ring.

The sounds of traffic rumbling nearby brought me out of my stupor. "I assumed she was going to finish the story today."

"Don't let your imagination run wild. She probably died of natural causes." Austin ran a hand down my arm before returning inside.

Trina's Trinkets was a popular tourist destination and stretch-pant clad middle-age couples strolled past, shaking their heads at the closed sign hanging on the door. The sign made my heart hurt. Trina's jewelry-making talent, combined with her jovial personality, made her a natural salesperson. Now she was gone, taking her gifts with her.

Sadness crept in, draining every other emotion, leaving me hollowed. I'd parked my car on a side street but couldn't remember which one. Uncertain, I shuffled uphill on Van Buren toward the Carmel Corn Cottage.

The words "A time to grieve is a time to feed" were engraved on my family crest.

As I passed Crystal's New Age Store, Crystal darted out, snaring me in a full body hug that had me gasping for air. We'd become fast friends when she'd moved into town because she bore a striking resemblance to me. Tall, blonde, and curvy, she'd been mistaken for me more than once before the townsfolk wised up and looked twice before addressing her by my name.

"You must be devastated." Hooking her arm through mine, she propelled me toward the open door of her shop. "Let me fix you up with some herbal tea."

Herbal tea wasn't going to fix what ailed me, but with no place to go and all the time in the world to get there, I figured a hot beverage wouldn't kill me. While she bustled around preparing the drinks, I rummaged through the drawers behind the counter, looking for whiskey. I didn't find adult beverages, but I discovered her stash of "herbs."

Spirituality was back in vogue, and Crystal had cornered the market by offering healing powders, palm reading, and tarot card readings. In the corner, she'd set up a round table covered in wispy fabric that lent a gypsy flair to the store. I suspected she supplemented her income by selling pot, but who was I to judge?

"I made Gingko Biloba tea to help with anxiety." Crystal sat the china cup on the counter, then waggled a handful of handmade tea bags in the air. "I'm sending these with you to help you get through the next few days. The taste is a bit bland, so add cinnamon or lemon peel."

I took one last look at the secret herbs in the drawer before picking up the cup and carrying it to the round table. "Ben thinks she died of natural causes, but I'm not so sure."

Crystal raised an eyebrow. "Why?"

Raising the cup to my lips I considered how much to tell. Deciding the gossip grapevine would have borne fruit before I finished my tea, I plunged ahead. "She left a note."

Her ringed fingers jumping rhythmically against the table sounded like bells. "However did she manage that?" Her lips tightened and her hands fluttered to her chest. "I'm sorry. I was just thinking of poor Trina trying to communicate while dying."

"She used eyeliner to write Arcana 2020 on a scrap of paper. Ben and Austin are looking for an address or someone whose name is Arcana." I sighed and closed my eyes.

Crystal leaned toward me. "I was teaching Trina how to read Tarot cards. She must've been leaving a clue."

"You know what Arcana 2020 means?"

"Not exactly, but she must have meant Major Arcana because there is no 20 or 0 in Minor." She leaped from her chair and sprinted to a stack of cards on a shelf, grabbed a set and raced back. "Major Arcana means big secrets."

I blinked hard, allowing time to process. "Big secrets. What about the numbers? Are two 20 cards possible?"

She shuffled through the stack, tossing out three cards. "No, there's only one 20 in a deck. I think she meant 2, 0, and 20. Major Arcana includes one unnumbered card — 0 — known as the Fool. He's the main character making his journey through the cards, learning life lessons known as the Fool's Journey." Tapping a card with a picture of a man in a dress carrying a knapsack, she said, "This is the Fool. He represents innocents, but some believe it's a nice way of saying he's stupid." She threw out another card. "The Fool card goes with the 20 card, called the Judgment card."

The Judgment card depicted an angel holding a trumpet and people rising from the grave with uplifted arms. "That looks ominous."

"The angel is Gabriel, and the people are rising to be judged." She lined the cards in a row, adding the 2 card at the end. "A three-card reading is called a no-spread spread, meaning these cards are telling something important about the past, present or future."

The 2 card had a picture of a woman in a robe holding a scroll with the letters TORA. "The Fool, Judgment — " I tapped the last card — "and this. What's this?"

She turned the card so I could get a better view. "This is the High Priestess. She's holding a scroll with the letters TORA, meaning the Greater Law or the Keeper of Secrets."

"What does it mean?" Tarot was complicated, and I was too rattled to grasp the explanation.

"The 20 and the 0 could mean a new beginning based on a new phase of life. Probably signifies her upcoming wedding."

I couldn't contain the frown. "She wasn't getting married. She broke up with Chet."

"Wh-what? H-how do you know that?" Overcoming her stutter, she managed to articulate, "Did she tell you?"

I nodded, my mind whirling. "Do you think the High Priestess signifies Chet's mother? She's a Circuit Court Judge. She paid for the reception, so she's gotta be ticked."

Raising her shoulders in a shrug, Crystal allowed attention to roam. "Probably. What else did she tell you?" She sharpened her focus, pinning me with her gaze.

The gossip mill was in a full gallop, but I wouldn't be the one to carry tales from the grave. "That was all. She asked me to meet at her shop so we could talk, but when I got there, she was — "

Dead.

Trina was dead, but I couldn't make myself say the word out loud. Chet's mother murdered her? The thought was ludicrous, but the cards didn't lie.

Trina left a message, and the message identified the person responsible for her death.

I stood, overturning the chair in my haste. "I have to tell Ben and Austin."

"Calm down. This doesn't prove anything."

"She was trying to communicate with me." I turned toward the door, but Crystal held up a hand.

"Wait. Let me give you something stronger than those tea bags." She took the bags off the table, rushed to the drawer behind the counter, and returned with another batch of bags. "These are more potent and will help you relax."

I snatched the tea bags, dashed out the door, and headed toward Trina's Trinkets, hoping one or both of the men were still there.

The cool autumn air did nothing to alleviate my heated skin as I jogged, *walked quickly*, up the hill and around the corner to the shop. Gasping for air, I tried the door. Finding it locked, I pounded on the glass.

The door flew open. Ben's wide shoulders and enormous frame filled the doorway. "Willow, go home and stop interfering."

"Where's Austin?"

Ben's chest heaved with the weight of his sigh. "At the coroner's office. I'm tying up loose ends and civilians aren't allowed inside." His phone rang and he dug it out of his front pocket with two fingers. "Chief Seastrom." His listened intently, then raised his eyes to meet mine. A minute ticked by and he scrutinized me as he talked. "Got it." He hung up and stepped from the doorway to stand in front of me.

The look on his face scared me. "What?"

"You mentioned the overturned bottles. I noticed a pool of saliva. Told the techs, and they tested the contents of Trina's purse. Found traces of batrachotoxin in a bottle of essential oils."

"Bah track o toxin? What's that?"

Instead of answering, he grabbed my elbows and pulled me to his chest. "You touch anything from her purse?"

His pine-tree-after-a-rain scent and left-over muscles from his military days sent shock waves all the way down to my toes. He liked to hunt, and he always smelled outdoorsy. I shook free of his grasp. "Of course not. What's that toxin stuff?"

"Deadly. Made from a poison pulled from the skin of a Golden Frog. Native to Panama and Colombia. Hunters use it to make poison darts. Can drop a man in a matter of seconds."

"So if I'd touched the oils, I'd be dead now?"

He stepped away and lifted his head as if considering my words. "True. Guess you're okay." Without another word, he turned on his heel and slammed the door, clicking the lock with force.

Someday soon, Ben and I needed a come-to-Jesus talk about our fractured relationship, but not today.

Too hyped to go home, too downhearted to socialize, I meandered toward the courthouse to confront Chet's mother, the Honorable Judge Sheila Wainwright. The closer I got to the courthouse stairway, my throat dried out and beads of sweat lined my forehead. Blowing through security, then taking the steps two at a time, I burst through the Circuit Court office, startling the clerks.

"I need to see Judge Wainwright." My words came out in a rush.

A girl whose face I recognized, but whose name I couldn't recall, looked me up and down as if I were deranged. "She cancelled all her cases and took her son on a surprise vacation to Belize." She parked her elbows on the counter separating us and leaned closer. "We heard Trina dumped him. You'd know if that was true, wouldn't you?"

"Trina's dead." I should've softened my delivery because the shocked looks on their faces indicated the gossip vine hadn't extended this far. "When did they leave?"

"A couple of days ago. Trina's dead? Suicide?"

"Of course not. Someone poisoned her." I hadn't meant to speak harshly, but I couldn't stand having anyone think Trina had taken her own life. I whirled and fumbled with the door, throwing it open with a bang. Heads turned as I charged through the hallway and down the stairs.

Outside, I sat on a bench to collect my runaway emotions. Murders were most often committed by someone the victim knew, and the suspect needed to have the means, the motive, and the opportunity to commit murder. Dating cops had lent me some insight. If Chet and his mother were out of town, they wouldn't have had the opportunity unless the poison had been placed in the bottle prior to their vacation. Pulling out my phone, I did a Google search, stalled a couple of times because of the spelling, and discovered batrachotoxin had a long shelf life.

My stomach rumbled. Inhaling deeply, I stood and beelined for the Carmel Corn Cottage, stopping in my tracks a few yards from Crystal's New Age Store. Up ahead was the unmistakable form of Chief Ben in a lip lock with Crystal. They moved apart and his deep laugh resonated. Hand-in-hand, they strolled in the opposite direction.

The urge to wallow in self-pity succumbed to the pain from the blow to my ego. Evidently, he had a type, because Crystal was nothing but a poor substitute for me. While I huffed and puffed, they walked down the hill and out of sight. I sprang into action, rushing into the Carmel Corn Cottage and buying the largest bag of double-dipped caramel corn along with a slab of fudge. The charming tinkle of the bell over the door set my teeth on edge, and I took an ineffective swing at it as I left.

Using my key fob as a car finder, I located my vehicle and began the long trek home, chewing on my treats *and* my life choices.

✳✳✳

The sound of a small engine woke me from my sugar-induced stupor. I'd finished the fudge, half the caramel corn, and three of Crystal's tea bags. By the time I located a robe and made it to the front door, the echo of the engine had faded.

My cabin was located near Story, a rural community separated from Nashville by winding roads and surrounded by a state park. The area was popular with hunters, but the lack of cell reception and the dense trees had sent more than one lost soul to my front porch searching for directions. Seeing nothing from the doorway, I went onto the porch to investigate. Stinging pain shot through my foot and up my calf. Hobbling back inside, I flopped on the couch and lifted my foot. Blood dripped onto the hardwood floor, and shards of glass protruded from my skin.

The cuts weren't deep, but there were several, all oozing nasty red. Using my fingernails, I pulled out most of the glass, but had to stop when I became light-headed. I rested on the couch and considered my predicament. The engine I'd heard sounded like an ATV.

Who had an all-terrain vehicle and would want to hurt me?

Nearly everyone in these parts had an ATV, but I could think of no one who'd want to harm me. My brain fritzed, and I shook my head to clear the cobwebs.

Did Trina think the same thing before she died?

My situation was dire. Holding it together long enough to get help was imperative, but my thoughts kept returning to Trina's cause of death. A poison used by hunters.

Ben's a hunter. Ben has an ATV. Ben has every reason to be mad at me, and he has means, motive, and opportunity.

The room spun and grew dark. I woke with my head on the couch and my foot dangling over the edge. The floor below me was crimson.

Way too much blood.

My cell was still on the bedside table where I'd left it last night, and the phone for the land line was a fuzzy dot outside of my reach, seemingly spotlighted by the afternoon sunlight streaming through the window.

The door splintered and Ben barreled inside, rushing toward me.

This time he's going to finish the job.

I crawled to the end of the sofa and curled up into a ball.

His boots thudded, then I was airborne.

✳✳✳

Hospital food was the worst, but I was glad fudge and caramel corn hadn't been my last meal. The scent of antiseptic filled the room, and Austin filled the cramped but functional chair at the side of my bed. The past few hours had dragged by with doctors of every specialty asking me the same thing, "What type of blood thinner are you on?"

The red stain on my bandaged foot had ceased to spread, but my head was in danger of exploding if I wasn't released soon. I spent a big part of the downtime using Austin's phone to search the internet about how to read Tarot cards.

My boredom was so great that I was relieved when Ben marched through the door, wearing an expression so sour he could've used it to make biscuits. He caught me staring, and for an instant his expression softened.

"I went looking for you when your office staff said you missed two appointments. Found ATV tracks in your yard. Matched them to tracks from Trina's place. What were you girls up to that got someone riled up enough to want to hurt you?" His face settled back into sourdough biscuit mode.

Having spent an afternoon fielding questions about my drug use, my stretched patience snapped, allowing my rage and frustration to escape with a hiss. "Nothing better to do so we broke out the voodoo dolls and summoned demons."

Austin's snort diverted Ben's attention. He inhaled deeply, gearing up for what I was certain would've been a scathing retort to end all retorts, but was cut off by the entrance of a nurse.

"Miss Blaine, you've been discharged."

A Lockheed SR-71 Blackbird could've crossed the Rio Grande in the same amount of time it took me to dress and climb into Austin's truck. On the ride home, we passed a metaphysical supply store and an idea struck.

"Austin, turn around. I want to buy Tarot cards."

He gave me the side-eye but pulled a U-turn and let me out at the door.

The medical boot I'd been given made walking easy. My purchase was made before he could park so he waited as I struggled into the truck's cab, then backed out of the lot and headed for home.

My mind reeled during the ride. Interpretation was key in Tarot cards, and I wanted to put the cards down and reevaluate my original connotation. The pain meds and the winding roads were not a good combo, and I was a bit woozy by the time we reached my driveway. Austin helped me from the truck, delivering me to the sofa where I pulled the coffee table closer and laid out the cards.

"Care to explain what's so important that you're jeopardizing your health by not resting?" Austin had gone into the kitchen while I was arranging and rearranging the cards, and he now stood with a steaming cup of tea.

I accepted the tea but set it aside so I could explain. "Trina's note indicated the Tarot cards 2, 0, and 20. At first I thought it was 20 and 20, but the same two cards don't make a spread." I went on to explain the meaning of each card and a no-spread spread. "Crystal and I read them to mean Judge Wainwright killed Trina."

Austin took a seat near me and picked up the High Priestess card. "You got that out of three little cards?"

I snatched the card out of his hands. "It's complicated, but I'm repositioning them to find out if there's another meaning. Trina wasn't experienced in reading the cards and now I think she was just giving me the numbers, not the order. The 0 card, the Fool, can go at the beginning or end, and it goes with the Judgement card. That places the Judgement card in the center." I slid the cards around on the table, forming different possibilities. "If I put the 2 first, and the 0 last I get a different meaning."

He leaned closer and peered at the cards. "What do the cards say with this spread?"

"I think the 2 means duplicity by someone who knows everything. 20 means crossroads of old and new, and a time to review decisions and actions." I wondered if Trina was pointing to Ben. He was undergoing a new phase in life with Crystal. He was a hunter, and he had an ATV. I didn't give voice to my thoughts. "The Fool. He's standing at the edge of a cliff, without caring that he can slip off. The Fool predicts a time of risks."

Austin offered a half-hearted, "Uh huh."

I turned the 2 card over. "Maybe Trina was trying to tell me Ben was at risk because of Crystal since she is his new beginning and he needed to review his actions."

"What?" He perked up. "Crystal and Ben?'

"I saw them together. They were pretty chummy. I think she meant Crystal was deceiving Ben."

Austin raised a brow. "That's a pretty big stretch."

I thought back to the stash of weed behind Crystal's counter. *Could she be part of a drug ring?* Given the availability of pot in the states surrounding Indiana, I dismissed the idea and reached for my tea. Austin hadn't known to doctor the tea with cinnamon and the bland taste gave me pause. "Gingko Biloba."

"Are you hallucinating?" He got up so fast the couch cushions came with him. "Let me take you back to the hospital."

I shrank from his reaching hands and grabbed my phone. "Gingko Biloba can cause bleeding. Let me Google it to be sure." A few seconds later I had the answer. "Yes. See right here — " I tapped the screen — "Gingko Biloba can cause bleeding, especially if a high dose is ingested. Grab a plastic bag from the pantry."

Austin tilted his head and squinted. "What?".

I yanked the tea bag out of the cup and shook it at him. "Ginkgo Biloba. Crystal gave me these. Take them to the lab to be analyzed. I think she tried to kill me."

Realization dawned and he became a blur of motion, securing a bag from the kitchen and zipping the tea bag inside. "I'll call Ben while I run this into town. Don't move from the couch." He jogged out the door and sped away.

I'd jumped to the wrong conclusion, and Crystal had encouraged me, but I couldn't figure out why. She knew the order she'd read wasn't right because she had the 0 in the middle and that card was always at the beginning or the end, never the middle. If Trina knew Crystal sold pot, she'd tell Ben or Austin, but most likely she'd do nothing because it wasn't hurting anyone. Unless it was hurting Chet.

All speculation came to a screeching halt when Crystal opened the front door and waltzed inside. "Didn't think your little boyfriend would ever leave. I need to get this over with and return to the shop." She held a small gun in her right hand and a reefer in her left.

"Are you going to kill me by 'blunt' force trauma?" My bravado was strong for a woman who couldn't run.

She laughed and held up the rolled weed. "Willow, always so clever. No, this is what the kids call Spice, synthetic pot, only my brand's doctored with mind-altering drugs. The little hayseeds in this hick town can't get enough of it." She lifted the gun in the air. "*This* is insurance in case you decide you don't want to have a little toke."

"That's how you killed Trina." Some part of my brain had put it all together and was screaming to stall.

"No. I wish I'd thought of that. Would have looked like an overdose just like those kids partying in the park." She moved closer. "My brother got me that frog juice from his job at the San Diego zoo. Wasn't sure how I was going to use it, but then Trina came along with all her questions."

"If I overdose, Ben and Austin will be suspicious." Stalling in real life was much harder than portrayed on TV.

"Spice can cause excess bleeding. Your blood is already thinned by the tea. This will put you over the edge, and the coroner won't have a reason to look for anything else."

A shadow of a man passed across the front window. In need of a distraction, I reached out. "Give me the doobie."

She smiled when she passed it over.

I sniffed. The smell was similar to pot. "Got a light?"

When she fished around in her pocket, Ben burst through the door and put her in a hammerlock. Within seconds my house was filled with officers, and a glaring Crystal was whisked away.

My hands shook as I passed the rolled-up Spice to Ben. "How did you know she was here?"

"Lucky guess." His regarded my shaking hands and he sat beside me. Taking my hand, he said, "Five kids overdosed in the park recently. This has been occurring more frequently in the past few weeks, so we suspected the dealer was someone new to town. When I contacted Judge Wainwright to tell her about Trina, she told me she'd taken Chet to rehab. She said Trina broke off their engagement because of his erratic behavior, which is consistent with Spice consumption. Trina knew about the Spice and probably guessed where it came from."

"How did you know Crystal would be *here?*"

"A few hours ago, a survivor told us where they'd made the buy. Got a warrant to search Crystal's shop, but the store was closed. When Austin called about the tea bags, I figured she'd come here to shut you up." He scooted closer and put his arm around my shoulders. "Guess she didn't realize how tough that is to do."

His touch calmed me, bringing back a memory. "I saw you with Crystal."

He ran a thumb over the inside of my wrist. "She reminded me of you. I wasn't ready to let you go."

I shifted my attention away while I considered his words. My spirits brightened. "This was fun. What about hiring me as a consultant?"

"No!" His voice echoed in the quiet cabin.

The 20/20 Club

by Mary Ann Koontz

Lizzy Jenkins was visiting the grave site of her recently departed mother when she almost stumbled over his feet. At first she thought he was a drunk who'd wandered into the cemetery and thought it a good place to sleep it off, undisturbed. But when her eyes traveled up his body, she knew otherwise. His black hair was standing straight up from his head, as though he had slid down into the position where he rested propped against a crudely made headstone. A knife protruded from his chest. She let out a bone-chilling scream, bringing Lindenwood Cemetery's groundskeeper running to her side. He immediately called 911, and helped Lizzy, who had turned as white as the corpse, inside the cemetery office. Soon, Fort Wayne police arrived on the scene and proceeded to get a statement from Lizzy, who was still in shock.

Arriving moments later, I received an update on Miss Jenkins' gruesome discovery from one of the uniforms, then drove the winding narrow road to the top of a hill beyond the center of the one-hundred-year-old cemetery. Large oak and linden trees protected those who rested perpetually beneath them, their roots tilting archaic stone monuments forward in reverent pose. Faded names and dates were century-old tributes of lives since forgotten. The crumbling stones made the modern granite tombstones that dotted the hills look like shiny baubles in comparison. I parked and walked the uneven ground until I reached the crime scene, partially hidden by a large angel sitting atop the monument of a nearby grave.

"This is a first," I said to the forensic photographer, who was already snapping photos of the victim. "Make sure you get the engraving nice and clear in the photos, especially the numbers 20/20."

"Sure, Wayne," came the reply.

I introduced myself to the cemetery's director, Sam Cutler. "Will you be much longer, Detective Nelson?" he asked. "We're supposed to have a funeral here in about an hour. The family's had enough stress in their lives without seeing this when they arrive."

"We're moving as fast as possible, but we don't want to miss any evidence," I said. "This is a crime scene, after all. Were there any staff on the premises last night?"

"No. The last person left around six-thirty," Sam said. "There's a fence surrounding the cemetery, but it's broken in several places. We were hoping to have repairs done next week."

When the photographer finished, I pulled on a glove and checked the dead man's pant pockets. A wallet containing 64 dollars in cash was inside. So much for robbery, I thought. The driver's license listed the man as Victor Pertoli, age 30, from Fort Wayne. I placed a call to the precinct to find Victor's next of kin.

I'd just hung up when Coroner Jan Rigsor approached the scene. "Sorry, I'd have been here sooner, but I was in court this morning testifying at a trial. I need to make this quick. A call came in on my way here about another dead body. Fortunately for you, that one's been dead for a while. So, here I am."

That explained her suit, I thought. "We feel honored by your presence," I said, giving her a mock bow. I stepped back to let her do her thing, before pressing, "Do you have an estimated time of death?"

"Hold on," Jan said. "What have we here?"

A tiny bit of white protruded between the lips of the victim. Snapping on a pair of gloves, she opened the man's mouth and pulled out a folded card. "This may prove interesting," Jan said as she bagged it and handed it to me.

I reached into the bag with a gloved hand and unfolded what appeared to be a business card. On the front was printed *20/20 Club* above a picture of Lady Justice clenching a sword in one hand, while holding evenly balanced scales in the other. The altered version, however, had her blindfold not only removed, but hanging from the tip of the sword. Also, an eye had been added to each of the balanced scales. *An eye for an eye*, I thought. Flipping it over, there was a handwritten note that read, 'In hindsight, he made a grave mistake.'

Jan finished her preliminary examination. "I need to get this man to the morgue. And to answer your question, I'd estimate time of death between midnight and 2 a.m., give or take. I'll know more after I do the autopsy. I don't suppose the card told you who murdered him?"

"Not exactly. Ever hear of the 20/20 Club?" I asked.

"Never heard of them," Jan replied. "It sounds like an optometrist's group."

"Not quite," I said. "Although, I imagine these club members like to think they see the law with 20/20 vision, unlike Lady Justice who wears a blindfold. Our victim appears to be an example of how they choose to mete out justice and balance the scales."

"So, you think this is the work of a vigilante group?" Jan asked. I nodded. "Great," she said. "Don't they know I have enough business?" Jan took off her heels and made her way back to the car, while the forensics team finished zipping the corpse into a body bag.

"Don't forget the tombstone as evidence," I said. The team scowled at me as all three men lifted the stone and manipulated a sterile bag around it before placing it on a dolly. Before they began the arduous task of getting it down the hill over tree roots and around graves, I asked, "Does anyone know what kind of stone this is?"

"Yeah, limestone," John Walsh replied. "My grandparents had it on the front of their house. There's a limestone quarry on Ardmore, south of town."

John had been with the forensic team the longest, and I liked to run hunches by him on occasion. "Why limestone?" I asked. "Seems like an odd choice for a tombstone."

John shrugged his shoulders. "Maybe because it's softer than other stones. You know, so they could engrave it easier."

"Makes sense," I said. "Thank you. So, it takes three individuals to lift the slab of stone, as you three just demonstrated. Either that, or two remarkably strong men, no offense, which means we're dealing with at least two or three collaborators in this crime."

"Guess so," John said.

The team staggered their load back to the SUV as I turned and studied the scene again. Why kill this guy in the cemetery, I wondered? I read the nearby tombstones. The victim had been positioned between two graves belonging to Harold Mason and Chris Sanders. I wrote down the names, along with their DOB's and DOD's. If only the dead could talk.

I headed back to the cemetery office where I learned that Miss Jenkins had been sent home after she'd calmed down enough to finish answering a few questions. I reviewed her statement, then called the precinct. The officer assigned the task of finding a relative for Victor was coming up blank, but he promised to keep searching. After disconnecting, I found Sam and thanked him for his cooperation. I left Lindenwood and decided to visit the Hanson Quarry in hopes of finding someone who'd recently purchased a single slab of limestone.

The main office was a short distance past the observation tower that looked out over the quarry. I went inside and spoke with the quarry's manager. Unfortunately, no such purchase had been made. "People seldom buy one slab," he said. "I'm sure I'd have remembered it." Still, he checked the receipts to verify it. "If they got the stone here, it's more likely they stole it in the dead of night. It wouldn't have been an easy task, but not an impossible one, either. We have security cameras, but not everywhere."

My phone rang, and I was surprised to see it was Jan calling. "Miss me already?" I teased. Her silence spoke volumes. "What's up?" I tried again.

"Remember the other body I told you about this morning?" Jan asked.

"Yeah, why?" I wondered how she'd managed to examine a second scene so fast.

"As it turns out, the body was only a couple miles from yours. It was a male. Hard to determine age yet because of decomp. The neighbors noticed a foul smell coming from an old abandoned building at the end of an alley. When the police investigated, they had to wear masks, but it didn't cover the stench. He must've been dead an entire week. If it weren't for the brick building and solid door, the neighbors would've noticed the tell-tale odor sooner."

"Sounds like you've had quite a day," I said. "But why call me?"

"The thing is," Jan said, her irritation palpable over the phone, "he was found hanging from the rafters. I noticed the familiar white paper as I approached the body. It was another 20/20 Club card."

Now, it was my turn to fall silent. "Text me the address. I'll be right there."

When I arrived at the scene, I discovered the extent to which Jan had downplayed the stench. I was forced to run in-and-out of the building to examine the crime scene. There was nothing unusual about the rope. It could've been bought at any hardware or big-box store. Nothing beneath the body provided us with any evidence either. When the body was lowered, I checked the jeans pocket and once again found a wallet with close to 100 dollars in it. A driver's license identified the victim as Hugo Mendez. I immediately called for a background check. His rap sheet was long, including a list of armed robberies for which he'd done five years before getting out on parole. He was released from prison three months ago. I took down his address and decided to swing by the place.

Hugo's home was only two blocks away. I stepped around toddler's toys as I approached the front porch. I rang the doorbell and waited. Moments later, a young woman with a child on her hip peered out at me. When I showed her my badge, her hand flew to her mouth. She let me in and placed the toddler inside a Pac'n Play along with a selection of toys. I asked if she was Maria Mendez, Hugo's wife. She nodded, her eyes wide with fear.

"He's dead, isn't he?" Maria asked.

"Yes, ma'am," I replied. I hated this part of my job. I tried to avoid telling her how he'd died, but she insisted. When I told her, she held her head in her hands. I offered to get her water, but she refused.

"I'm so sorry for your loss," I said. After she'd gained her composure, I asked, "Did you ever hear your husband mention the 20/20 Club?"

Maria frowned. "No, why?"

I told her about the business card found on him.

"Can you tell me what was going on in his life recently? I know he did time for armed robberies."

Maria glanced over at her child. "Money's been tight. It was all I could do to feed my son, let alone myself, while Hugo was in prison. My parents tried

143

to help, but they had very little money to spare. On our last visit with Hugo, before he got out, he gave me the name of a guy who could loan us money. I told him no, we'd get by, but eventually I gave in.

When Hugo got out, this guy insisted on a return on his investment. Hugo couldn't repay the loan. The guy threatened to kill us unless Hugo did some robberies for him."

"What's this guy's name?" I asked.

"He went by Jersey," Maria said. "I only talked to him on the phone."

"I'll need his number, along with the places Hugo robbed and the dates." I handed Maria a pad of paper and pen. She scrounged through a kitchen drawer and found the number, then added the robberies to the notepad.

"Is there anyone else who might want to hurt your husband?" I asked.

"No. He was a good husband and father. He even helped the neighbors fix their fence a couple weeks ago. There were never any bullets in his gun. He couldn't hurt anyone. It doesn't make any sense. Hugo was making money for Jersey, so why would Jersey want to kill him?"

I couldn't argue with her logic. I gave her my card in case she thought of anything else. On the back, I included the number of someone who could help her with financial aid.

Back at the precinct, I searched the backgrounds of the two victims, but couldn't find any overlap. Next, I entered the names from the two tombstones that Victor had been positioned between. The first, Harold Mason, was 55 when he died. His background was unremarkable, with no priors. There were no relatives listed that I could find.

I entered the second name, Chris Sanders. He was only 19 when he died, still living with his parents. He was found shot around 10 p.m., along with the manager of a convenience store on 7th Street, during an apparent robbery. The only suspect, a man who'd been previously arrested with Chris for robbery, was never convicted of Chris's murder. I searched further and discovered the other man was Hugo Mendez. I mulled the new information over, then decided to pay Chris Sanders' parents a visit.

Mr. and Mrs. Sanders were cordial enough, but I knew my visit was forcing them to recall memories they'd just as soon forget. It had been a little over a year since their son had died, not nearly enough time for their grief to have passed. I wondered if there ever was a period of time when grief released its grip, or was it like the tide that ebbed, only to come roaring back?

I asked about their memories of Chris. He was a sweet child, but his teenage years were rebellious. They hadn't been concerned until the day his mom found a wad of bills in his drawer while putting away his clothes. When they'd questioned him, he insisted he'd been doing odd jobs to earn it, but they found too many holes in his explanations. Then, he was arrested for robbery at 18, barely an adult as far as the courts were concerned. Hugo Mendez had been with him, and the family blamed Mendez for steering their son astray, ultimately holding him responsible for Chris' death. They were sure he'd been with their son in this last robbery as well.

I asked if they had a picture of Chris. Mrs. Sanders retrieved a framed family photo that hung in the hallway and handed it to me. I stared at the sibling in the picture.

"Who's standing next to Chris?" I asked.

"That's our other son, Victor," Mr. Sanders replied.

"Forgive me for asking, but does he have the same last name?"

"No," Mr. Sanders said, looking puzzled. "My wife's first husband passed away when Victor was 10. He was 11 when we married, so we gave him the choice of keeping his dad's last name or using mine. He chose his dad's – Pertoli."

That would explain why we hadn't located the family of Victor Pertoli, our first victim. They had different last names. "So, Chris and Victor were half-brothers?"

"That's right," Mr. Sanders said. "The two were very close at one time. The past few months before Chris died, though, they argued a lot. I'm not sure what about." A shadow crossed Mr. Sanders' face. "Why do you ask?"

"Did you ever hear either of your sons mention the 20/20 Club?" I needed to get as much information as I could before throwing added grief at the couple.

Mrs. Sanders' eyes lit up. "Yes. Victor dropped a card with that name on it when he was here last. I didn't get a good look at it, because he snatched it out of my hand."

"Did he tell you anything about the club?"

"He said it was a grief support group. I tried to ask him more about it, but he changed the subject. We were happy he was getting help. He became so withdrawn after Chris died. Our whole family's been devastated since …" She couldn't finish the sentence.

"When did you talk to Victor last?" I asked.

"He was here for dinner last Sunday, a few days ago," Mr. Sanders said. "He seemed happier than we'd seen him in a long time. We assumed it was because of the support group." He looked at me with suspicion. "Why are you asking all these questions about Victor?"

I hated giving them the news about their second son's death. They would never be the same, I thought. They'd lost two sons in a little over a year's time. No parent should have to go through such grief.

The Sanders' gave me permission to search Victor's apartment and handed me their spare key. When I asked if they'd like to be present, they declined. Mr. Sanders merely asked me to return the key when I finished.

Victor's apartment was on the west side of town. It was in an old home that'd been divided into two apartments. His was on the upper level. The door was ajar, and I entered with caution. Someone had beat me to the search and had gone to great pains to be thorough about it. The difference was whoever ransacked the place seemed to have been looking for something specific, so they had the advantage over me.

Stepping gingerly across the floor, which was littered with the contents of Victor's shelves and desk drawers, I put on a pair of gloves and shuffled through some of the debris. I picked up several books and checked the spines. All were various titles on justice. I moved to the bedroom. There I found the mattress upturned and drawers pulled from the dresser, then dumped onto the floor. When I examined the dresser, I noticed a cord dangling free at the back of it. I followed the cord up to a lamp that sat atop the dresser, its shade askew. It seemed odd that it wasn't plugged in. I tilted the lampshade up and found a pamphlet wedged into its seam. I wiggled it carefully until it came free. How ironic, I thought, reading the brochure. It was a list of dates and times for an anti-violence group. The next meeting was tomorrow afternoon.

I grinned. Maybe I was the one who had the advantage now.

***

The following afternoon, I stopped at the courthouse and found Room 108 on the main floor. A small group of people had begun to assemble, and I hoped I didn't reek of cop. At 44 years of age, I found it increasingly difficult to be cool, especially when I had a teenage son who reminded me constantly that I wasn't. Today, I would settle for not having the appearance that screamed cop. I grabbed some coffee from a table at the back of the room, and then took a seat in one of the 10 chairs that'd been arranged in a circle. At two o'clock, when the meeting was scheduled to begin, I noticed there were three empty chairs.

The group expressed surprise at the absences. It wasn't like Antonio, who normally led the group, not to show. One girl commented that Suzanne told her she'd definitely be here, but she wasn't. It was the first meeting John had missed as well. They hadn't noticed that a fourth person was missing, probably because I was occupying his chair. A guy named Jake finally realized it and asked if anyone had heard from their newest member, Victor, who'd joined them a couple months ago. No one had heard from him. They'd know all the grizzly details tomorrow, I thought, now that Victor's family had been notified of his death, thanks to me.

The meeting commenced without those absent, and I listened as each member present introduced themselves and revealed the parent, sibling, or spouse who had been lost to violent crime. When it was my turn to speak, I made up a name and a brief story. I had many to choose from, but fortunately none of the stories were mine. By the end of the meeting, I'd managed to garner the last names of the missing members, along with bits and pieces of their stories.

Arriving back at my car, I scribbled down notes. Antonio Vasquez, a police officer whose wife was killed in a drive-by meant for a neighborhood gangbanger. Suzanne Mitchum. Her dad was killed by his business partner. John Williams, whose brother was killed in a car-jacking. All three had one thing in common. There had been no convictions in those cases. I took a deep breath. Were these the members of the 20/20 Club? Motive: check, except for

Victor. If these were the club members, why kill one of their own? He'd been a card-carrying member. Had Victor threatened to expose them?

I returned to the precinct to learn more about the three members. A background check on Suzanne showed her to be a black, 28-year-old female. She'd testified she'd overheard her father's business partner, Martin Billingsly, arguing with her dad, Parker Mitchum. On the day he was shot, Mitchum accused Billingsly of embezzlement. The evidence was said to be circumstantial, and Mr. Billingsly walked away from the trial with a clean record.

Curious, I entered Martin Billingsly into the system. His obituary came up. It stated he'd died January 6, 2018, in a car accident. I brought up the police report on the accident. Martin's car was believed to have slid off an icy road into a pond. His watch had stopped at 11 p.m.

I moved on to the next 20/20 member, John Williams. His data showed him to be a white male, age 27. He had three sisters and one brother, Jerome. I typed in Jerome Williams. An article about a deadly car-jacking came up. It seems two men had attempted to steal the vehicle that Jerome was driving. When he refused to get out of the car, Jerome was shot and killed. There'd been no eyewitnesses or video cameras in the area. Word on the street was Nico Reed and Sean Donner had been heard bragging about their new ride which they'd sold for parts in a nearby state. There was no conviction.

When I entered the two names again, two obituaries came up. I double-checked the date of death on each and sat back in my chair. Both died on March 20, 2018, exactly 10 years to the date that Jerome had been killed. I checked the circumstances of their deaths. Nico had died of an overdose of heroin, and Sean had suffered a massive heart attack.

This was too much of a coincidence, I thought. But Martin Billingsly died on a different date than Suzanne's father, Parker Mitchum. I keyed in Parker Mitchum again and reread the coroner's report. Time of death was estimated around 11 p.m. That was the same time Mitchum's watch had stopped. Another coincidence I wasn't buying. There was no mention of a 20/20 card being found in any of the three reports, though. So, what changed prior to Hugo and Victor's deaths? Why the sudden need to draw attention to their deadly acts of justice?

I checked the death linked to the third member, Antonio Vasquez. I found only a short article on his wife Ana's death. There wasn't much for the reporter to say since no one seemed to have seen or heard anything. That is, except for Antonio, who was present when a bullet slammed through the front of his home and lodged in Ana's heart. He'd held her in his arms and watched her die before the ambulance arrived. He reported hearing tires squealing following the shot but had seen nothing. According to the article, he suspected his neighbors knew more. They were too fearful of being targeted themselves should they say something. Everyone guessed they'd shot into the wrong house. I knew that until Antonio learned more, there wouldn't be another body in this instance. But he was a cop, and apt to find a way to get information, even if it took years.

That left Victor Pertoli, a new member of the 20/20 Club. Only he and Hugo had the 20/20 Club calling card on them. Why had the club members gone from secretly balancing the scales of justice to letting the world know? And something was off about Hugo Mendez and the robbery where he'd reportedly shot Chris, Victor's brother. It gnawed at the edge of my subconscious, and it stuck there. I decided to call Maria.

"Maria, this is Detective Wayne Nelson," I said. "We met the other day."

"Yes, I remember," she said.

"When I spoke with the Sanders family, they blamed Hugo for their son's death. But something about that didn't sit right with me, and I was hoping you could help me find out what it is," I said.

"That's easy. He didn't do it," Maria said defiantly.

"How do you know?" I asked. There was silence. "Maria, I'm trying to clear his name on this, and maybe it will help me find his killer as well." Maria sighed.

"Okay. The night of that particular robbery, my husband was somewhere else."

"Where?" I asked. "He had no alibi at the time."

"That's because he was on the opposite side of town," Maria said, then hesitated.

"Doing what?"

"Robbing a gas station," Maria finally said. "He was afraid he'd go back to prison, and they didn't have enough evidence on the other robbery that night to convict him. So, he stayed quiet. I'm sorry about the Sanders boy, but there's no way Hugo was responsible for his death. Besides, he never used bullets in his gun."

"Thank you, Maria. You've been a big help," I said.

I pondered this new information. The first time the 20/20 Club decided to leave a calling card, they may have killed the wrong guy. They hadn't been so careless in the past. I needed to find out how they were communicating. It wouldn't have been safe to talk at the anti-violence group, although I guessed that's where they'd met. I needed to pay the FWPD Cyber Division a visit.

Jason was a fresh-faced kid who didn't look a day over 18, but he swore he was 25. Although he was the youngest, I knew he was the best tech in our Cyber Division. I'd no sooner briefed Jason on what I was hoping to find when his fingers were flying across the keyboard. "Let's try a screen name they might have used to set up a private chat room," Jason suggested.

"Try the obvious, 20/20 Club," I said.

"I found it, but it was closed out."

"Can you tell me the date the account was set up, and the date it was closed?" I asked.

"Hang on," Jason said. "It was set up November 20, 2017, and closed on, hey, a week ago."

So, it'd been set up shortly before the first "accidental" death had occurred. Plenty of time for the members to have planned the first murder, Martin Billingsly, the following January. "It was closed the same day Hugo was killed. Interesting," I said. "Can you tell me who set up the account?"

Jason worked his magic again. "It was set up by Antonio Vasquez. What a coincidence, there's an Antonio Vasquez that works for the FWPD." He glanced up at me.

"Not a word about this," I warned. Jason shook his head. "Can you see if Antonio set up a new account for a private chat room?"

Jason hurriedly entered more information, clicking through one pop-up box after another. At last, he said, "There are 10 new accounts by Antonio Vasquez. It's a popular name.'

"Eliminate those not in Fort Wayne," I suggested.

Now they were down to three. I stretched my back, trying to think. "Can you bring up the screen names on those accounts?"

Jason brought up three, but only one stood out, *Hindsight*. "That's it!" I said. "Now, I have one more favor to ask . . ."

I'd just returned to my desk when my phone rang. "Detective Wayne Nelson," I answered.

"Detective, this is Sam Cutler, the director at Lindenwood Cemetery."

"Yes, I remember you. How are you?"

"I'm fine," Sam said. "I wanted to call because something came up that's probably not important, but you said to call if I remembered anything new."

"That's right," I said. "What is it?"

"I forgot to tell you we have a security guard that we share with other nearby businesses. He has a schedule that enables him to patrol each place. The night the murdered man was left in our cemetery, our security guard said he patrolled here between 10 and 11 that night. But the owner of the insulation business across the street, who shares the security guard with us, said he saw the guard's car at the cemetery well past midnight. He remembered thinking it was odd at the time because it wasn't the guard's usual schedule. He said it had to be around 12:30 because he'd left a wedding reception 20 minutes earlier. He'd stopped in to pick up some work for the next day so he could work from home in the morning. I'm sure it's nothing, though. The security guard has seven years of experience working with the FWPD."

I gripped my phone hard. "What's his name?" I asked.

"Antonio," he said. "Antonio Vasquez."

I thanked Sam and disconnected. Checking the clock on my phone, I realized I needed to move it if I didn't want to be late to a very important meeting. I touched base with my boss briefly, who informed me that Tony, as they called Antonio in the squad room, left 10 minutes ago. Thankfully, the captain had stalled him with an important envelope that needed to be dropped off ASAP to someone at the courthouse. It was bogus, but I was grateful the captain had bought me some extra time.

I parked behind the cemetery main office next to the surveillance van.

Numerous bugs had been planted in the chapel, so I slipped in my ear buds and grabbed my binoculars. I was thrilled Jason had found the group's meeting place after scrolling through their chat room site.

The first to arrive was Antonio. He unlocked the gate to the cemetery, closing it after he'd pulled through, but leaving it unlocked. He drove to a small limestone building, that Sam had told me dated back to 1895. Located near the center of the cemetery, it was called The Chapel of the Woods. Antonio pulled out his set of keys he'd used as a security guard and unlocked the main door. A second car pulled in, followed soon after by a third. Suzanne Mitchum and John Williams glanced around, then entered the chapel as well. A fourth car pulled up and the driver got out, but unlike the others, he took a deep breath before entering. I listened closely.

"Okay, Jake," Antonio said gruffly, recognizing him from the anti-violence group. "We agreed to meet with you, so what's with the email you sent us, 'I know what you did, and I want in?'"

"How'd you know how to find us?" John added, moving toward Jake.

"I got suspicious when those suspected of murdering your loved ones suddenly had accidents or committed suicide," Jake said. "So I did some snooping and found your private chat room."

"I don't trust him," Antonio said, as he rushed forward and patted Jake down. "No wire and no weapon," he said taking a step back. "So, this is the way you choose to ask to join us?" he sneered.

"How else was I supposed to approach you?" Jake said. "But I've got one question before I can commit. Why the change? You had a good thing going. Your victims each died with no one the wiser. Then, I read in your chat room that you started leaving cards. Why? Wasn't that risky?"

Suzanne spoke up, each word punctuated with venom. "That was Victor's idea. We didn't know he'd left the card on Hugo's body. It wasn't his call to make."

"Shut up!" Antonio yelled at her.

"Is that why you killed him?" Jake asked.

"That, and finding out he had us kill an innocent guy," Suzanne said, ignoring Antonio's warning.

"But how did you know he was innocent?" Jake prodded.

John Williams clenched his fists. "Because Victor was high that night and looking to steal money to supply his habit. He and Chris decided to rob a convenience store. After getting the cash, Chris went to the car. That's when Victor started waving his gun around and shooting at random. He didn't know Chris had reentered the store, until he fell to the floor motionless with blood pooling around him. The store manager screamed, and Victor panicked. He killed the manager, who he thought was the only witness."

"But he wasn't the only witness." Suzanne said. "We found a junkie who shot up regularly behind the store. The night Chris died, he was in the store's bathroom and cracked the door enough to see it all go down. He ran out the back before the police arrived."

"Victor's family hated Hugo Mendez already, so he was the perfect patsy for the murders," Antonio seethed. "He used us. He used the 20/20 Club to kill Hugo and further cover up his involvement in Chris' death."

Suzanne shook her head. "Not only did he bring us unwanted attention but he defiled our club's purpose for justice. Victor killed Chris at the convenience store on 7th Street, and the body was found around ten o'clock . . . "

"Which is why you murdered Victor on July 10th," I said. They turned to see who'd spoken. Antonio reached for the weapon he had tucked into the back of his jeans. "I wouldn't," I said. Six police officers entered the chapel, weapons aimed at the three. "Nice work, Jake," I said. "If you ever want to give up your day job, call me."

"But Antonio checked you for a wire," Suzanne said.

"Detective Nelson had the entire chapel bugged instead," Jake explained.

The officers moved in and cuffed the three suspects.

I strolled over to face the now guilt-stricken individuals, who'd attempted to play God in meting out their own form of justice. "So much for your 20/20 vision for justice," I said. "In hindsight, I'd say you all made grave mistakes."

I nodded at the officers, "Get 'em out of here."

Tailor-Made for Murder

by C.L. Shore

Daniel Ruiz sat staring at the swirling hollyberries and mistletoe on the kitchen tablecloth. He stifled his urge to vomit. He'd already puked several times, his stomach couldn't possibly be holding on to anything.

The uniformed woman sitting beside him put a hand on his arm. "Daniel." She moved her face closer, trying to look into his downcast eyes. "We need to go downtown. To the station."

Daniel didn't feel the January cold as he took a seat in the squad car. He paid no attention to the snow-packed city streets. Instead, he replayed his memory of the last 90 minutes. Less than two hours ago he'd been euphoric, counting himself lucky to be walking out the door of the St. Vincent Emergency Room at 7:38, just minutes after his night shift ended. He knew the day shift would be having a harder job on New Year's Day. Sure, there had been a couple of car wrecks with smashed up people coming in on the night shift. But they didn't hold up the nurses too much, they'd either be treated and released or sent to the OR. Overnight, he'd dealt with one of each type. But the day shift? They'd be dealing with hangovers, dietary indiscretions, holiday gout . . . problems that were sometimes tougher to figure out.

With the New Year's Eve shift qualifying for a double bonus, night shift plus holiday pay, he'd willingly signed up. He and Tiffany would use the extra money to celebrate her birthday on January 7. They'd enjoy a quiet evening at a special restaurant without having to battle the crowds. And the inebriated.

When he'd approached the duplex door next to the driveway, something appeared to be off. The door was slightly ajar. His first thought was Tiffany was up and had seen him pull his black Saturn into the drive. But a dark kitchen greeted him, there was no coffee on. He thought he smelled the faint aroma of cinnamon, though.

"Tiffany?" No answer. "Tiff!" His nursing shoes squeaked as they moved quickly over the vinyl floor and into the hallway leading to their bedroom.

She's sleeping in a strange position. Her face looked straight up at the ceiling, her body twisted to the side, legs covered by the comforter. She was wearing her black-and-red flannel pajamas, her "lumberjack PJs" as she called them. As he approached the side of the bed, he saw that her pajama top was open and her eyes were, too. A chain of tiny red spots dotted the pillowcase.

He remembered screaming and feeling his knees buckle. His neighbor on the other side of the duplex ran in, a burly guy in his late 30s. "What's going on, man?" he said, winded. His focus moved from Daniel on the floor to Tiffany on the bed. "Oh, man! I'm calling the cops."

And the cops had come, of course. Cops and more cops. He'd been asked a few questions, as had his neighbor. Evidence was being collected, and they were readying Tiffany's body to leave the duplex. He wanted to kiss her one last time, but the cops said no.

At the station, they explained he wasn't under arrest but they wanted whatever information he could give them. Daniel said he had no problem with sharing information. They swabbed his cheek. The two detectives asked questions, many of them probing. Was he having an affair? Was she? Anyone at his workplace who had an obsession with her? Was Tiffany pregnant? Did anyone have feelings of revenge toward either of them? A jilted lover in the past?

No, Daniel had said. No, no, no, and no. They'd been married two years, money was tight, but that was temporary until Tiffany finished school. Only a few months, and she would have graduated. And they'd hoped to have a baby sometime in 2021. Overall, things were good, even great. He looked down at the worn square of vinyl flooring in front of his chair.

"Daniel." He felt the touch on his arm. The same female officer, Detective Black. Her voice was warm, soothing. "Is there anyone I can call for you?"

"My sister." Daniel rattled off a number, his brain on autopilot.

The officer managed to jot it down. She walked over to a phone hanging on the wall and punched in the digits. Daniel heard her speak to someone, but he didn't focus on the words. He looked at the clock – 11:30 a.m. on January 1, 2020. Just over three hours since he walked through the door to the duplex unit he shared with his wife Tiffany, and found her dead.

"Your sister's on her way." Detective Black removed something from her pocket. "Here's my card. If you have any concerns or additional information, please call."

Maria tumbled into the room minutes later. Daniel stood and she pulled him into a tight embrace.

"Daniel," she said. "Oh, Daniel, Daniel . . . "

"Who could do this to Tiffany?," he asked when Maria released him from the crushing embrace. "She was nice, kind, sweet . . ."

Maria shook her head. "Daniel, you're right. I was so happy for you when you met her. She was the perfect person to be your wife. But sometimes goodness in one person brings out the evil in another."

Daniel took a small step back. "That's such a sad thought. But it feels like the truth. Nothing else makes sense."

Maria grabbed her brother's hands. "You're coming home with me now. I'll kick your nephews out of your old room and you can have privacy. Tomorrow, we'll try to go through some things. Now, you need rest."

Daniel flinched at the thought of staying at a home with three noisy boys and an overweight husband who drank beer from his recliner through every televised football game. But he couldn't remain at the duplex with the yellow tape over the door. "I want to stop by the duplex first. I know I can't go in. But I want to check out my car, make sure it's locked. I don't think I can drive today, though."

"Of course not. You got your keys?"

Daniel nodded. When Maria pulled into the duplex driveway, he got out and was relieved to see his car was locked. Actually, it was *their* car, his and Tiffany's. Working night shift allowed them to get by with one vehicle, another way they'd saved money. He unlocked the driver's side door and slid behind the wheel. He looked in the glove compartment. Nothing unusual there – just the registration and insurance verification. He checked the pink envelope in the door where Tiffany kept her university parking pass. A small blue card was wedged at the bottom. It almost looked like a ticket, but one long edge was perforated. It had been ripped off something else. A receipt. He slipped it into his pocket. He looked over the rest of the car's interior before locking it and returning to the passenger seat of Maria's SUV. It only took her a few minutes to reach the three-bedroom ranch she shared with her family.

The house was quiet on their arrival. Maria got her kids up and out of their room with promises of video games in their pajamas, at least until their father wanted to watch college bowl games. She brought Daniel a plate of huevos rancheros and a small household fan. "To drown out background noise."

Daniel wasn't sure if he could eat, but he polished off the eggs and settled down on top of the lower bunk in the same room he'd occupied his junior year of high school, when his parents had business back on the island. His mind rehashed the last 24 hours, then the last week. The thoughts kept coming faster until his mind numbed and he slept.

***

Daniel woke up in darkness. The Rose Bowl was over, and Pedro, his brother-in-law, snored in his recliner. Maria roused her husband and sent him off to bed before setting a plate of back-eyed peas and tamales in front of Daniel. "Eat," she said. "You need to take care of yourself."

Daniel told her the boys could have their room back. He'd slept enough, might nap on the couch later, but he planned to make some lists. Lists of things about Tiffany and things they'd discussed in the last month. "Maybe that will help us figure out who killed her."

Maria nodded before leaving him in the family room alone. He polished off the food before finding a pencil and a discarded envelope under the coffee table. He printed "Tiffany" at the top of one sheet and began a list. "Beautiful. Polite. Good figure. Sweet nature. Good singing voice. A student. Creative. Managed money well."

Tiffany had managed the household expenses and paid the bills. They'd bought most of the Christmas gifts for their family members from Konrad's

Department Store because Tiffany had received a 30-percent-off coupon in the mail. Not only that, they had received 120 dollars in Cold Cash coupons based on their holiday spending. They'd agree to split the reward as their Christmas gift to each other. She'd hinted that she'd spent hers on something that he would regard as a gift as well. He'd find out on her birthday. One week into the new year.

Daniel hadn't thought about that too much, until now. He still had his sixty-dollars-worth of coupons and planned to use them to buy her a birthday gift.

Tiffany had received her grades from the downtown university via email, just prior to Christmas — 3.63 GPA. She was majoring in elementary education and planned to do her student teaching in Speedway, beginning in mid-January.

Daniel started another list of people that Tiffany interacted with. Family members. Classmates. Teachers. A few close friends from high school. Perhaps people she interacted with in the business world? Her hair stylist, maybe. He doubted there were any others. Surely, she didn't shop anywhere often enough to be a "regular." Except maybe the grocery store, but that was a big chain store where individual costumers would be unlikely to be noticed. Except Tiffany was young and very pretty.

He remembered the receipt and retrieved it from his pocket. The small piece of cardboard measured about one by three inches. The date 1/2/2020 was handwritten in ink across it. Tiny red letters in the left-hand corner read *A-One Tailor*. Nothing else. No address or phone number. As far as he knew, Tiffany had never been to a tailor.

His mind rebelled at so much scrutiny. He stretched out on the couch until Maria woke him up. "It's eight-thirty. Pedro's off to work, the kids went to school. Let's think about what we should do." She started the coffee maker and popped a couple of breakfast pastries in the microwave.

Daniel showed her the receipt. "I found this. It has today's date on it. No address for the business, though."

"That's easily solved." Maria took out her cell phone. "There's a business with that name not too far from the university downtown. Near 10th Street."

"Let's go." Daniel felt energized, at least there was a clue to follow. He was desperate to make sense of the senselessness that had assaulted his life.

"Okay. By the way, Tiffany's parents have been calling. They want to see her, of course. And they want to know about a funeral. I told them it was a coroner's case for now. Can't do much until the autopsy is complete. That might be today."

"Thanks for talking to them. I don't think I could manage it right now." Maria had offered to take his cell phone and handle all calls as long as he needed. A very sisterly offer.

Traffic was a little heavier on the first workday after the holiday season. But the university was still in its midyear break, and there was ample parking in front of A-One Tailor, a small storefront on the ground floor of an older apartment building. The Chinese good luck cat with its moving paw was featured in the front window, along with several Asian-looking long gowns. A bell tinkled as Daniel pushed open the door. A woman wearing a tunic over a full skirt came to the counter. Her long black hair was pulled into a knot at the crown of her head. A few locks hung free. "Can I help you?" she asked. Her voice was soft, but clear.

Daniel scanned the long rows of garments in clear plastic hanging behind the woman. "I found this receipt with my wife's things," he said. "We came to pick up whatever she left and pay for it."

"Ah. Yes, Miss Tiffany. I remember." The woman had a slight accent, but she spoke English fluently. She ran her hand down the row of garments across the back of the store. "Here." Whatever was in the bag was simple and black. Daniel wondered if it could be a choir robe. "Ten dollar."

Daniel had a ten in his wallet. She made out a handwritten receipt. Daniel laid the clothing across the back seat. "We'll take this home and figure out what it is when we get back to your place."

Maria started the ignition. "Okay."

Once back in Maria's kitchen, Daniel removed the plastic from the garment. It was a dress made of slinky black fabric. There were slits in the sleeves and up the side seams from the hemline.

"Wow, this looks like a sexy little number. A little black dress." Maria picked it up. She read the label inside the back neckline. "Apartment Eleven. One of Konrad's clothing lines."

At least some things are starting to make sense, Daniel thought. This is how Tiffany spent her Cold Cash, and why she said it would be a gift for him, too.

"Let's see how it would look on a person," Maria said. "I'm a little bigger than Tiffany, but this fabric is stretchy."

She took the dress from him and disappeared into her bedroom without waiting for an answer. Daniel struggled with an unfamiliar mix of surprise and disgust at his sister's action, but she'd disappeared with the garment before he'd had a chance to react.

Within minutes Maria returned. The dress was at least one size too small for her, fabric meant to drape was stretched to the limit. The slits revealed glimpses of upper arm and thigh. Tiffany had it shortened, most likely. She planned to wear it at her birthday celebration. Daniel shook his head. For the first time, he felt like crying, but he held it in. He'd wait until he had privacy.

"Thanks for letting me see what it looks like on a person. I'd like to put it back in the bag now."

Maria was built like a shot putter. Her muscular and big-boned frame was a contrast to Tiffany's petite and delicate physique. Tiffany had been a decent runner in high school. Occasionally, she'd talk Daniel into doing a 5K run with her, if he had the weekend off.

Maria disappeared to take off the dress. Daniel heard his ringtone coming from her purse and retrieved his phone. He didn't recognize the number but answered the call. "Detective Black here," her voice was business-like, but gentle. "We're almost done with the crime scene processing. You can move back after 4 p.m., if you feel up to it."

"Thanks. I may do that."

Maria returned to the kitchen, dressed in her own clothes. She handed the black dress to Daniel. He put it back on the hanger, noting a red-blond hair caught in the zipper pull. He slipped the dress in the bag and hung it in the coat closet. He'd return it to the duplex later that day.

***

161

Daniel's hands began to shake as they turned the corner a block away from his residence. He pulled his keys out of his pocket. "You sure you want to do this?" his sister asked.

"Maria, I can be alone in the house now. There's more I want to think through. If I need to come to your place later, I'll phone you. I can handle any calls from Tiffany's mom and dad now, too."

Maria didn't look convinced, but she didn't argue. "Whatever you say. Just call if you need anything. Please."

"I will."

Maria gave him a quick hug. The afternoon sun cast a few bright patches on the white snow, but stark shadows from telephone poles cut across the yard as she drove off. Daniel unlocked the door, went to the living room, and sat on the couch. He allowed the tears to flow until they stopped of their own accord. Then he stretched out across the cushions and fell asleep.

He closed the door to the master bedroom after waking a few hours later. He took the black dress, which he'd draped over a chair, to a closet in the second bedroom. Tiffany had referred to the eight-by-twelve space as her office. It was her domain at least three-quarters of the time. She used it for studying and paying bills. Her computer had been on the desk, but the police had it now. Actually, it was *their* computer, but she used it most of the time. Daniel knew she had a Facebook account and at least two email accounts, one for school and one for personal use. He also had an email account for work, but he never used his personal one. They'd agreed when they'd married that they would share all passwords, and he had hers written down, somewhere. He hadn't thought about ever needing them, but now they could be important.

Daniel sat at the desk. Her textbooks were neatly stacked to the right of the computer area. A small bulletin board on the wall held a 2019-2020 calendar and various notes. All but one seemed to pertain to assignments and deadlines. The exception displayed a handwritten seven-digit phone number. He'd check that out later.

✳✳✳

Breakfast318. How could he have forgotten Tiffany's password? Breakfast for the obvious connection to her name and the movie, 318 stood for March 18. That was the first day they'd breakfasted together as husband and wife, after their "crazy St. Patrick's Day wedding" as she'd called it. He had to smile a little. Irish jigs and salsa music. Yeah, it was crazy.

He used his cell phone to open Gmail and signed in using Tiffany's password.

There was nothing unusual in Tiffany's Inbox or Sent mail. Communication with family members and friends, plus the occasional advertisement or communication from her dentist's office. He decided to look at her Trash. Several emails there from one source: The Pirate King. They began December 26 and ended December 30.

"You looked so cute, modeling that sexy dress. I want to take you out. Wear that dress for *me*. The Pirate King."

The other three emails were in the same vein, except the last one was more aggressive, castigating Tiffany for not responding. "What! You think you're too good for me?" It looked like Tiffany had opened them all but responded to none.

Daniel felt his heart drop before his blood began to boil. He'd seen the little platform, flanked by the triple mirrors. The Pirate King had probably watched Tiffany model the dress at the tailors. With her strawberry blond hair and slim figure, she probably looked appealing.

He jumped up from the computer and ran to his car. It took him exactly 15 minutes to walk through the door at A-One Tailor.

"Hello?" the Asian woman's eyes flashed their recognition. "One minute." She held up her hand in a "stop" gesture. After checking a customer out, she came back to Daniel. "You have question?"

"I do. I came to pick up the black dress yesterday, remember? My wife, the person who brought the dress in, was murdered. I need to know what clients were in your shop when she tried on the dress for you."

"Ah. Let me think. I might be able to remember this information, but I feel better talking to police about it."

The police. "Have the police been here?"

"Not yet. But I heard story about your wife on the radio. Police may be coming to talk with me."

"Okay." Daniel didn't know how to proceed. "Can you tell me if they do come?"

"Maybe. I have your phone number."

"Mine?" *Why did this business owner have his number?*

"Yes." She rattled off seven digits.

"Oh. Yes, that's right." Daniel let out a pent-up breath. The number she'd recited was their landline number. Of course, she'd need contact information for her customers, in case they didn't pick up their clothes. "You seem to have it memorized."

She shrugged. "My talent. I remember numbers very well."

Daniel struggled for something to say. "Well . . . if the police do come about my wife's case . . . I would appreciate it if you call me. You can leave a message if I'm not there."

She gave a quick little nod of her head. Almost a subtle bow. "Yes."

Why didn't I give her my cell phone number? The thought hit Daniel as he balanced on the build-up of icy snow to unlock his car. He dismissed the thought quickly. *Probably just as well. Not sure I'd want my cell phone number in her mental Rolodex.*

Daniel showered and changed clothes when he arrived at the duplex. He found some leftover enchiladas in the refrigerator, and he chopped up some lettuce and tomato for garnish. The place was too silent, but he couldn't bring himself to watch TV now. He found himself crying. Tiffany had bought this lettuce, made these enchiladas. He let the tears flow for a few minutes. *Enough. Save your tears for something more than lettuce.*

His cell rang. Maria.

"Hey, little brother. How are you doing?"

"I think I'm making a little progress. Found a clue. Did Tiffany ever mention The Pirate King to you?"

"Yeah! I should have thought about that! Someone with that name was sending her creepy emails, like a cyberstalker. Except, she thinks she saw him in person, too, at the tailor's. He watched her try on that black dress. She said he stared at her, made her feel uncomfortable."

"That name, The Pirate King. I looked it up. It's a character from The Pirates of Penzance. Obviously, not a real name – or title."

"Yeah. Tiffany said whoever came in after her brought in a costume including a shirt with puffy sleeves. He said he needed it altered quickly, was going to be in a play."

"Hmm." Daniel was starting to feel his skin crawl. "Okay. Thanks for the info. I'm going to do a little research tonight. Try to find out more about this weirdo." He heated the enchiladas in the microwave and found a cold beer in the fridge. He needed to chill while he considered his next move.

Phone records seemed like an obvious place to start. He placed his dirty plate in the sink and rinsed it before heading back to the computer. He had never scrutinized their phone records before, but he'd set up accounts and passwords for their joint cell phone account and their landline. He found his small notebook where he'd recorded all the info.

It was an easy matter to scrutinize the incoming calls on Tiffany's cell and the landline. Most were family. A couple on her cell were repeated numbers starting well before the end of December. Daniel assumed these were classmates or friends. He wrote down the unfamiliar numbers and would try and search Tiffany's contacts later. The landline contained incoming family calls and a few from 800 and 877 numbers. Cold advertising calls, most likely.

He looked in vain for Tiffany's cell. He didn't go into the master bedroom and he wondered if the police had it. He looked at his own phone and found two messages from the IMPD. He'd call them in the morning, probably would be good to exchange some information. He'd find out if they had Tiffany's cell. And he'd tell them about The Pirate King.

***

He woke up with sunlight streaming in the living room window. He'd slept from midnight until eight o'clock, almost unbelievable, given the circumstances. He reached for his cell immediately, but it buzzed before he could dial the police. The screen read "Unknown." Ordinarily, he wouldn't answer it, but he took the call. "Hello?"

"Daniel Ruiz? This is Detective Black of IMPD. I have some information for you and I'd also like to ask you a few questions. Would that be okay?"

"Sure. I really want to talk to you, too." Daniel hoped she'd listen to what he'd found out. She arrived with a junior partner, a young man with oily skin who looked to be about 18 years old. He was introduced as Detective Briscoe.

Daniel led them to the living room. "Sorry, I should have put on some coffee, I guess. Truth is, I just woke up when you called."

Detective Black waved her hand, as if to dismiss his concern. "Believe me, we're plenty caffeinated." She sat on the opposite end of the couch and turned to face Daniel. Detective Bristow sat in an overstuffed chair on the other side of the coffee table. "Let me tell you what we know. Then you can fill us in with anything you've found out."

Daniel nodded and she continued. "The autopsy has been completed and routine toxicology was done as well. Those results will take a while to get back. But we know the cause of death was due to lack of oxygen. Smothering."

Daniel felt the nausea he'd experienced a few days ago return. He took a deep breath.

"The way her pajama top was opened suggests a sexual motivation. But there was no sexual assault. Tiffany put up a fight, we found some dried blood and skin under several of her fingernails. This, of course, is evidence. We also found a couple of dark hairs on her pajama top."

Daniel unclenched his fist and sighed.

"Do you have Tiffany's cell phone?" Daniel asked.

"We do. And the computer, of course. We've started to go through her communication. Anything you want to share?"

Daniel told them about the dress, the tailor, and the emails from The Pirate King. Detective Black was interested. She asked to see the emails, and Daniel opened the files on his phone. He told her about the tailor and going down to pick up the dress, then his return visit to try and get information about The Pirate King. How the tailor refused, but said she'd talk to the police.

Detective Black raised her eyebrows and nodded her head. She looked at Detective Briscoe. "Looks like we need to make a trip downtown. Thanks, Daniel. We'll talk to you later if we have something. If you think of anything else, please call."

***

Daniel sat on the couch for a while after the two detectives left. The information about smothering nauseated him. He'd been processing that Tiffany was gone, but really hadn't given much thought to the *how*. He'd been more immersed in the *why*. The sexual nature of the crime distressed him, but he felt relieved that she hadn't been raped.

He shook his head. While the detectives were busy, he'd do some research with the unidentified phone numbers. He doubted if any would lead anywhere, but the task would keep him busy. His mind went into the time-defying zone of his phone screen. When his cell phone rang, two hours had passed.

It was Detective Black. "We're close to your place. We'll stop by in five."

Daniel raced to the kitchen to make coffee. He needed some himself. He found the canisters of creamer and sugar and put them on the table just as the knock came on the door. He gestured to the two detectives. "Come in and have a seat."

Detective Black pulled out a kitchen chair and slung her jacket over its back. "Yes, I'll have coffee now. To warm up." Detective Briscoe nodded and grabbed a mug, adding cream and sugar. He sat more tentatively, without removing his coat.

Daniel realized he was still wearing the clothes he'd slept in and hadn't had anything to eat or drink all day. *These guys are probably used to seeing weird things from the survivors of crime.* "What'd you find out?"

"We spoke with the seamstress. She did tell us about the Pirate King guy, although she knew nothing about his using that name. Her hesitation about providing the info to you was due to the fact that our Pirate King is a minor. He dropped off a costume for a school play to open in early January. Junior or senior in high school, tall, thin, and freckled. He was at his cousin's in Detroit over the new year. That can be verified. So, he's not our killer."

"How about those creepy emails?"

"Our cyber sleuth is on that. He may have info before the day is out. He'll find out where they originated, and we'll follow up." She sipped the last of the coffee. "I'd like to have that dress you picked up from the tailor. You'll get it back."

167

"I thought the tailor was creepy. She knew our home phone number by heart!" Daniel almost yelled as he walked to the closet and retrieved the dress. Could the owner of A-One Tailor be a serial killer? She'd probably know a lot about people. The clothes they brought in would probably reveal a lot about their owners. Maybe she looked at every customer as a possible victim.

The two detectives took off. Daniel heard nothing from the police that evening or the next day. Maria said Detectives Black and Briscoe came over to interview her, though. Daniel used the time to talk with his supervisor. He felt he needed at least at least a week before he could resume a shift in the ER. Maybe more.

The next morning dawned with bright sun and frigid cold. Daniel woke thinking about Tiffany and the birthday celebration they'd planned. He jumped when he heard a knock followed by the creak of the kitchen door opening.

"I've got cinnamon rolls!"

Maria. Daniel calmed at the sound of her voice. She did have a key, after all.

His sister peeked her head into the living room. "I'm going to put some coffee on. I thought maybe you'd like company."

"Thanks, Maria. You know how to be considerate." She smiled before reaching for the coffee.

His cell rang. *Unknown* flashed on the screen. *The police.*

"Detective Black here. We just drove past your duplex, saw your sister is there. We have some new information. Okay if we stop by?"

"Sure." Daniel hung up and Detective Black strode into the kitchen less than a minute later, followed by Briscoe. Maria stopped scooping coffee from the Maxwell House can, her arm frozen in midair.

"Why don't both of you come and have a seat in the living room? We'll share what we've found out with both of you. That is, if it's okay with you, Daniel."

"Of course. You can tell Maria anything." He looked at his sister. She gave him a tentative nod.

Detective Black waited until Daniel and Maria sat on the couch. "We found where the Pirate King emails originated."

"Really!" Daniel inched forward on the sofa. "Does that point to a suspect?"

"We think it does. We also talked to the tailor again and looked at that dress. Three hairs were caught in the back zipper pull, one blond and two black. There was also a long, black hair clinging to the hemline."

"I think Tiffany had the dress shortened," Daniel offered. "Most off-the-rack dresses were too long for her."

Detective Black nodded. "The hair near the hemline is coarse and straight. Asian. Not necessarily surprising since the dressmaker worked on the hem. That leaves us with the two black hairs near the neckline."

"Maria tried on the dress for me after we got it at the tailor's," Daniel explained. "I think the dress was a surprise for me. Tiffany and I were planning a special night out on January 7, Tiffany's birthday."

"So, here's what we've got. The Pirate King emails came from Maria's family computer. The dark hairs on the dress neckline matched the hairs on Tiffany's pajamas. We also noted scratches on Maria's right wrist area yesterday."

Daniel felt the sofa cushions shift. Maria had inched forward to the very edge of the couch.

Officer Briscoe leaned forward. "And those drops of blood, on the pillow case? The preliminary tests showed similarities to your blood, Daniel."

Daniel felt his biceps tighten. *The cops think I killed Tiffany?*

"But," Detective Black interjected, "the blood came from a female."

A female, a female. And not the tailor . . . Daniel felt his mouth go dry. He had the sensation of retreating down a long tunnel, observing his environment from a distance.

"Is there something you want to say, Maria?" This came from Briscoe.

Maria tensed before her body went limp and she flopped against the back of the couch. Then she sat forward, clenching her fists.

She looked straight ahead, at a blank spot on the wall. "I thought of the Pirate King messages as a joke. Tiffany seemed a little creeped out by someone at the tailor, and I decided to send her a couple of scary emails." Maria paused and looked down at her lap. "But when I got here New Year's morning . . ." She put her face in her hands. She made no sound, but her shoulders shook.

"Daniel," Maria lifted her head and spoke in a tender tone, tears cascading down her cheeks. "That year you lived with us in high school, I saw you change from a little scrawny boy into a strong man. I knew you needed a strong woman to make your life complete."

She directed her gaze back to the hands in her lap, shaking her head. Her voice became louder, her speech more rapid.

"That Tiffany. She thought she was so perfect. She thought she could make you happy, but she didn't fool me. She couldn't even make cinnamon rolls! Your favorite. New Year's Eve, I stayed up late to get them started and got up early to bake them. She was playing the pampered princess, staying in bed. So, when I came in – she was asleep and I thought . . . I could just take care of this right now. Daniel would be so much better off without her lazy little self . . . " She chuckled, a low throaty sound, before erupting into tears. Daniel retreated farther down the tunnel, but Maria's laughter followed him and echoed in his head.

Daniel wailed. He tried to say "why?" but his lips couldn't form the word. The cry of a wounded animal came from his lungs. From his soul.

"Oh, she put up a fight. A little one." Maria crossed her arms and laughed. "Tiffany was so pitifully weak. Not fit to be the mother of your children, Daniel."

Cuffs were applied, rights were recited. Briscoe took Maria out of the room, through the kitchen. It happened in a fast blur of activity. But it was slow-motion, too. Like a bubble separate from his full awareness. Daniel hadn't fully processed Tiffany's absence yet, now this . . .

He felt a touch on his arm. Detective Black.

"Daniel." She tried to look in his downcast eyes. "Is there someone I can call for you?"

MD 20/20

by Hawthorn Mineart

The Tense Man in the alley again tonight. I seen him there 4 nights now, but he only seen me the once. He a white man who wear a black jacket and cap, and sometimes have a black cloth that cover his neck and his chin. The numbers 2-1 are on back of his hand. I pass him on Thursday when me and Mogen went out looking for Mr. Orange. Mr. Orange been gone since Monday, which I writ on my calendar since I got a calendar now so I know which days are. Mr. Orange goes away for a while sometime, so we don't worry usual. But Mogen misses his friend, so I tole him we go looking round the soccer park. I nod at the Tense Man on Thursday, so he know I'm not a bother, but he get real mean. So I leave him be on Friday and Saturday and just slink by and look at him instead.

Now it Sunday night, and the Tense Man is looking again at the little house at the end of the block. He just stand and stare at the window, looking at the light. It worry me, like the numbers on his hand are a worry. There a new little family in that little house, mom and dad and tiny baby. Mom and dad are young too. They just move in Monday. Before that the house empty for near a year. Before that people met there but didn't nobody live inside. Long time back it was a pea-shake place. I bought tickets there from time to time when I was young, before I joined up and went away.

The Tense Man stand with his shoulders all hunch up and legs bent, like a boxer 'bout to throw a punch. But he don't move. Don't seem right for a house with a baby, so I watch, and he watch, and Mogen watch too, but he real quiet standing next to me. He a good dog about not making no noise when we don't need no noise. Stand about knee high with curly gray hair, same as mine. But Mogen have a big friendly smile sometimes, and I don't like smiling much. I pull back on his collar, but he don't need me to tell him something wrong with the Tense Man. Mogen stand about the same way, like he got his wind up too.

We watch for while, but nothing happen, so we go on to the soccer park. I walk Mogen round the edge so he can do his business and not mess where kids go play. Then we hunt for Mr. Orange, but we don't see him. He not in the park, or on the walkway they pave over where the trains used to run. We look neath the underpasses of the interstate and make our way back home a different way than the Tense Man. Me and Mogen get settle back in at our spot, but I can't fall to sleep, and he can't neither.

I get a thought, so I get out my paper and pencils and I draw a picture of the Tense Man and I write the story of how many nights he wait outside the little house. I get Mogen on a leash cause we about to talk to a lady in the middle of the night and I don't want no problems. I take my drawing and head down to see if the Tense Man is still there. He is. Still watching, still tense. So we skirt by and go cross the park and the walkway to the building where the Milk Factory was when I was a boy. The building was crumbling down for a long time — most of my memory — but a man done fixed it up now and he use it to park his cars. There is a Security Lady who guards them at night. She real young, too, and pretty, but tough-like, enough to guard buildings. Remind me of my Aunt Shirley, who was tough, too. But Security Lady always nod at me and smile at Mogen, so I know she know what good is.

The building have a few lights on, so I think she probably there. She there most nights. Sometimes she come outside to check the front, but at different times, so I never know when. It's a warm night, though, and dry, so me and Mogen can wait on the concrete ledge across the way. We good at sitting enjoying. The moon always changing, but it always nice to look at. Tonight there some clouds, but not many, and they don't cover the moon none, so it look like a picture in a frame. Cars go by on the interstate; people always going and going even in the nighttime. Seem like a lot of doing when should be sleeping but I can't talk 'bout that myself.

Sure enough, the Security Lady come out to check the building and see me and Mogen. She nod at me, but I start up, so she stop.

"I got a worry, and I think I should get some help," I tell her. I don't talk to people much, so that's a lot of words for me, and I stop.

"What do you need?" she asked.

"There's a man hanging 'round a little house, couple blocks away. He don't look right. An' there's a baby in there." I hand her the drawing, and she hold it up to the light near the door and look and read. Then she look at me in the eye for a long time, then look at Mogen. He sits down and look at her serious, no smiling, and she decide.

"Give me a minute, then you can show me," she said.

She goes back in and shut the door. Take several minutes, and then she come back out and lock up, make all kinda beeping noises and such 'til the building locked up tight. Then I walk her back across the walkway and the park, and down the block. Under the street light I see she got lines on her forehead, even though she young. She carrying a gun on her belt. We come around the garages from the proper direction until she can see the Tense Man without him see us.

He standing where he always do, under the eave of the garage across the alley, looking from the shadows at the window of the little house. I imagine if you look from the little house you couldn't see him hardly. But we could see him. He shifting from one foot to another, smoking a cigarette. We was stopped around the corner from him, so he couldn't hardly see us, and we watch for a long time.

Then Security Lady turn to me and say, "You go home. You have a place?" I nod, because we do now, me and Mogen and Mr. Orange. "I've got a friend who can take care of him. You go."

We leave her and walk quiet back to our spot. Our spot is the garage of the Quiet Lady. She talk me into sleeping on the couch in there one night when it rain and my tent been torn by mean kids. Then she give me a key so I can come back. I try not to take it, but the Quiet Lady look so sad, so I agree. She quiet, and I am too. I try not to be a bother to her. When I walk around in the day, new things appear in our spot some days. Dresser with shirts and pants.

A microwave on top of the dresser. A mirror. Small refrigerator with food next to the dresser. Calendar with dates crossed off and a pencil for me to do. A clock plugged in. I try to give her money but she just put it in the dresser. Seven months gone by, we stay here. It got cold outside, and some gentlemen came and sprayed foam on the garage walls of our spot. Blankets on the couch. A space heater with a note 'bout not leaving it on all the time. When I leave, I fold blankets and put clothes away. Quiet Lady park her car on the street in front, leave garage to me, so I keep our spot clean. I wash up at the hose outside sometimes, but I shower down at the Mission on Delaware.

Mogen and me settle into our couch when we get back, but I can't sleep. I worry now 'bout the Security Lady. I leave him on a blanket on the floor and I go back out and down the alley. The little house is two blocks north, just off Tinker Street. Tense Man is not there, but driving slowly through the alley is a police car. Inside is a Cop Lady and a police dog. Cop Lady have red hair, all pulled back and thin face. Dog is a German Shepherd. Cop Lady see me even in shadows and stop to shine light at me. I walk over so she can see me because don't want trouble. She relax when she see me walk out, so she must be looking for the Tense Man.

"Are you Ward?" she ask. I nod. Don't know how she know my name, but she do. "You saw the white man with the tattoo out here?" she ask, holding up my drawing from Security Lady. I nod again. "I'm going to drive through the alley a couple times a night for awhile so he doesn't come back. You need to stay away, okay? I don't want him to see you and think you're the reason I'm around. He's dangerous."

I do what she say. Go back to our spot to sleep and stay away. More days pass, and I stay away so I don't cause trouble. But Mr. Orange still gone. Me and Mogen go further away during the day looking. This the longest he away from us. I worry we gonna find him on side of road, but we don't.

***

One night late we asleep, and I smell smoke. Dreams don't have smell, not for me. I know this ain't no dream. I get up and check around, but it not our spot on fire. I put Mogen on leash and we follow our noses, see what's burning.

I see the light from the fire and hear the roaring, but it further off than I think at first. Ten blocks east, hugging the side of the interstate is the house where the fire is. We get there and stand in an empty lot watching. The police and fire trucks are around, but they standing back letting the house burn up mostly. Maybe it too far gone already. I recognize this little house, too. Another pea-shake place, dirty white paint. Always had shingles curling up on the roof and a janky porch tilted loose from the house. It's done fall off now; flames climb up and up from the roof with embers floating in the air. The interstate in the background, cars still whizzing by like nothing going on. The air is too hot, like sun burning my face, and the smoke make me cough.

Mogen is crying little sounds. He don't like this fire, he tugging toward home. He pulls me near into a sign planted at the edge of the empty lot. It's the same as several planted in empty lots on this little block. White, with logo of three rectangle shapes on it, each a different color green, and two names — Plank & Van Hassel. No saying what the sign is for. Supposed to know already, it seem to me. Sign's not for me then, cause I don't know.

I give in to his tugging, and Mogen pulls me in direction of our spot, but as I turn I see something I don't want to see at all. The Tense Man is there, standing off away from the burning house, but he ain't looking at it. He looking at us, me and Mogen. An' he don't want to see me no more than I wanna see him. He start toward me and my knees start to wobble. But he don't get far before he see something over my shoulder, and he turn around and move away fast.

I turn to see what he afraid of, and it's the Cop Lady in her car pulled up next to us, with her dog beside her, window down. Tense Man is still moving away fast, not looking back. I tell her, "That's the man watching."

"Go home. Go home now. But not the way he's going," she said, picking up her radio. I move off, pulled by Mogen, and I hear her talking into her radio, but I can't tell what she's saying over the sound of the fire. We don't see the Tense Man at all on the way back to our spot, and the air gets cooler and the night gets quieter the closer we get. The smoke still hangs about though.

***

Still haven't found Mr. Orange, but I don't go out at night. Four weeks and five days since we seen Mr. Orange. I draw a picture of him to put on the lamp posts, but I don't know how to make more yet. I might ask the Quiet Lady, so I put it in my pocket for when I see her. Mogen and I walk during the day, but we look around corners first.

I don't want to see the Tense Man at all, even from far away. It's been four weeks since we first saw him on that Thursday. My head started hurting again sometimes. I'm thinking he set that fire. I worry more and more about the baby, but I'm too afraid to go check on the little house with the baby in it.

I leave Mogen in our spot while I go down to the Mission to get a shower, cause they don't allow dogs at the Mission. They giving out new ball caps that say "Ignite" on them. Seem like a funny idea to have on my head, but I guess I don't have to look at it. They have a meal for us, and new socks, too. The Quiet Lady gave me socks, though, so I gave mine to one of the others. He might not have a spot.

Just up the block from the Mission I saw that sign again. Painted big in the glass window of a building, three green rectangles and "Plank & Van Hassel." This time they tell what they do. "Real Estate Law." It's a nice sign. The different greens are pretty and I'm happy to know what they do finally. My brain been working on that puzzle too long.

I stood too long looking at the sign because I realize that the people inside the window looking out at me, too. A gray hair man in a business suit, and a Fat Man with a red face and a t-shirt that say "Indy Chicken" on it, and the third man, one who just walk into the room — the Tense Man. He recognize me, and I recognize him, and both of us freeze in the spot, don't know what to do. He can't come after me on the street in front of people, though. He say something to the other two people, and the Fat Man leap up outta his chair like he gonna come for me, but the Tense Man stop him. Then they all start yelling at each other. I turn quick and try to get out of sight. Go back to the mission for a bit and wait for a hour. I worry they come in after me, but they don't. Play checkers a bit, then leave by the back way. I don't see any of them as I slink back to Mogen, staying in the alleys and shadows. I get to the garage and lock it up tight behind me.

Something wrong with the Tense Man and the fancy sign being together, and the Tense Man near old pea-shake places. And one a them on fire. I think I should tell the Security Lady, or the Cop Lady, but I don't know how to explain it. I draw a picture of the sign and the man, but I don't think it explains. I decide to go over to the Milk Factory building and look for the Security Lady after it gets dark. Mogen wants to go with me, but I make him stay. He whines though, after I shut the garage door and lock it up. I have my picture with me, and I slink along, staying out of sight mostly as I cross the soccer park and the paved walkway to the Milk Factory door. I sit outside for a long time, not out in the open, but in the shadows of the building. But the Security Lady never come out. I'm too scared to stay longer, so I leave the picture under a rock near the door and head home.

The Quiet Lady left me meatloaf in my little refrigerator. It's the exact same as my mama used to make, and I heat it up in the little microwave and eat it and it reminds me of being a boy and sitting at my mama's table. Being told to eat my green beans first before I eat the meat parts so I don't skip the greens. My mama went to heaven a long time ago, but I eat the green beans first because maybe she looking out for me and know how to scare the Tense Man away. My head hurt a lot more now, and I don't know how to stop it. I got hit on the head back in the army, so long ago I don't hardly remember it anymore, but it still make me stop in my tracks now and again.

I settle in with Mogen and we lay there with the lights off. He lick my face and it makes my head hurt less. I almost fall asleep when I hear a clank sound outside, like a metal can hitting something. And a curse, like a man swearing. Then I smell gasoline, sharp and clear, and I know right away what's going on. I gotta get the dog out of the garage right away. I scramble to unlock the door, but Mogen is already leaping at it, and as soon as I get it open he's out going after whoever is outside. I realize when I hear the screams that it's not the Tense Man at all. It's the Fat Man with the red face from the window of the business. Mogen has his arm in his mouth, and the man is on the ground screaming high and fearful like he gonna die, rolling around trying to hit my dog. The lights come on at the back of the Quiet Lady's house and she come out sudden, phone to her ear, screaming into it, and I realize she got a gun in the other hand, too. She waving it around and it's clear to me she have no idea how to use it, but the Fat Man don't know that. He crying now, and Mogen does let go of him, sitting on the grass like he done nothing at all. The man bleeding everywhere, and crying at the Quiet Lady, and gasoline spread all over the side of the garage, making the air smell sharp.

A police car came screaming up the alley then, lights on, and the siren flips on sudden toward the end. The Quiet Lady steps back and drop her gun gently into the grass of the backyard. The Cop Lady still in the car, and she get out with her dog; she never saw the gun. The sound of another police car is in the distance. She look at me, and I see she have my new drawing in her hand.

"What's going on here?" the Cop Lady says over the Fat Man's crying. He look at the new Police Dog next to her like he afraid of another bite.

"This man was pouring gasoline on my garage, and my father's dog attacked him," the Quiet Lady says loudly.

"I . . . Mr. Ward is your father?" the Cop Lady says, confused.

"Yes. And this is our dog," the Quiet Lady says to her, pointing at Mogen. I just stand there, because I don't know what to say, and it was her house anyway.

"Can you tell me your name?" the Cop Lady asks the Quiet Lady.

"Julia Ward. This is my house. My father and his dog live with me." I still don't know what to say, so I don't say anything, but the air leaves my lungs for a bit before it rushes back in. I never asked her name and I'm not sure why I didn't. I'm not sure she owes it to me.

"This man was trespassing?" The Cop Lady asks about the man bleeding on the ground.

"Yes. He's a stranger. I've never seen him before," the Quiet Lady – Julia — says.

"He's a friend of the Tense Man. The one who stands around. I saw them at the real estate place near the mission," I manage to tell the Cop Lady. She look at the gasoline on the garage, and the man on the ground, and the can laying on its side in the yard.

"Sir, you are under arrest for attempted arson, trespassing, and whatever else I can think of to charge you with," the Cop Lady says to the Fat Man. She tucks my drawing into her pocket and forces the Fat Man onto his face by pulling his arm behind him. He still squealing and crying. The other police cars arrive then, but she gets him handcuffed and laying on his face so when they come up, they know who to pull up and throw up against the police car while they call for an ambulance.

A man cop come over then and ask the same questions, but now the Quiet Lady standing in front of me, with Mogen pulled up next to her, and she say the same things loudly that she tell the Cop Lady, and I still don't have to say anything until they ask "How did you discover what he was doing?"

"I was asleep in there with Mogen, and I smelled gasoline," I tell the Man Cop.

"You were sleeping in the garage?" the Man Cop asks, like he don't believe me.

"It's his man cave; he likes to be alone sometimes," Julia says. "You know how men are." The Man Cop laugh and write stuff down and tell her, "Okay, Ms. Ward. If we have any questions, we'll call you." He hand her a card and she take it. Eventually the ambulance come, and the crying Fat Man get loaded into it, and the Cop Lady and her cop friends go away.

We are left in a empty backyard.

"If you could pick up that gasoline can and put it somewhere, I'm going to spray off the garage. Then you can tell me who the 'Tense Man' is," Julia say to me. We do what she say, and when she done spraying off the garage she wash Mogen's face too. Then she sit down on the edge of her porch. She's wearing a night gown and a long robe, and fuzzy slippers on her feet, which Mogen sits directly on top of, like they his own feet.

I remember the gun in the grass. I pick it up and open it up. It not loaded. I set it down on the porch next to her and then sit down myself with it between us.

"You learn how to use that if you gonna have it in the house." I tell her. "It not safe."

"Maybe you can teach me. Now tell me who the 'Tense Man' is. And who that man was," she says to me, pointing out into the grass.

So, I tell her about Mr. Orange being lost and the house and the family with the baby, all the way up to seeing the Tense Man and the Fat Man at the law office. I say more all at once than I said for a long time. Sometimes I have to stop because I remember smells or sounds and I have to think about them awhile before I can get words again. In the end she knows all of it.

"I want to talk to the security guard woman. I think I owe her a fruit basket. And the cop woman too. Now I have something to ask you. Do you remember Margaret Cooper? She was my mother."

As soon as she says it I realize where I know her face, and my heart leap up like it trying to jump outta my chest. I can't say nothing; I just nod.

"Well, she told me a Robert Kent was my daddy. He was never around. But after my mama died, my auntie told me you were my father and you were in the Army. My birth certificate says my last name is Ward. Do you think that could be true?"

I don't have any words at all. I just start crying like a baby. She looks like Margaret, but she also look like my mama. I don't know what to do. That must be answer enough for her, because she seem like she heard a yes out of me.

"I looked for you, and the VA said you were hurt in the war, but that you were here in town. The Mission told me where to look for you," Julia said.

I just cried some more, because it was too much to think of.

"It's okay," she told me, "It's been a long night. Maybe you can get some sleep, and we can look for Mr. Orange tomorrow together. But I would like for you and Mogen to sleep in the house. I have a security alarm."

***

I sleep like the dead on Miss Julia's couch, and so does Mogen, so much that we don't even hear the knocking on the front door until Miss Julia answer it. She already dressed and ready for the day. I get up in time to see the Security Lady standing there. She speaks to Miss Julia.

"Hi. I'm Lea Roquera. I work security for Robert Fordham at one of his buildings across the Monon Trail near here. I heard from my friend Officer Ryan that you and your father had some events last night. I met him a while back and wanted to check on him, if that's okay?"

"Certainly. Come in. I heard all about you last night. But he calls you 'the Security Lady' so I'm glad to hear your actual name." She steps inside and Julia shuts the door after her.

"I guess I never actually introduced myself to him. Oh, hello, Mr. Ward," she says, as I make my way to the front door, Mogen padding after me. I nod, because words are not really coming to me at all. Mogen's tail wagging like it going to fly off any second. She tells me her name again, and we shake hands.

Julia is impatient. "So, apparently there was a man trying to set fire to my garage last night. I guess because my father saw something about an arson fire and put information together?"

"I think that's exactly what happened. I called Molly — Officer Ryan — and sent her over here when I found this outside my door. You drew this, right, Mr. Ward?" She had the drawing I did of the sign and the Tense Man. I nod.

"I thought she was answering my 911 call," Julia says.

"That may have been the second car that came. Officer Ryan has been working on several arson cases with Fire Department investigators. Because of your father's observations, she suspected the man your father calls 'the Tense Man' was setting them. When I showed her this, we agreed she should come see your dad. Police have been thinking the arsons were gang-related and racially motivated, and that's likely true. But the man she arrested last night implicated a real estate law firm as well. That's thanks to your dad making connections."

Julia put her hand on my arm like she's proud of me, but I'm still trying to figure out what's going on. Miss Roquera can see I need help. "The man you call 'The Tense Man' is Jason Green," she says to me. "He's a white supremacist gang member. He was hired to set fires by the man from who came here last night, Ernest Shepford. Shepford was hired by a real estate law firm to get people to sell their property for a new housing development. All the land they're trying to get is owned by black families. Shepford and Green were trying to scare them into selling. We'll see if the real estate firm knew what they were doing."

All of the pieces snap into place in my head finally, and I understand. I think I might have figure it out if I had time to think. "The Tense Man and the Fat Man were at that place yesterday." I pointed out the drawing. "I saw them, and they saw me. But the family with the baby?"

"We think that's another property they wanted. But the owners fixed it up and rented it out. Green may have been trying to figure out whether to carry out his arson plans anyway. It's a good thing you noticed him and said something. That family may owe you their lives."

"I was looking for my cat." I tell her, and she looks surprised.

"My father has an orange cat named Mr. Orange. He's been missing several weeks." Julia says. I take my drawing of Mr. Orange out of my pocket and hand it to Ms. Roquera. She smiles.

"I know where your cat is, Mr. Ward. I think you should come with me. I can show you."

She drive me and Miss Julia to the Milk Factory and unlocks the door and lets us inside. A very thin man with wire glasses is inside the building reading papers at a desk. He surprised to see us.

"Mr. Fordham, this is Mr. Ward. He's been looking for his missing cat. I thought I should show him where she's been all this time."

"Ah. Pleased to meet you. I think you may be surprised." He nod and go back to his reading. Ms. Roquera take us past the entryway and into the large factory space. Spread out across the floor are cars of all kinds. I count more than thirty, all of them fancy.

"Is that a Maserati?" Julia asks.

"It is. This is one of the rarest car collections in the world, actually," Ms. Roquera says in a low voice. We follow her to the end of the row to a large basket. Inside is Mr. Orange curled up, with seven tiny orange kittens. "Your Mr. Orange is actually Mrs. Orange, Mr. Ward. I hope that doesn't upset you."

I kneel down and pet her head, and she rub against me in her basket like a queen, smug, like she fool me all this time. Well, she did. I guess it ain't too hard to do. I been surprised a lot.

"Her real name is Orange Jubilee anyway, so I guess she don't need no new name. But I don't think I can take care of all these kittens," I say, because that is a lot of mouths to feed. Miss Julia already give me a lot of pet food. I pet one little kitten, and they all start crawling over my hand like they need me.

"How about if I keep her and the kittens here until they're bigger, and when they're ready, maybe one of these boys can come home with you? Mr. Fordham is fond of her and would like to have her live here and chase mice." I nod, because he got enough money. She can have a real nice home and family in his garage instead of mine.

182

"Wait a minute. Did you name your pets after your liquor?" Miss Julia asks, and I know she thinking about the bottles in my refrigerator. "Mogen David, Orange Jubilee?"

Ms. Roquera is figuring it out, too. "Mogen David 20/20. That's original," she says, laughing. "My dad's pets would be Schlitz Malt Liquor."

"Didn't think I'd have to explain it to no one," I said. But I see the way Miss Julia's eyes sparkle when she laugh, and I guess I'm glad I have someone to explain it to now.

Dingo Dan

by B.K. Hart

February 29, 2072   7:36 a.m.

"Hey kid, what's your name?" Detective Rebecca Logan asked as the teen walked away.

"Rice."

"Your mama named you Rice?" She tilted her head.

"No," he spat, his face working to hold back words he would have said had he not been speaking to a cop. "My mama named me Jason. My last name is Rice."

"Cough up your digits. We could have more questions."

He tried some evasive maneuvering, but she pried his address and phone number out of him. Forcing one of her cards on him, she told him to call if he thought of anything else.

"Logan?" he asked, studying her card. "Like the X-Man . . . Wolverine?"

She hissed and clawed the air with her non-existent fingernails.

He sneered and shuffled off muttering, "That be more like a cat."

She stifled a grin and slapped her notebook against her thigh.

"You the new girl?" Detective Denver McNulty approached her, one hand out, the other hefting what appeared to be a heavy black field kit. He was slender, hair trimmed neatly and tight to his scalp, dressed in casual khakis and a blue button-down shirt. His shoes were worn black sneakers which might have passed for dress shoes from a distance. Police officers never knew when they might need to take off at a run.

Detective Logan's eyes narrowed. "Girl?"

"I mean girl as opposed to boy. You know, the new kid. Not that you're a kid or anything." He stumbled around, tripping over his tongue, making the situation more awkward. "Not saying you're an old lady either . . . I'm just saying . . . Why don't I start over?"

He wiped his sweaty palm on his dark blue slacks feeling more like the new kid than the new 'detective.' "I'm McNulty. Are you Logan?" he said offering his hand again.

"McNutty?" she asked.

"Ah," his smile was easy. "So, you do have a sense of humor. They sent me down with the field kit. With the shutdown, it's hard to get any field equipment. Dispatch said you called in a body but didn't have any tools to process the scene."

"That about sums it up. Central sent a couple of droids, so I had them secure the area while I knocked on a few doors. The body is relatively fresh, less than four hours. Hasn't gathered too many blowflies. Livor mortis is starting on his face and neck. I didn't want to roll him over or move much until I could get some proper readings and pictures. Limbs were beginning to stiffen as I arrived on the scene."

"Not your first dead body, then?"

"Walk and talk, detective." Logan led Denver back through Mass Avenue Square to where she had left her two droids on duty. "I've been here two weeks. I can't get a field kit. I can't get a camera. I can't get a laser stick. I have a pair of metal cuffs, and a few flexicuffs, from my old job in Kenosha, as well as my magic stick. Luckily, my phone has a camera app. I'm skilled at hand-to-hand. I'm smart. I'm relatively young, flexible, and in good health. Otherwise, I would call this government strike bullshit and tell the powers-to-be to stick this job where the sun don't shine."

"I feel that way even when there isn't a shutdown, detective. What have you got so far? I can't get you a field kit, but I have one, so you get me."

"Deceased currently known as Dingo Dan. Associates think he might be from Australia. Said he's been in the area a couple of years and for a while his nickname was just Double 20."

"I don't get it?"

"I didn't either. Apparently when he first showed up, he'd wander around mumbling about how he'd been here since 2020." Rebecca turned to the body, pursed her lips and shook her head. "There is no way in hell this guy is 70 years old, or even 50 if he happened to be born around or in 2020. My best guess is age 34 to 38, though it's hard to tell under all the blood and bruising. Based on the elasticity from the backs of his hands, and the lack of creasing around the eyes, I'd say no more than 45. Now that we got your handy dandy field kit, you might be able to get more information."

Denver knelt beside the body, removed an enhanced biometric reader, gloves, and stereopsis goggles from his kit. The goggles functioned as a dual purpose, enhancing the static area being observed, and simultaneously documenting the sequence of discovery electronically. Denver began his exam.

"Mass Avenue is climate controlled. The medical examiner is going to need to do a more thorough exam when he gets the body. Right now, the time of death is right around three this morning. Prints register to a Dan Ingino out of New York. He's been missing since 2070. That's interesting. According to our database, we had a missing person report filed on this guy. He disappeared following a SkyIndy concert where he was the bassist. Band called Acentria."

"I know that band. It's a throwback metal band. Give a guy some credit, man!"

"I give you credit. Did I say you couldn't have credit?"

"No," Rebecca kicked his foot. "The name of their song was 'Give a Guy Some Credit, Man.' It's kind of thrash rock." She flicked a switch on her phone, and loud screeching noises emitted from her speaker.

He ignored the distraction as he carefully pushed up the shirt on Dingo Dan's arm exposing a tattoo high on the wrist. His goggles locked in. With only an edge exposed, the goggles could recreate the fully inked pattern through the shirt. "He has a full sleeve."

"Tat?" she asked. "You got an extra set of those goggles?"

Denver looked up at her, overhead light bright in his eyes making him squint. "You should meet my daughter. Kati's 16-ish, meaning she rarely acts anything less than 30-ish. Pretty much likes anything she thinks will drive me crazy or baffle me beyond measure. She would likely love that, uh . . . music."

She flicked off the music bringing back the relative quiet of the morning.

"Anyway, Dan Ingino. I wonder why he didn't come up as a match when they put him in housing? Seems as if he disappeared two years ago and showed up on the streets here. Housing Authority should have matched him."

"Not necessarily. You aren't required to be registered to gain housing in this city. They provide a unit based on your need. If you show up and ask, they give it to you no questions. You get a chit. It's almost as good as witness protection. I mean, if you didn't want to be found, that is. Mr. Dingo must not have wanted to be found."

Rebecca bit her lower lip and squinted around at the surrounding apartments. The street was enclosed from 10th Street south to Pennsylvania creating an indoor mecca, filled mostly with apartments for displaced workers. Soup kitchens were on every block, along with laundry facilities, a coffee house, shoe shops, a couple of recycled clothing stores, and at least three clinics. She might have only been in town a couple of weeks, but she'd learned early that the city had a unique way of supporting what would otherwise constitute the homeless population.

"The chit is good for housing and food. I presume the clinic, too?" she asked.

"The chit gets you a job in any storefront along the street here. They're all chit hires. It's the only requirement for housing here. You show up, get your chit, and it's preloaded with twenty-four work hours. Go to any of these places, work your hours and everything is free in exchange. Food, medical care, clothing, housing."

"Does it work?" she asked.

Denver shrugged. "The area is mostly self-contained. Very little crime. Residents clean the streets. Take out the trash. There's a list on the square of specific duties which can be performed while here on the inside to earn the 24. The rest is free time. Some people teach. Classes are free. Teaching counts toward hours. Everyone benefits."

"Sounds like Utopia," Rebecca said, then turned pointedly. "Crime-free, except for the dead guy."

"Ten bucks says the perpetrator isn't from here," Denver said stretching his hand out in the bargain.

"Do I look like a fool?" she grinned. "Grammy used to say, 'Rebecca Sue, I might have raised a fool or two in my lifetime, but I ain't raising you to be one. So, straighten up or get the switch.'"

Her smile faltered.

"I didn't leave much behind in Kenosha. She never gave me the switch either, but she sure liked to threaten it. Anyway, I got a lady over in 1103B who says her kid knew Dingo pretty well. Smart kid, she says. He was at school when I was knocking on doors earlier, and he's supposed to return home around noon. Name's Floyd Houston."

"Well then, I suggest we get the examiner here to pick up our stiff. Then find a cup of coffee while we wait for Floyd. I can let you pick my brain on how to be more efficient in your position."

"You mean how to do my job with a toothpick and sharp poke to the eye? Because I'm telling you, I am not digging this strike. Makes me want to punch someone in the throat. I thought it was illegal for public servants to go on strike."

"It is." He made a calm down motion with his hands. "Nobody is on strike exactly. We are currently experiencing an increase in sick day usage. It's that joker in the White House who isn't allowing certain federal and state agencies to pay their employees. The Senate gets paid, Congress gets paid, the president gets paid. The shutdown means right now, you and I work for free. Some people find this a bit unfair."

"It only lasts about three weeks though. The first week, we take the hit. The second week Congress gets suspended. By the time it reaches the president's pockets, they get it together. Suddenly the politicians are all buddies again, and everybody gets their back pay."

"True, but it's a temporary measure. In six months it happens all over again. People are sick of it. Shutdowns would have more impact if they suspended the president's check first, Congress second, and public servants third."

"Preaching to the choir, brother."

They waited another 45 minutes for the coroner to show up. By then

Denver had sold Rebecca on the fresh cinnamon rolls they'd been smelling from Millie's Bakery Bocado around the corner. Other than confirming the body needed more extensive scrutiny back at the morgue, the examiner didn't have much to add. Though he did say the damage could have come from a beating, but the way the body was laid out, it might have also been a fall. They all looked up. The maximum height in the Mass Avenue Mall was five stories. There were rafters throughout the structure where additional beams helped keep the indoor structure secured and supported the roofing, lighting, and other maintenance access points. Catwalk crossbeams and larger platforms interlaced so small groups of people could gather.

"So, there's a possibility he was hanging out in the rafters and fell?" Rebecca asked.

"Or was pushed." The coroner ran a wrinkled hand across his white, prickly chin. "The thing is, he ain't bloody enough."

Denver had noticed. "I thought maybe he took a beating but didn't really break the skin much, only … I don't know. What about you, newbie. Any ideas?"

Logan narrowed her eyes on Denver then switched her gaze back to the body and pursed her lips. "Okay. So maybe he was dead already, then got pushed from the rafters?"

They all shifted away from the body as a couple of droids arrived and prepared the body for transport. They moved with quiet efficiency, and Rebecca watched with a perplexed frown.

"That's another thing I don't get. This city invests in droids for assistance, to do grunt work, ticket vehicles, monitor crime scenes. Why don't they equip them with the field kit supplies? Fingerprint readers? Camera equipment? You have an entire mini-city within the undercity of SkyIndy dedicated to taking in what would otherwise be homeless individuals, but you don't trick out your droids so they could be useful in, say, strike conditions?"

"Good point, for most of it. Though we find droids don't rank well on the empathy and sympathy scale so they're not ideal for canvassing."

They were hit with a double dose of cinnamon as Denver pushed open the glass door to Millie's. Rebecca paused for a moment in the doorway and took a couple of deep breaths. It calmed her. She could smell the coffee under the sugar, the butter, and the yeast. It was lucky for her she worked this district and walked nearly ten miles every day. A few extra calories weren't going to hurt her or slow her down.

Denver checked his watch. "Looks like we have about thirty minutes before we head back to 1103B? Coffee?"

"Strong, with vanilla cream. No sugar. I have a feeling I'll be getting plenty from the Danish."

Out of habit, Rebecca scanned the square through the glass pane. There wasn't much pedestrian traffic. No motorized transportation was allowed inside the enclosed mall area. She watched a thin blond girl on a skateboard blowing a big pink bubble as she swerved gracefully down the sidewalk. Across the street stood a couple of guys Rebecca would describe as goons if she were in her old neighborhood. They were dark-suited, SkyIndy logo on left breast pockets. Sunglasses when none were needed. Paunchy in the midsection. Looking a tad out of place in her opinion. The teen she questioned earlier was near the same corner, backside to her, but she recognized the hoodie.

The roll came out warm, sitting in a puddle of butter, with cream cheese icing melting across the top. It sat by itself in a ceramic dish nearly touching the rim around the outer edge of the plate.

"Do I eat that or just slap it on my hips since it's going to end up there anyway?"

"This is why I only got one." He placed a second plate on the table and patted his belly. "I can't afford to consume a whole one, either."

While they got down to the business of consumption, Denver placed his communication unit on the table. He tapped into the district database and pulled a virtual screen open so Rebecca could see what he saw. He accessed a professional dossier on Daniel Ingino. They browsed his bio, found a minor mention to the band Acentria, and what amounted to a résumé.

"Looks like he owned his consulting business. Seemed like a pretty smart guy," Denver said.

"Yeah, so how does a guy . . . Oh wait, scroll back," she pointed to space in the air. "Says his girlfriend reported him missing. She lives in Georgia though.

Didn't you say he was from New York?"

"Well, born in New York. Moved to Georgia after college. Can't say I blame him. I've never been to SkyYork. I hear it's fancier than our overcity, and I've heard a lot of ugly stories come out of the underside there."

"Kenosha was too small to need a skycity, Milwaukee could have but didn't. I went to SkyChi many times. They don't do a very good job of lighting up the undercity, if you want my opinion. Darkness breeds bad behavior in the hearts of humanity."

"Hunger breeds bad behavior in the hearts of humanity," Denver corrected. "Indianapolis is progressive about taking care of its people. Other cities study our design and layout, what the city vision was back at the turn of the century. The urban wars destroyed infrastructure in most of the major metropolises. Everywhere across the U. S. Here too. Have you made it to the dump over by Washington and West Streets?"

"No, that's out of my jurisdiction. And, frankly, touring the city dump isn't my idea of a good time."

"Isn't anybody's idea of a good time. Interesting fact, that location is where all the state government buildings used to be. When the bombings began with the urban wars, an extremist group got it into their heads that the government center was designed to be quarantined from the rest of the city. It was connected to hotels, the Circle Center Mall, all the way over to Market Street by underground tunnels. Most of the tunnels are still functional to a degree. We still have people who live there, but we try to get them up and in the Mass Avenue complex. I heard they had skywalks even before they built SkyIndy, but most of those were destroyed as well. The extremist group believed when Armageddon came, all the state officials were going to hole up in the government center and lock down access to the tunnels, crosswalks, hotels and attached restaurants, and mall. They would be self-sustaining. Leaving all the little people outside to suffer through the apocalypse."

"That would be a jerky thing to do."

"True. Also, true, all these areas were attached. It turns out most of them had life support systems built into them. They even connected to one of the largest, most affluent, hospitals at the time. Now, the government buildings are the city dump."

***

February 29, 2072 12:36 p.m.

They entered a neat living area and were offered a seat while Mrs. Houston rousted her son out of the shower. It would only take a few minutes, she assured them. The apartment was compact but not as small as one might imagine. Apparently, the city made accommodations for individuals who came with children. Room designs were done accordingly. If Vivian Houston had birthed more than one child, she would have been given a unit with additional bedrooms, bunkbeds installed free of charge.

A young boy about 10 years old boldly approached Detective Logan and held out his hand. "Hi, my name's Floyd. Floyd Houston. But I prefer to be called Fifi."

Rebecca's eyebrows shot up in surprise, charmed, yet stifling a laugh. "Fifi," she repeated dryly. "Did your mother tell you why we're here?"

"Yeah, she said you found Dingo Dan. He was my friend." Floyd sat down on the floor next to the coffee table, chin dropping for a solemn moment as if in prayer. "He was a cool guy. Watched out for me, you know?"

"You know why anyone might want to hurt him?" Denver asked gently.

The boy shrugged and shook his head. "Not really. I mean, the guy was a genius, you know? He was way big into lighting and design."

"How long have you known him?" Rebecca asked.

"He showed up a couple years ago, maybe?" He looked at his mom for confirmation. "Wasn't it about the time I was taking that Russian class? Spring of 2070, right?"

"You took Russian?" Rebecca asked.

"Yeah, I have an aptitude for languages. I was placed in special classes when I was in preschool and knew most of the basics of Spanish, French, and common romance languages. You know, numbers, letters, hello, goodbye, thank you . . . basics."

Rebecca looked at Vivian Houston who simply shrugged. "What can I say? My kid's not normal. He's a friggin' genius. I have no idea where he gets it."

193

"She used to put headphones on her belly and play me Mozart when I was in the womb," Floyd said casually.

"Seriously?" Denver asked.

Floyd looked at him. Very quietly he said, "You aren't really that gullible."

"Hey, it's plausible. I've heard many strange stories in my lifetime as a detective."

"I gotta get to work," Vivian cut in. "You know the rules, Floyd. Nobody in the house. Leave me a note with a destination if you go out. Present company excluded."

"Fifi, Mom! Yish," Floyd protested.

Rebecca tapped her notebook. "Fifi, if you knew Dan Ingino so long, do you know why he was here? In the assisted housing sector?"

"Well, he was messed up when he got here. Hit over the head. Couldn't actually remember who he was or where he came from."

"But he said he was from Australia?" Denver asked.

"Australia?" Floyd looked from Denver to Rebecca and back again. "Why Australia?"

"Well, I interviewed a few people on the street who said he was from Australia, hence the name Dingo Dan."

"Nah, that's not it." Floyd leaned back on his hands tilting his whole body back so he could look up at the ceiling. "People can be stupid. He was always Dan Ingino. People had never heard the name 'Ingino' so his name sort of got bastardized into Dingo and it stuck."

"No foul language," Vivian called, slamming the door behind her as she left.

"Mom, when the word is used that way it means . . . " Floyd waved his hand around as if plucking it out of the air. "Ah, never mind."

"So, you always knew his real name?" Denver clarified.

"From about the third week or so he was here. At first, he didn't know anything. He just kept mumbling stuff about 2020. Being stuck here. He's lucky he was in our district when he was attacked. They don't ask many questions, just administer treatment and send you off. Course, he didn't have any place to go, so they sent him to the chit office. It was weird in the beginning, like he didn't know who he was but didn't want anybody else to know either. I think even subconsciously he was trying to protect himself in case the attacker came back for him."

"You say he was smart?" Rebecca cut in.

"Sure was. He had this whole," Floyd hesitated, looking down and away from the detectives. "He seemed to know stuff about light control systems. So, sometimes I would help him with his programming. We would hang out at the library. A couple times he came to my school."

"Programming? Like computers?" Rebecca repeated, eyebrows arching.

"Programming is just another language. Piece of cake if you have the skills. I'm slow cause I don't really type so fast. I'm getting better, though."

"What kind of stuff would he need programming for?"

"Oh, you know, stuff." Floyd averted his eyes. Then, thinking of a better response, looked up and met Denver's eyes. "Like he helped tweak the mall lighting so it would more closely match the circadian rhythm of real daylight. It had something to do with biorhythms. Dan noticed the light stayed constant in the mall. I mean, it dimmed at night but not to like, nighttime dark, like outside the mall. Though, I hear that's kind of artificial too because SkyIndy blocks natural light to the surface."

"Okay, go on. All probably true. You helped him change the light cycles with a program?"

"Sure, there are maintenance types of jobs posted in the square every week. Some are ongoing like HVAC, and toilet work . . . Nobody wants to do toilet work." Floyd said this matter-of-factly. The boy was so serious. Neither detective laughed but they exchanged a look between them.

"I don't have an address for him in any of my inquiries. Do you know where he was living?" Rebecca said.

"Yeah, he lives like two floors up. 3102A. Three for the third floor. A means it's on the right side of the hall. 102 means unit one, housing up to two persons. I can't understand why they didn't just use a dash. Like our apartment would be 11-3B and Dan's would be 31-2A. Would it be so hard to figure out?"

"I didn't realize they had a numbering system on the address labels," Denver commented.

"It was part of the Bicentennial Agenda they started at the turn of the century. When they planned the groundwork for most of SkyIndy. Built into the program was a design to address the homeless population in Indianapolis. I only know this because my Current Affairs class did an in-depth analysis of the Plan 2020 as it was presented back then and how it has been modified to meet the current needs of the city. Oh, in fact, that's why Dingo Dan was here."

"What? Why? I have clearly missed something." Rebecca said, pen pausing in her notes. "Dingo Dan was here for a concert in SkyIndy."

"Well, he was, but he also had a meeting during the Indy 2020 Plan Semi-centennial. You know, 50-year celebration we just had in 2070. Golden Jubilee." Floyd looked back and forth between them. "Did you live here two years ago?"

"No."

"Yes."

Floyd looked exasperated. "We figured it out. Dingo Dan and me. He'd been stuck here since the Golden Jubilee. The city's 50th anniversary of their visionary planning legacy. It was a huge deal. That's why he kept saying since 2020. It was all he could remember at the time."

Floyd waited.

"So, we should check out his apartment," Denver said slowly.

Floyd threw his hands in the air, let out a grunt and fell to his back on the floor.

"Fifi," Rebecca said, hiding her amusement. "Why don't Detective McNulty and I run up to Mr. Ingino's apartment. We may come back and see you later. Possibly tomorrow after we've had a chance to get more information from the coroner and see what the domicile reveals. Would that be okay with you?"

"Whatever." He scrambled up from the floor. "I'm not sure I can tell you anything else useful though. Except for the big guys."

"What big guys?" Rebecca said.

"Big guys who were asking around about him. If you see a couple of guys in suits, it could be them."

"I saw a couple of guys in suits." Rebecca got up and went to the window. It was a bad angle on the wrong side of the building. "Hmm, well. I saw some suits down near the coffee shop. Can't see them from here."

***

February 29, 2072   14:47 p.m.

"What do you make of this?" Rebecca asked referring to the mostly empty room. There wasn't a thing here one might call a personal keepsake. It wasn't hard to tell because everything had been turned over, opened, spilled out, and scattered across the floor.

"Looks like someone else beat us here," Denver said.

"I don't get it. Guy disappears. Hides under the radar for almost two years. Then suddenly shows up dead. His apartment ransacked. The kid said he'd been beaten the first time. And it looks like he was beaten a second time. For what. What am I missing here?"

Denver prowled the edges of the room, touching the wall, squinting into wall vents. Rebecca set a chair upright and plopped down on it. The furniture was mismatched, as if pieced together based on discarded remnants from other people's lives. Not a knickknack in sight. A few things had been broken, cord pulled free from a toaster, like from rage instead of searching for hidden belongings. Denver was flipping over a kitchen drawer, dropping knives, forks, spoons back into it still looking.

"What are you looking for?"

"Not sure. Flash drive, memory stick, magnetic disk, IBM Atom? Hell, I would be happy with a notebook or insurance papers, anything that told us something about this guy. Go check the bathroom. Toilet. Ceiling tiles."

Surveying the mess, Rebecca rose from the chair and put her hands on her hips, shook her head and wandered off to the bathroom. There was nothing in the places Denver told her to look. She was surprised at how clean the area was for a single guy living alone. It was almost like he was trained to hit the toilet. She closed the commode lid and sat on it to peer under the sink and piping. Denver came and stood in the doorway.

"Well? I'm out of ideas."

"Maybe because there isn't anything here," she said, then tilted her head and squinted. She lifted her head and looked over the top of the sink, then dropped it to peer below the sink, then over the sink again. Slightly off. "Huh."

"Something under the sink?"

197

"Nope." She stood, walked over and stepped inside the tub. She passed her hands down the tiles, pressing gently, then took an index finger and pushed on a tile three from the bottom. It released a soft click and slid out of the wall. "Well, isn't that nifty. Who'd think of a tiny drawer behind a bathroom tile?"

They removed the contents then receded back to the living area where Denver had righted a small two-top table. Rebecca straddled her chair and began sorting through the pile. Cell phone; needed access. Small round glass chip. Several 4x6 sheets of paper with schematics hand-drawn on them, and what looked like hieroglyphics down the side but was more likely Dingo Dan's shorthand.

"We should take these down to the lab," Denver suggested.

"If they are all on strike, it won't do us much good."

"I told you, it's a shutdown. Besides, I know how to run a lot of the equipment. And, I'm pretty good with Aircrack. I might be able to get into the phone with the right tools."

✳✳✳

February 29, 2072 16:16 p.m.

They were about a block away when Rebecca stopped in her tracks. Something. When they had left the building, she had noticed something. It was the teen. Rice. He had been slouched against the building across the street from the apartment. As soon as they appeared, he had straightened up, turned away, and began texting. She had seen him too many times today. Near the body this morning, near the goons this afternoon.

"That's not right." She turned and began sprinting back the direction they had come.

"What's not right . . . hey?"

A minute later and she would have missed seeing Jason as he disappeared into a clinic. She was breathing heavy when she grabbed him by the elbow.

"Hey, man. What are you doing?"

"The phone," she demanded, hand out. "Let me see the phone."

"Yo, Wolverine." The kid laughed a little. "I know my rights. You got a warrant?"

"How about I arrest you for murder, or maybe accessory after the fact?"

They were attracting attention in the lobby of the neighborhood clinic. The waiting room was small with only a few patients. Two doctors poked their heads through swinging doors at the end of a short hallway due to the commotion. Denver was bent at the waist, winded from the run, but dragged a pair of flexicuffs out of his back pocket as he tried to recover.

"I didn't kill anybody." Jason dropped the defiant stance and looked scared. "Couple guys asked me to keep an eye out for you, that's all. I did what they asked. They give me couple of chits. No big deal."

"Phone, now." He lifted his phone and Detective Logan snatched the device from his hand. "So, you told them when we left the building. And? What did they do then?"

"I don't know. I didn't see them," Jason protested.

"Where were they when you last saw them?" Denver asked.

"On the corner. They said they were going for a sandwich or something."

"You stopped watching us once we left the building," Detective Logan stated.

The detectives looked at each other. "Fifi!"

They sprinted down the sidewalk. As they neared the apartment, the entry door flew open and Fifi came flying out, sailing over the steps, and landing on the concrete in a crouch before them. The door banged open again revealing the brawny men from the corner. They moved quickly and hit the top step as Denver and Rebecca came sliding to a stop at the foot of the stairs. Fifi bounced from foot to foot then darted away toward the coffee shop.

Rebecca slid out her magic stick. In Kenosha, it had saved her more than once, just like magic. A little flip of the switch and a nice little jolt sang down the prong, temporarily stunning up to a 300-pound animal. Or human. Goon Left decided she looked like prey. She zapped him. He was the first to fall. On his way down to belly flop on the pavement, she whipped out flexicuffs and slapped them around his wrists.

Meanwhile, Goon Right sidestepped Denver, elbowed him in the kidney and was in the process of turning to fire a right hook toward the disadvantaged detective. Denver dropped to the ground and swept his leg out, under, and around Goon Right who looked surprised as he flipped onto his back, flailing like an overturned turtle. Goon Right grabbed Denver's pant leg. Denver just managed to get himself standing, and down he went again. Rebecca winced as grunts exploded out of both men. Denver flung himself, off-balance, landing in the middle of Goon Right's chest, who began a labored wheezing cough. She waded in, cuffs in hand and secured the second man.

***

February 29, 2072 19:16 p.m.

"If you knew what they were after, why didn't you just tell us when we interviewed you?" Detective Logan asked.

"You didn't ask." Fifi shrugged as if it was all the answer required. "I didn't know for sure, but after he did the presentation to the city last week, Dan started getting really paranoid again. He thought someone was following him."

"And this presentation was about a prototype which would piggyback on a Polaris 3D Complete mobile app?" Denver clarified.

"Yeah, we've been tinkering with it down here in the mall. See, you could control everything from one central unit or a mobile application if you wanted. Administrators could use it for crowd control, population monitoring, or crime watch. It's a very sophisticated add on; works in conjunction with your current lighting control system. The real gem buried in this was that it had a unique interface with green space horticultural lighting, which could make a non-growing space a viable platform for centralized farming."

"When he was beaten up the first time, this was because he showed the technology to city planners who were going to buy his prototype."

"It's what we think, anyway. The mall started using similar technology, and it triggered Dan's memory. He had locked up his gear for the concert topside. Then he got beat up and couldn't remember where he hid it. When the city began phasing in the dimming features for the mall, he remembered where he secured his stuff. We started working on the lighting systems in here right after he started remembering his programs."

"I don't get it." Denver scratched at his chin. He had a purple bruise on his cheekbone, just beginning to darken. "They couldn't find his prototype, so they killed him and pushed him off the rafters? How does this complete their end game?"

"I pushed him off the rafters."

"I beg your pardon?" Detective Logan asked after a stunned silence.

"He liked to go there and think, get away from people. I don't know where they beat him, but they cut him bad. I don't think they meant to kill him, but he crawled out on the rafters and he died. I knew nobody would find him for days, maybe weeks. When I found him before school today, I pushed him off the rafters so somebody would call the police."

"Well, Fifi. I don't think we can arrest you for accessory. Since he was already dead. Desecrating a body . . . " Detective Logan teased.

"I've been thinking. About the Fifi thing." The boy turned his head thoughtfully. "I'm not really digging it, you know? I think I want to be called something else."

"Yeah, like Floyd, maybe?" Denver suggested with a touch of humor.

"I was leaning toward professor."

Cipher

by Elizabeth San Miguel

My dearest Tamara,

When I first learned I was dying, I knew I wanted to do something special for you. I put all my receding energy into this trinket you hold. I left something for you. Something you want more than anything else in the world. Knowing your puzzle-solving skills, I thought you might enjoy one last game. Don't guess. If you put in the wrong code, the clue inside will be destroyed. The correct code will lead you to what you most desire. You have 40 days to take a whack at it. Afterward, your gift will go elsewhere.

All My Love,

Deborah

"Bitch, I hate puzzles." Tamara looked around hoping no one gathered around the grave had heard her. She received the letter and puzzle box just before the start of the funeral. Tamara had not wanted to read the letter in front of the lawyer nor Deborah's husband. Poor Wade was probably the only person who would actually miss her.

Tamara looked over. Wade sat graveside listening to the service. Such a sweet man to have lost two people he had loved so much in one lifetime. He looked exhausted, and Tamara wondered if he had been crying. Deborah didn't deserve his tears. Neither had Liv. But Wade, like many good people who never saw bad in others, was unaware of his epically poor choice in women. At least he had the solace of a job he loved. After two long years, his primary concern could again be the sick children he treated in his practice instead of a terminally ill wife.

Tamara, seated under a shady tree in back, looked at the puzzle box in her lap. The box was actually a six-inch long cylinder with wheels on either end and a button to push when you wanted to try your luck and see if you'd figured out the code. Four spots to put in numbers and letters. Intricate carvings covered the box. Tamara had to give Deborah props for her woodworking skill. The puzzle box was a fine example of her best work.

Tamara wanted to destroy the box, but dire consequences awaited if she did. Tamara wished again that Deborah, who had died only a week before, could be brought back to life. Not for grief. Rather, Tamara wanted to kill Deborah, slowly, painfully, just as Deborah had done to her for the past 12 years. The beautiful object d'art was one final twist of the knife.

"She spent the last three months working on that cryptex." Wade stood over Tamara.

"It's over?" Tamara jerked and looked around and saw everyone heading toward their cars. "She would have hated hearing you call it a cryptex."

Wade shook his head slightly and looked down. "It's not my fault everyone read the Da Vinci Code and knew where she got the idea. And cryptex sounds better than Crypto Lock Box. We're heading back to the house. Are you coming?"

Tamara smiled and got up. "You want me to?"

"Of course. You were her best friend, after all."

Tamara opened her mouth to ask if he, Wade, wanted her there at the house. But the point was moot. She would go, and she hated herself a bit as she followed Wade like a puppy.

"I've been trying to figure out the code. I can't imagine it has to do with base math, but the first two boxes are 0 through 9 and then A through J and the second two are just numbers."

"If you want to stay after, I'd be happy to look at it with you. Maybe we can figure it out. What base would it be?"

"Base 20 since it's only through J." Tamara just knew she was so good at base math she didn't even have to figure anything out.

"Yeah. It's hard to think of Deborah doing anything with base math. She wasn't even that great at base 10. Could barely figure out 10 percent to get a sale price." Wade smiled.

"Oh my God. Do you remember that shirt I used to wear all the time? *'There are 10 kinds of people in the world, those who understand binary and those who don't.'* No matter how many times I explained to her 10 in base 2 equated to 2 in base 10 she would ask what the other eight types of people were. What killed me is Deborah seemed to expect praise for subtracting 2 from 10." Tamara laughed and shook her head.

Wade sighed and smiled. "Sounds like her."

As strange as it sounded, base math was how Tamara and Wade had become friends. She, Deborah, Wade, and Liv often hung out together at bars when they were in college. Wade would buy Tamara a shot for every math question answer she got right. Perhaps it wasn't the best idea to ply an alcoholic with shots, but what did they know.

"Man, how many times did we have to get your drunk ass home?" Wade shook his head and smiled.

Tamara's heart fluttered when she realized they were sharing a memory. She had loved Wade for a long time. Despite repeated attempts to stop her stupid crush, she never managed. After all these years, she doubted she ever would.

At Wade's house, Tamara ended up taking on the role of hostess. Once everyone else had left, she started to clear away the mess. Tamara often looked at the bottles of liquor. Just one little taste. She had given the stuff up 12 years ago. Even so, when she was around it, she wanted it.

"What's in the letter she left you?" Wade was sitting at the table sipping a mug of coffee.

Tamara thought about it, shrugged her shoulders, and gave him the letter to read. He looked at Tamara, his eyes crinkled. "What *do* you want most in the world?"

She wished she had the guts to tell him she wanted him. But Tamara knew Deborah's letter did not refer to her unspoken and unrequited infatuation.

Tamara shrugged her shoulders. "Nothing she had to give. I don't know what she means." *Liar. Liar. Pants on fire.*

"Do you want some help?" Wade's left eyebrow raised a tad.

She nodded her head, went to the table, pulled out the puzzle box, and handed it to him. "Be careful. If it's handled too roughly it might break the glass inside.

"The box has a glass vial with either vinegar or some sort of mild acid in it. It probably has a small sheet of very delicate paper in it with another clue on it. Put in the wrong code, push the button, it breaks the glass and destroys the paper. Put in the correct code, it's like a key, it'll open up the box without breaking the vial."

"Are you forgetting I watched her make those things for the past decade." Wade looked intently at the box.

"Uh, sorry."

He looked at the box and frowned. "I never understood why she liked Mayan art so much. The whole culture was so violent."

Mayan. Yes, that was it. The images carved into the cylinder were Mayan. Of course. Tamara slapped herself on the forehead. "Geez, I wonder if that's a clue."

"What? Why she loved Mayan art? I don't think – of course, you've known her such a long time . . . "

Tamara shook her head. "No, I mean why she decorated it with Mayan symbology."

"Tamara, how long did you know her?"

"I wonder if this is writing?" Tamara stared intently at the cylinder still in Wade's hands.

"Tamara?"

"Hmmm?"

"How long did you know Deborah?"

"Uh, we were in kindergarten when we met. We were both awkward and gravitated toward one another. I helped with her math homework and she'd stop anyone bigger from picking on me. Which meant everyone."

Wade jerked straight up in his chair. "She protected you?"

Tamara nodded her head. "Yeah. She was the only one allowed to bully me."

"Oh. And you two ended up going to the same college?"

"Uh-huh. You know this. That's where we met you and Liv."

Wade frowned.

"I'm sorry. I shouldn't have mentioned . . . I'm so sorry." Tamara wanted to bang her head into the wall.

Wade was silent, then shook his head. "It's okay. It's been 12 years. I should be over it by now. Right?"

"Do you ever really get over things like that?"

Liv and Wade had been high school sweethearts. They weren't engaged when she had met them, but they were well on their way.

"It was a surprise when they found . . . God, there I go again. I should just have a foot permanently placed in my mouth." Tamara lifted her right foot and wiggled it.

Wade shrugged his shoulders. "When they found her body. I, uh. I was shocked. I had hoped . . . No reason for her to leave, but you still hope. Stupid." Wade clutched the puzzle box firmly.

Tamara worried it might break. She took it from his hands and looked at the box. "I wonder if these are words carved into the box. Mayan words, maybe?"

Wade crossed his arms in front of his chest and leaned back in his chair. He took several deep breaths. After a moment, he sat up straight and picked up the brightly colored coffee cup from the table and swallowed the last of the now cold coffee. "She was into their art. Do you know if she was interested in the writing as well?"

"They're sort of the same thing, I think. I mean the images aren't abstract. They represented phonemes, if I'm remembering correctly. Or, was that Egyptian? Ugh, all I have to go on is some television documentary. She won't have made this easy." Tamara made a mental note to start researching Mayan writing.

"No, she never made anything easy."

Was that a note of derision in his voice? Tamara gazed at Wade. He looked back at her.

"Why did you — uh — never mind."

"Why did I marry her?"

Tamara nodded.

"She was pregnant. I wanted children."

"Ah. If she hadn't gotten pregnant, you probably would not have married?"

"No 'probably' about it."

"When she lost the baby though, you didn't get a divorce."

"No, I mean, I thought, if she had gotten pregnant once she could do it again. But then she didn't. It's pointless to think about now." Wade rubbed his right index finger around the rim of the mug he was still holding. "Tamara, she was pregnant, right? That wasn't a lie?"

Tamara looked back down at the puzzle box which was Deborah's actual baby. She was unsure what to tell Wade. "She told me she was pregnant."

Wade threw his mug shattering it against the wall. "She's dead now. Will you *please* tell me the truth."

Even though Wade had not thrown the mug in her direction, Tamara crouched down and covered her head, waiting for a blow. Wade rolled his eyes. "I'm not going to hit you, Tamara."

Tamara looked up at Wade. "I didn't know. I didn't find out she'd lied until after you were married. I thought you both were happy and it was uh, just a matter of time before she actually got pregnant. I didn't say anything. The last thing I wanted was to make you unhappy, Wade."

Wade looked at Tamara for a moment longer. He then got up and got a broom and dustpan and started sweeping up the shards. "I'm sorry, I didn't mean to scare you."

Wade's reaction stunned rather than scared her. If anyone had ever asked her about him she would say he was easy-going and kind. Always, unfailingly kind.

Tamara slowly got up. After loosening her grip on the puzzle box, she knew she would have to be more careful. If she broke it or failed to figure out the puzzle, her life would go from bad to not worth living.

"I think I'll go home now. Please let me know if you need anything."

Wade kept cleaning and didn't look as Tamara left the house.

***

Thank heaven for Google. After hours of searching, Tamara had finally deciphered about half the glyphs on the puzzle. No sentences but glyphs for water, rain, lightning, and of course, death.

Tamara recalled the lake less than a mile from the craptastic house she and Deborah had rented during college. The night Deborah was not so subtly referring to on her puzzle box had been one of the worst storms of the decade. Tamara remembered Deborah expertly backing the little hatchback up to the dock where one small boat with a tiny engine was tied up. Rain came down in waves with bright flashes of lightening that blinded them. Rolls of thunder rattled their bones.

How did the joke go? A good friend will help you move. A great friend will help you move the body. Tamara had always thought of Deborah as a great friend, an annoying one, but a true one. She was no friend at all. Deborah hadn't killed Liv directly, but she deserved part of the blame.

***

"Liv seems sweet." Tamara had just met Liv and Wade a few days before at a show of student artwork where two of Deborah's pieces were on display.

"Seems . . . being the operative word." Deborah's chin went down and one eyebrow up as she got ready to dish. "She said some catty things to me about you after that boyfriend of hers paid you so much attention."

"She did? His focus was on her. He barely noticed me."

Deborah shrugged. "I can only tell you what she said to me."

"What did she say, specifically?" Tamara was intrigued.

"She said you were mousy and unkempt."

209

Tamara was stung and confused. "Why did she suggest we hang out? I'm meeting her and Wade at the library in 30 minutes."

"You? Just you?" Deborah frowned.

"No. Open invite. We're going to see *As You Like It*. You don't like theater and I didn't think you'd want to go. She called me mousy and unkempt?"

"Well, she didn't use those exact words, but yes. I might like it, you don't know."

Tamara shrugged her shoulders and sighed inwardly. She did know. Deborah did not like the play, but this is how the unlikely friendship began for the quartet.

Wade often came to the bars with math problems already worked out to see how far in her cups Tamara would have to be before she started getting answers wrong. Turned out it was pretty damn far. Wade always credited Tamara with his learning base math after spending so much time working on equations and answers to ask her in bars. After Wade read out the problem, Tamara spat back the answer, downed a shot, then moved on to the next equation. He bought the occasional drink for Deborah, but his attention was on Liv because he loved her, and Tamara, because her ability fascinated him. Deborah was the odd man out.

***

"I think Liv is pregnant," Deborah said. She and Tamara were having a rare night with just the two of them.

Tamara just wanted to watch television, but her heart sank at the thought of Liv's pregnancy. "Oh, well, she and Wade will probably get married then."

"I think it's someone else's."

"Oh?!" Tamara was embarrassed at how happy that idea made her.

"Yeah, but I think she's going to tell Wade it's his."

"Oh." Monosyllabic much? Tamara rolled her eyes at herself.

"Look, don't freak out. But I saw her studying up on poisons. I'm not sure, but I bet after she marries Wade, she plans to kill him. His family is so rich."

"Don't freak out! Really? Why in the world do you think Liv would do such a thing? And who the hell else's baby would it be? It has to be Wade. He'll be over the moon." Tamara resigned herself to their marriage.

"Just some things she said. She mentioned a cousin who married a rich guy."

"What cousin? Who cares if she married a rich guy?" Tamara just wanted to watch TV.

"The husband died. And she said it like she wished the same thing could happen to her."

Tamara tried to think of a single time Liv had ever said anything about another guy. She had to admit, she spent most of her time talking to Wade. Liv never seemed to mind. "When do you have all this time to talk to her? She has never said anything remotely like that to me."

"She says plenty to you. You just don't remember."

"Why wouldn't I remember?" Tamara crossed her arms in front of her chest.

"Don't get snippy. How many times have you woken up in your bed with no memory of how you'd gotten there? All those drinks Wade buys for you, what do you expect?"

Tamara's heart skipped a beat. Was Liv evil and was Tamara too drunk too often to notice? If Wade were in danger. What could we do? "We should report her to the police, then."

Deborah rolled her eyes. "And tell them what? I don't have any proof. Just suspicions."

"Maybe you're wrong, then." Once Tamara saw the look on Deborah's face, she wished she could pull the words back. Never tell Deborah she's wrong, especially when she was. Tamara hoped to shut down Deborah's coming storm by distraction. "Well then, you need to tell Wade."

"Me? You think I should tell him. He won't believe me. I'm not the one he fawns over and buys drinks for."

"He won't believe me, either." Tamara doubted Liv's guilt, but she didn't know her well.

"Well, don't blame me if they get married and then he *dies*. I tried to warn you." Deborah went to her room. Tamara thought she had said her final word, but she came out a few minutes later. She was holding a piece of paper, torn at the top. Deborah didn't say anything, she just held out the paper for Tamara to take.

Need to find out which poison to use to kill bf/husband soon after marriage. Must be doubts as to cause of death. What books to use for reference?

It was in Liv's handwriting.

"Where? Where did you get this? What is it?" Tamara's stomach sank.

"I tore it out of her notebook. She's always writing things down." Deborah sat down on the couch.

"This will count as proof. Let's go to the police."

Deborah shook her head no. "Already tried."

"You took this to the police? What'd they say?" Tamara looked at the paper again.

"Well, to a friend of mine. A policeman. He said we'd need more but keep the paper. If Wade dies, we'll have proof of what happened." Deborah took the note back, folded it, and placed it in her pocket. "You should tell Wade. I'm sure he'll believe you."

Tamara thought incessantly about what to do. Even with the note, she had a difficult time believing Liv was evil. Instead of warning Wade, she first wanted to talk to Liv. Maybe there was an explanation for the note. Deborah was probably full of crap.

Tamara arranged to speak to Liv alone, which took more effort than expected. Wade went with her everywhere. Tamara was so nervous she decided a shot of liquor might take the edge off. Or a few. Her next memory was feeling the floor shake after hearing a loud clap of thunder. She had no idea where she was because she was either blind or it was completely dark. Her stomach clenched as a flash of lightning illuminated the room. She was in the front room of her house and someone was lying on the floor near her.

Okay. Not blind. She needed light, but the whole house was dark. Nausea had her hoping she wouldn't vomit. She wasn't sure how long she lay there before the lights flickered on. She looked at who was next to her. It was Liv. Mangled. Wet. Bloody. Dead. Tamara looked at the bloody hatchet lying next to Liv.

"Oh, no. No. No. Liv. I'm so . . . oh please God. Please." Tamara leaned over Liv's body and cried. The door opened and Deborah, dripping wet from the storm, and thankfully alone, looked at the gory scene. Her jaw dropped and her eyes widened.

"I thought you were just going to talk to her."

Tamara began sobbing. "I don't know what to do." Tamara tried to take in air. Great gulping sobs echoed out of her.

Deborah just stood there a moment. "She should disappear."

"What?"

"She was going to kill Wade. Let's take her to the lake. No one is out in this." Deborah gestured to the windows indicating the weather outside.

"We can't do that. It's against the law."

Deborah didn't respond. She just looked at Tamara.

Deborah took over. She made Tamara put on gloves. They wrapped Liv up in a surprisingly strong vinyl shower curtain and tied the package closed. Once outside, Deborah produced a tarp and some rope from the back of the car. They had taken everything out in a boat, coming close to death with the waves on the lake all but capsizing them. A few concrete blocks to weigh her down and she disappeared into the lake. Tamara wanted to join Liv at the bottom, but Deborah kept her alive by reminding her that Wade was now safe because of her.

When they got back to their house they cleaned like never before. Liv's blood had been contained in one small area and had soaked into a rather small rug with a waterproof backing. The rug went into the lake as well. They had gotten away with it. Even after exhaustive searches, no evidence was found that Liv had ever done anything other than walk away. Except she walked away without taking anything with her.

And then, yet another unexpected thing happened. Suspicion fell squarely on Wade. However, he was so broken up at her disappearance, he did not stay a prime suspect for long. Tamara wanted to be around Wade but feared she might confess to him. She chose to avoid him.

Deborah ended up comforting him in every way possible. And their "shared" grief at Liv's disappearance led to a relationship. When Deborah feared Wade would leave her, she became miraculously pregnant. A quick wedding and a miscarriage later and Deborah was determined to live happily ever after, which included having her very own servant.

Deborah had kept the hatchet and gloves Tamara wore that night. With her fingerprints and Liv's blood, it would be all that was needed to convict.

At first, Deborah would ask little things of her. If Tamara balked, she would start murmuring the Lizzie Borden folk rhyme under her breath. Tamara had no idea how many times she had struck Liv, but given the general absence of blood, she guessed it was far fewer than 40.

Tamara's memory of the evening never returned. Her brain provided no glimpse of the horrific death. Tamara had wanted to move away from both her and Wade, but Deborah insisted she remain.

Then Deborah had gotten sick. For two long years, Wade and Tamara took care of her. All seemed lost, and Deborah was told to prepare for the end. Even so, Deborah never tired of having Tamara at her beck and call. Tamara looked forward to her death. And now, Deborah managed to punish her one last time and make her work to get the bloody hatchet back. Tamara had to figure the puzzle out. Her only act of rebellion had been refusing to answer Deborah's phone call the night before she passed.

Tamara continued to work on interpreting all of the Mayan glyphs, but then she realized not all of the images were Mayan. There were Yoruban images and Bhutanese writing. The writing just translated to the number 40. The Yoruban images were beautiful but were not writing and thus didn't translate. Tamara figured 40 was what she should put into the box. She had mentioned 40 days in her letter. The 'take a whack' phrase in the letter also made her think of the Lizzie Borden taunt.

Tamara put in 4 on the right and 0 on the left. But it didn't look right. Why have four spots? She had to get this right. Her heart pounded. If wrong, her life was over.

She put her finger on the button, breathed in, and was about to push down when she wondered, why Yoruba? She thought back to what she knew about each. All three cultures were geographically located where the weather was usually hot. She knew most writings all over the globe started as an accounting system. Number systems varied across the world depending on many factors. A place in Spain, where most of the people were born with six fingers, had a numbering system based on the number 12. After a quick search, she confirmed Mayan, Yoruban, and Bhutanese cultures all used a vigesimal number system. Base 20. Hot weather cultures would use fingers and toes. Could Deborah have actually done something with base math?

She looked at the box and changed the display to 20^{20}. Which was 40 in base 10. It looked correct. She pressed the button and it popped open. In it was a paper-wrapped key with the name of a bank on it, and all she needed to know to get into the safety deposit box.

It only took a few minutes to get to the bank and open the safety deposit box. Inside, was the hatchet and the gloves and the note in Liv's handwriting about poison, and a notebook. On the notebook cover, also, in Liv's handwriting were the words: *Story Ideas & Notes.*

Tamara opened the notebook to a page where half the page had been torn out. She matched the torn note to the page. Tamara broke out in a cold sweat. No. No. Please. She looked through the book. Liv wrote down story ideas. Tamara knew she was an English major, but she never equated it with fiction writing.

One last item was a piece of letter-size paper. On one side, in the middle, was typed: *Now who's the dumb one?*

Tamara had killed an innocent person. She knelt down under the table and covered her head with her arms and began rocking back and forth. Tamara gulped, trying to get enough air. Her only solace all these years was that she had protected Wade from Liv. But then Tamara noticed the other side of the paper.

On it was Deborah's writing. Shaky. Tamara guessed it was written near her death. The first line was a date. It was, in fact, written the day before she died.

Tamara,

I'm so sorry. I set this all up thinking you had killed Liv all those years ago. I haven't looked at the hatchet for 12 years. I just now noticed the finger impressions are much too large to have been made by your hand. I swear, all these years, I thought you had killed Liv. I have no idea who might have killed her. I will try to call you and maybe we can figure it out together. Please forgive me for how I have treated you all these years.

All my love,

Deborah

***

Who the hell killed Liv, then? Tamara locked all the items back in the box and left the bank. She needed to think. She couldn't just give the hatchet to the police. After all, how would she explain where it came from?

For the first time in 12 years, Tamara not only had a drink, but she got well-and-truly drunk. She ended up at Wade's house and knocked on his door at three in the morning.

Wade opened the door, rubbing sleep from his eyes. "What is it? What's happened?"

She threw herself into his arms, stood on tiptoe, and kissed him. He pulled back.

"I love you. I've always loved you. I know you're sad Deborah died. I'll give you your space I promise. She was not a good person. I'm not a good person either, but I'm not as bad as I thought."

Wade stepped back from her. "What are you talking about?"

"Liv. I'm talking about Liv. I didn't kill her."

Wade frowned. "Did you think you had killed her?"

"Yes. Deborah found me. I was so drunk. I don't remember anything, but I thought . . . I must have killed her."

Wade looked at Tamara, his head cocked, listening, but still confused.

"I think I need some coffee. God, I think I'm drunk from your kiss. You'll probably need some too." He turned and walked into the kitchen.

"Uh, yeah. Coffee." Tamara felt confused. She thought Wade would be thunderstruck. Instead, he just seemed a bit bored.

She sat down at the kitchen table and he made coffee for them both.

Wade gingerly drank his. "Okay. Why did you think you'd killed Liv?"

"She made plans to see me. I was going to ask if she planned to kill you. But I got drunk before she arrived. The next thing I know, I'm lying beside her and she's dead. I thought I must have killed her." Tamara paused. She felt sure Wade would get angry since she had known all these years Liv was dead. But nothing. He just sipped his coffee and looked at her.

"Then Deborah came in and saw what happened. Instead of turning me in, she helped me dispose of Liv's body." Tamara continued on when Wade didn't react. Tamara decided she must be more intoxicated than she realized.

"After all that, what made you decide you weren't a murderer?" Wade asked.

"Deborah's note."

"The note the lawyer gave you?" Wade finally showed some emotion, even though it was mainly confusion.

"No, the one in the box."

"The cryptex? You got it open? Can I see?"

"I didn't bring it with me. No, the other note. She wrote me a note the day before she died. She realized the handprint on the hatchet was much too large to be mine. Someone else killed Liv."

Both of Wade's eyebrows went up. "You have the hatchet?"

"No. I mean Yes, but No."

"Yeah. Drink more coffee and try again." Wade pointed at her mug.

Tamara lifted and took another swig.

"I don't have it on me. The police . . . "

Wade stood up. "You gave it to the police?"

"Not yet." Tamara looked at Wade and the other shoe dropped. Once again, Tamara couldn't believe what a bad judge of character she was.

"Oh, good. Because I would like to give it to them." Wade sat back down and took another sip of his coffee. He looked at the cup, and for a moment Tamara thought he might fling it like he had done before. After thinking for a while, he just shook his head. "Damn. I have to admit, waking me up at 3 a.m. That worked very well. Was that your plan?"

Tamara sat there gobsmacked. She knew she needed to say something, but what? She was in deep shit.

"You shouldn't kill me." Tamara felt completely and totally sober. She

217

wanted to live. Tamara wished desperately that math skills would translate to her being able to talk her way out of this. But no.

"Why?" Wade actually seemed curious.

"Because the hatchet and letter are in the same place as before. If you kill me, then in 40, well no, no, 35 days the information will go to the police. If those are your fingerprints, then that's pretty much of a slam dunk murder rap."

Wade looked at his coffee almost as if he were waiting for it to give him an answer. "Well, I'm sort of in a 'damned if you do and damned if you don't' situation here. If I let you go, then what's to stop you from giving the evidence to the police?"

"I'm sure I can come up with something that will work for both of us. Just answer me this. Why did you leave the hatchet?"

"I hadn't planned to leave it. I was going to slime it up with blood and put your fingerprints on it. Damn lights went out. I left it there by accident. When I went to go back for it, Deborah was there." He shrugged his shoulders. "And I never could find the hatchet afterwards."

"Why did you kill Liv? I would've sworn you loved her."

Wade's nostrils flared. "I did love her. I still do. But she wanted to leave me. Me! I thought she might be going to see some other guy. But she actually ended up at your house. She saw me and started yelling at me and saying that I was smothering her, and she wanted to be alone. I offered her marriage and family. I wanted children. What is it with you women not wanting kids? I don't get it?"

Tamara, up until five minutes before, would have happily married him and given him as many children as he wanted. But, what with his crazy showing, she felt chagrinned. Murder was what it took for her to finally get rid of her crush.

Tamara knew she must still be somewhat drunk when she heard herself say, "I would have had your kids."

His eyebrow raised. "You want to get married and have kids? Is that what you meant by something for both of us? Liv was always trying to push us together. You know after she met you she said how she loved how tiny and cute you were. A tiny, sweet mouse. She thought it was wonderful that you could just wash your hair and comb it out and it would look wavy and free."

Tamara's jaw dropped. "I guess that's one way of saying mousy and unkempt."

"What?"

Tamara shook her head. "According to Deborah all those years ago, Liv called me mousy and unkempt."

"Deborah. I picked the wrong one." Wade looked at Tamara, assessing her. Once, Tamara had longed for Wade to look her way, but now she felt sick. "Why did you pick her?"

"She was the only one who didn't look at me like I was guilty of Liv's death. Even you shied away from me." He frowned.

Tamara wanted to yell at him that she felt guilty and couldn't face him.

"But you did kill her, and you were planning to frame me for the murder."

Wade laughed. "Well, no one likes to be suspected and I didn't plan it."

Oh well, since he didn't plan it. It's all okay then, Tamara thought.

"Yeah, so here's what is going to happen. You're going to give me money. We'll start with ten thousand and go from there. It won't ever be more than you can afford. In return, I won't give the hatchet to the police."

Wade grimaced like Tamara had just kicked him in the nuts. "Where's the benefit for me?"

"I just told you. I won't turn in the hatchet. It'd be awkward to explain anyway." Tamara's heart pounded but she tried to look as if she didn't care.

"You don't love me anymore?" Wade's disappointment surprised Tamara. She considered how to answer. Finally, she shook her head no and then shrugged ever so slightly.

"I bet given enough time you could love me again."

"Sure."

Tamara considered a career change to professional poker player when Wade let her leave. She drove directly to the nearest police station.

It's All Relative

by S. Ashley Couts

In the gym, a basketball hit the floor, making a kid named Blaze a little jumpy. It was late, and he shouldn't have been at his hallway locker outside the gym. But he was too afraid to leave. He had a stalker – a guy had been watching him, asking about him – his friend Ashton had told him.

Blaze unlocked and opened the locker, and a barrage of clutter tumbled out – books, drawings, other personal belongings, even clothing. A book tipped over from above, nearly hitting him, and he shoved it aside. That's when he saw the note, the page folded as a four-pointed star. He picked it up and turned it in his hand. Each corner had a word.

I. Hate. You. Blaze.

Thanks a lot, Stella.

She was one of his few friends, so he stuffed the note in his pocket and sighed at the mess. He was too tired.

After re-stuffing his locker, Blaze walked the hall searching for a way out of the building. Most of the doors were locked with chains across them and the new security system activated. But that wasn't his greatest concern at the moment.

His greatest concern was the stalker.

Ashton was a big, scary dude. In addition to selling weed in school, he had his hooks in a lot of poor kids for loans dealt out at lunch. Loans with high interest and heavy penalties for failing to repay.

But against all odds, he was also Blaze's friend, though hardly a good one.

"Look at it like you got a bodyguard, man," Ashton had said, giving a laugh that freaked Blaze out.

Finally making it outside the building without setting off an alarm, Blaze pulled up his black hoodie, which made him feel anonymous, and skulked off, his torn shoes making floppy sounds as they scraped the wet pavement.

It was raining again, sprinkling – but not hard.

It had been a crappy day from the very beginning, though not an unusual one.

The foster baby had kept him up all night. He'd wanted to catch some winks during his early morning classes, but the teachers would have none of it.

At lunch, he had to deal with Ashton's demand for pay-back on his huge lunch loan. Blaze would have forfeited the meal – some white soupy shit they passed off as real food – but he was starving. His foster mother, Judy Hogmann, had been on a rampage, saying he was the reason the baby was up all night. She loved taking meals away as punishment, so he hadn't any breakfast.

Being in the Hogmann house was a living nightmare. But he had been in so many homes, he didn't know anything else.

There were eight children, ages three to 15, in the foster home. And like parasites, Judy and Melvin Hogmann made a living off them. He claimed a bad back, so he couldn't work. Judy claimed her bassett hound as a "service animal" and in public hobbled around with a cane and wore a leg brace.

Though he was tired and still hungry, Blaze didn't want to go back there, but he couldn't immediately decide where to go.

This day, no, all of 2020 so far, had sucked.

Rain hit his back. He kept to the shadows, jumping at everything that seemed out of place. There, in the shadows, he thought he saw the guy who'd been following him. Blond and kind of tall.

Both the rain and his fear of a stalker motivated him on where to head next. Jerry's Pool Hall.

Blaze liked hanging out in the dark, smoky room talking to the owner, Jerry, a 60-ish retired military vet who loved to give advice to anyone who would listen, especially Blaze.

"Sometimes I wish my real father was alive," Blaze said.

"I get it, son. What you got there is a pipe dream, isn't it?" the old man said through the haze. "It makes sense to be longing for what you never had."

"Can we play?" Blaze asked, indicating the pool table.

Jerry picked up a cue stick as Blaze, cue stick in hand, positioned himself on the other side of the table.

"Maybe you should just try your imagination. In your mind, he can be anything you wish him to be," Jerry said, but then added sadly, "Of course, in reality, he could be some terrible person . . . just cooling his heels in lockup somewhere."

Jerry hit the cue, which rolled across the table and hit its mark with a small thwack. The red No. 3 ball rolled, bounced off a felt-edged wall, darted back across the table, and fell into the pocket.

Jerry and Blaze re-positioned themselves around the table accordingly.

"I always say, let sleeping dogs lie," Jerry said, as he eyed his next shot.

"It would be cool if he was a war hero or something," Blaze confided. He had one hand in his pocket and pulled something out.

"Like I said. Pipe dream," Jerry said, viewing him skeptically. But then he stood up as he noticed something. "What's that you got there in your hand, Blaze?" He walked around the table to the boy.

"It's some sort of military ribbon, I think. I've had it forever. I keep it in my locker, and it fell out today," Blaze said. "This paper, too. It's a hate note from my girlfriend, Stella."

"Let me see that," Jerry said, reaching out his hand. "No, not the note. The other thing."

Blaze handed it over, but his attention was on Stella's note. "She hates me."

"I seriously doubt that," Jerry said absentmindedly as he examined the ribbon. "Mind if I hold on to this for a while?"

Blaze didn't hear the question. His brain was elsewhere. "Ashton claims this tall, blond guy is stalking me."

Jerry laughed as he pocketed the ribbon. "Why do you listen to Ashton anyway? He's a jerk in my book."

"Yeah, I know. A Prize A jerk."

They continued playing until it was dark outside, and then Blaze left the pool hall.

✳✳✳

In front of him, the house loomed like a big hulking shadow. Through the walls, he could hear the calamity inside. The baby was screaming, and there was a huge ruckus of bumps and thumps as if the whole house would burst at the seams. The prickly evergreens surrounding the house epitomized how he felt about the whole thing.

Blaze was late, and would surely pay, so his only option was to sneak inside. He grasped a rusty drainpipe, maneuvered up onto the side of the porch and across to the hinged doggie door. It was nasty and clogged with mud and hair, but it allowed even big dogs entry into the house.

His fingers barely fit under the opening and, with slight difficulty, he managed to wedge them through. Suddenly, he felt something – the dog's black snotty nose. But it was when he heard his name that he froze.

"Blaze. I won't be sorry to lose that one," Judy said.

"Who's coming for him?" Melvin asked.

"Someone from the children's home."

"They'll eat him up there." The man laughed.

"Who cares?" she said. "The best part for us is we get someone new."

"Yeah. One kid is a brat, shuck 'em out and get another," Melvin said. "So, what time does he go?"

Blaze never heard the answer. He crawled backward from the doggie door and off the porch. He looked around, ducked back through the bushes, and ran down the street. It wasn't like he hadn't been in this predicament before. In fact, he was a bit relieved. This was the worst foster home ever.

At the corner, he stopped running and took out his phone. But it was still dead. It was hopeless.

Fortunately, it had stopped raining a while ago, but it was very late. The big clock outside the bank read 12:20. Blaze walked around looking for a place to crash and ended up at a McDonald's on Shelby. His lunch money for the week amounted to $10 and some change. He pulled that out.

Stella's note, folded like origami, came out with the money. He held it in his hand. For a moment, it seemed to burn into his palm as if it were poison. He turned it over and over, feeling each edge. Then, finally, he unfolded it and read.

No surprise. She wanted to break up. Because of something Ashton had said.

How could a guy be both a friend and a jerk at the same time, Blaze wondered?

He ate a burger and some fries then walked over to Garfield Park where he pulled off his sweatshirt, found some free newspapers from a box at the corner, and wadded them into a ball for a headrest.

With the sweatshirt covering his head, he crashed on a bench in a gazebo, well-hidden from view from the street.

⁂

Blaze slept fitfully but woke with a start when he heard a vehicle pull into a nearby parking lot, which was close to the tennis courts. It was Ashton.

Blaze collected himself and walked over. "How'd you find me?"

"I stopped by the house and they said you hadn't come in. So I thought, where else could the idiot be?"

Ashton put his fat arm around Blaze's small shoulder and pulled him along. "Where we goin'?" Blaze asked.

They walked toward the Jeep.

"To get something to eat," Ashton said. "Your stalker is still around. I saw him. Was gonna confront him if I saw him again today, but when I stopped by your house and you weren't home I got me an idea."

"Should I call the cops on the dude?"

"Woah, I don't think you want to do that. For your own good, man, you best leave this one alone. I guess you got yourself into something here, pretty boy. Now it's on you if they're coming after you."

Blaze stared at him in surprise. "Hold it, dude. I have no idea what you're talking about."

"Look, you don't want to talk about it, it's cool man."

"You're a jerk and you don't know shit about anything," Blaze said angrily.

As he got into the Jeep, Ashton said, "What I know is I gotta plan. But let's eat, first."

***

They chowed down on a few burgers at McDonald's and then headed to Ashton's house.

Ashton had a room up in the rafters, and it was his domain. Signs on the wall outside make clear who was boss. "STAY OUT OR BE KILLED" was the most prominent warning. Entry was by invitation only. The rafter room was stifling hot, but two exhaust fans kept the heated air blowing.

Ashton was in a good and generous mood, and offered to share a joint, which Blaze declined. Ashton opened a bar containing his stash of candy and chips, then reached into his personal freezer filled with Mountain Dew.

Petty crime and extortion at school had its rewards.

Ashton sprawled in his huge, purple beanbag chair with an open bag of Cheetos on his belly. Blaze sat in the big brown beanbag chair, his skinny arms hanging like oars over the sides.

"You got to face it, man," Ashton said leaning back in his king-size chair. "Most people hate you."

"You're stupid, Ashton," Blaze said defiantly. "Go screw yourself."

"I'm serious, Blaze. Admit it. You have the worst luck of anyone I know." He punctuated this statement by toking a joint and plunging his hand into a bag of chips, while flashing a crooked half-smile.

"So, let's just look at the facts here," Ashton said through a mouth full of smoke and Cheetos. "And I say this as kindly as I can. If we count your friends, what do we get?"

Blaze gritted his teeth. What could he do? He was captive.

"Go on," he said dejectedly.

Ashton shoved the chip bag to the side, held up his chubby, orange-colored fingers covered in Cheetos dust and started to count.

"One," he said. "Old Mrs. London in social studies likes you. A little. Maybe. That's sad, man. Really sad. A broken-down teacher is your only friend."

He hooted.

Scowling, Blaze snatched the bag from him. "Not true. Stella likes me."

"Recant. Stella liked you. You broke her heart. Now she hates you, Stella hates you, dude. Thanks to me."

"Okay. Get to the point, you have a solution to my problem?"

"I do. But I gotta' warn ya, you won't like it."

"What choice do I have now?"

"In my opinion, slim to none."

The room was silent for a moment.

"Okay, what?" Blaze said.

"I can kill you," Ashton said with a straight face.

"Yeah, right." There was a long moment of silence before Blaze laughed nervously and let out a small choking sound. "Are you for real?"

Ashton looked at him for a minute then said, "Okay. I'll sweeten the deal. I'll also erase your lunch debt. Zip, zip, gone. Just like that. But, still, you gotta die."

"I don't want to end it all just to get out of owing you," Blaze said.

"It's the stalker I'm thinking about," Ashton said quickly

"What about the stalker guy?"

Ashton laughed.

"Stupid question. If you're dead, who's he gonna stalk? Me?" He leaned forward in his chair, grabbed Blaze's bag of chips and dumped them onto the floor. "You're really dumb, man. Look, it's like this. I'll tell Stella and some other kids at school you're missing. Maybe even that something bad happened to you, like you got kidnapped by a stalker. They can put up missing posters around town. But you're gone. Dead."

"So, I don't really have to die?"

"No, but everyone . . . like your stalker . . . thinks so. You go into hiding. And I can arrange it. I'll talk to Stella." Ashton smiled and leaned back into the beanbag chair. "Or I could actually kill you."

"No, that won't be necessary," Blaze said, warming to the idea of escaping his stalker. "Let's talk about the plan."

✲✲✲

Although it was a ruse with the truth known to only a few, word of Blaze's disappearance spread rapidly. Soon the story of the missing kid went viral and was picked up by the media. There were pictures of Blaze on posters which were shown on TV.

Gossip and rumor regarding the sad and tragic end of the kid named Blaze were everywhere.

Social workers soon arrived at the Hogmann's house, evaluated the situation, and immediately took all the foster children, placing them in other homes. The police quickly followed, asking Judy and Melvin Hogmann serious questions that they could not adequately answer.

Television cameras were at the house when the police carted both off to jail, leaving the neighbors to care for the snotty-nosed dog.

Blaze, in the meantime, hung out mainly in the garage of a vacant house across the street from Stella. Turns out she didn't really hate him.

Stella would visit him, mostly when her parents weren't home or were asleep, taking him food, snacks, clean clothes, and other provisions, though she wouldn't stay no matter how much he begged.

Blaze would only go out well after dark, hiding in bushes at the end of the block as he waited for Ashton in his jeep. They would sit in the park as Ashton updated him on what was going on.

***

After a couple of weeks of searching for the missing child, the investigation narrowed down to two people, Ashton Bowers and Stella Hopewell.

Police Detective Harriette Appleton called Ashton in for questioning. He arrived with all the youthful overconfidence of someone in deep water who was unaware that they were about to drown.

"*What can I do for you*, detective?" Ashton said with a smirk, a gold tooth exposed by his crooked smile.

Appleton had researched his bio, from his baby booties until the moment he swaggered into her office. He needed a smack-down, and it was coming.

"You've got quite a history," she said, looking up from the rap sheet.

"I didn't come in here to talk about me."

"I see you live on Tabor. That's near the projects. Lots of drug action there."

"Your point? You racial profiling me?" Ashton said. "I'd hate to think that."

"Get off it, white boy. You look like a user is all."

"Lady, I'm just trying to help you find my friend. I was hoping to cut through the bull."

"Okay." She put her pencil down and looked at him. "Where is Blaze?"

"The last time I saw him he was with a blond guy."

"Now that is bullshit, and you know it. When we find him, and we will, and we get your fingerprints off his dead body, you're going to jail," she said, then paused before adding, "For a long, long time."

Ashton's smugness disappeared.

"So help yourself, kid. Tell me. Where's Blaze?"

***

After lunch, Stella was called down to Miss Pickett's office at school and was made to wait outside. She didn't want to answer any more questions. The whole Blaze-thing was going to mess up her entire life.

Across from her was a huge, colorful poster meant to encourage positive thinking. It said, *Do the thing you think you cannot do.*

Through the door, Stella could hear Miss Pickett's voice. It sounded like trouble.

But Miss Pickett flung the door open with a cheery welcome and Stella rose to enter the office. As usual, Miss Pickett offered Stella chocolates from the fishbowl on her desk, which Stella refused, not because she didn't like chocolate, but because she felt it was a bribe.

The counselor cleared her throat and said, "We need to talk about that boy you've been hiding, Miss Stella."

Stella's eyes widened. She shifted in her chair and looked toward the window.

"Come on. We know you know something. Just give up your friend and you can go back to class," the counselor told her.

"I really don't know where he is," Stella said in a small guilty voice.

"Are you sure? The police were here a while ago with some interesting information they got from Ashton Bowers. Maybe you have something more you want to tell me? We can help Blaze, you know."

The 15-year-old girl hung her head.

***

A few weeks later, Jerry, from the pool hall, met Blaze at Sheriff Charles Hampton's office. Blaze looked like a different person, having spent the past week in a clean, comfortable and welcoming foster home, with people who seemed happy to see him.

They gave him new clothes and got him a haircut. He looked so different – in new jeans and plaid shirt, with his hair slicked back – Jerry barely recognized him.

"You got your wish, son. I'm so happy for you," Jerry said.

Blaze shook Jerry's hand. "You will always be my friend. I can't thank you enough for bringing my family to me."

"Hey, kid. That wasn't my doing. That was the United States Marine Corps and their records department," Jerry said. "I just followed the trail about that stalker you mentioned and went to the Corps with that ribbon you left with me. It all led, not to a stalker, but to your birth father who was, yes, in the military. And your Grandpa, too. So, you get double for nothing."

He gave the kid a back pat.

The sheriff took Blaze and Jerry to a reception at the American Legion Hall, where they could view the displayed medals that had been earned by Blaze's newly found family during their military service careers.

The room was filled with people who had touched Blaze's life. Blaze looked around, but the one person he wanted to see was missing.

Up at the front, Sheriff Hampton gently put his hand on the shoulder of a tall, blond man, and made the introductions.

"This is my son. His mother and I adopted him when he was 15. He had just gone through a sad time and was grieving the loss of his first-born child. He'd hooked up with a scared girl who had given birth to his child out of wedlock."

The sheriff looked at Blaze and smiled.

"My boy grew up to be a fine young man. Please, meet my son, Major Ryan Blaze Hampton, a decorated Marine."

He was the blond man Ashton called Blaze's stalker.

"I guess I scared some kids, I'm sorry. I learned about my own son years ago and I have periodically been looking for him. But my search was always interrupted when I got sent to remote places for the military. So, I guess I *was* inadvertently the stalker," he laughed. "I didn't mean to scare you, Blaze."

Just then, the Legion Hall doors flew open and Stella rushed in. She spotted Blaze and headed straight for him.

"Oh, Blaze, can you ever forgive me for ever believing Ashton?" she asked.

"I don't know, Stella. But 2020's looking up. I suppose we can talk."

The Release

by Ramona G. Henderson

I woke up covered with perspiration. It was the same nightmare I'd had for weeks where pages were flying off a calendar as I frantically tried to stop them. No matter how hard I tried — they flew faster and faster into nowhere. 2020 was approaching, and with each day, I became more fearful because Gioe was set to be released on the 15th of January 2020. Every night I checked the handgun concealed in my headboard to make certain it was loaded. I practiced the moves of grabbing it quickly. The alarm system had been updated, but I knew I couldn't rely on it. It was a lesson I had learned the hard way 14 years ago.

***

It happened about a year after Wade and I were married. Between Wade's income and my inheritance, we had more than enough to invest in a nice house. Three months after we moved in, Wade had a business trip. He would be gone several days so I asked Grammy Sue to come and spend the week. I took some unpaid vacation days so we could spend time picking out paint colors and draperies and come up with ideas for furnishing the house. She was much better at decorating than I was, and I knew it would make her happy to be asked to help.

I picked up Grammy Sue at the airport and took her to a nice restaurant for dinner. It was only seven o'clock when we got home. Grammy loved the house.

She went from room to room, and I could tell she was already thinking of decorating ideas. We were tired so we had a cup of chamomile tea and went to bed. I had forgotten to turn on the alarm system. I got out of bed and shuffled sleepily to the foyer where the keypad was mounted and set the alarm.

I had worked twice as hard the past few days so I could take the vacation days without getting too far behind and had no problem falling into a deep sleep. I was abruptly awakened in the middle of the night. A large hand was covering my mouth and pressing so hard I was unable to scream. He was on top of me and pressed the flat side of a knife blade against my face.

His voice was deep. "Don't scream or make any noise. If you do, I will slit your throat."

At first, I was frozen with fear. Then I felt my body trembling. I tried to think what I could do, but I had no weapon. Wade's gun was locked securely in its box on the closet shelf. It had been there since my brother, Mark, and his wife and children had visited. Why hadn't I thought to put it by the bed while Wade was gone? Then I remembered Grammy and hoped she wouldn't wake up. I prayed he didn't know she was in the house. I started second guessing about the alarm. *I set it. I know I did. How did this intruder get in without making a sound?*

"Please, just take what you want and don't hurt me. The jewelry is in the top two drawers of the lingerie chest. My purse is on the chair. Please take it and go."

"What would be the fun in that? I'm not interested in money. Just relax and enjoy this."

I'm not sure why, but I couldn't submit to him. I just couldn't. I fought him. I grabbed one of the king-sized pillows and forced it between us. It protected me from the first thrust with the knife. My resistance must have startled him because I was able to roll off the bed and grab the metal shoe storage tray that was beneath it. It protected me from getting slashed the second time. I leapt into the walk-in closet and locked the door. My hands were trembling, and I was so frightened that I couldn't remember the right numbers to open the gun box. He began to kick the door, and his foot went through it. I backed into a large box of things to be donated to charity. Wade's old baseball cleats were sitting on top of it. I took them, slid my hands into them and flipped the light switch off with my elbow just as he broke through the door. He must have turned on a lamp in the bedroom because there was enough light for me to make out his outline in the doorway. As he lunged at me with the knife, I slapped the sides of his face with the cleats as hard as I could. I ran as fast as I could into the living room and headed for the guest room. Grammy was standing in the hall. She gasped at the sight of blood on my nightgown. I was so adrenalized I hadn't realized I'd been stabbed.

"We have to get out of here, Grammy."

She had her cell phone in her hand. She whispered, "When I heard the noises, I called 911."

"Thank God."

We were almost at the front door when the intruder blocked our way. His face was covered with blood. "All you had to do was cooperate. Now you're going to die."

As the intruder stepped toward us, a police officer slipped through the front door and came behind him with his weapon drawn. "IMPD. Don't move. Put your weapon down. Put your hands on your head and get on your knees now."

Another police officer entered the room. He looked at us. "Is anyone else in the house?"

I said, "No, at least there shouldn't be."

One of the officers cuffed the intruder while the other one yelled for someone outside to check the premises. The intruder was taken away while the remaining officer checked every room in the house. A female officer entered the front door. She approached us and introduced herself as Officer White. "An ambulance is on its way."

I was still clutching one of the baseball cleats. She took it from me. "Ma'am, you're losing a lot of blood. Can you walk to the bed?" I started feeling faint. I held onto her as she helped me into the guest room and onto the bed. She got into her first-aid kit and retrieved a thick bandage and pressed it against the wound on my stomach to slow the bleeding. Grammy Sue was watching. I saw her clutch her chest and drop her phone.

"Help her!" I screamed.

Officer White turned just as Grammy collapsed. She spoke into her radio. "We have two people in need of an ambulance. Repeat, two in need of medical assistance. One stab wound. One possible heart attack."

I held the bandage to my wound as the officer attended to Grammy. The EMTs arrived within seconds. They performed CPR on Grammy and used a defibrillator. We were taken to a hospital emergency department where we were separated. I never saw Grammy Sue again.

* **

I was examined and taken to an operating room. When I woke up in the recovery room, I asked about my grandmother, but no one seemed to know anything. They kept saying they would try to find out. I finally stopped asking, fearing that they did not want to tell me the truth.

The pain medication caused me to fall asleep, and I was out for several hours. I woke up in an intensive care room. I dozed off and on throughout the day. Wade arrived in the middle of the afternoon. As soon as he was notified about what happened, he took the first flight he could get out of London. I started crying as soon as I saw him. He held my hand and kissed me. "I'm so sorry I wasn't there for you, Tracy."

"It's not your fault. You couldn't have known something like this would happen."

"Why didn't you have the alarm on?"

"It was set. I don't know why it didn't go off. He must have tampered with it somehow."

"Well, the police have him, and you're going to be all right. That's the important thing."

"Wade, have they told you anything about Grammy? I don't even know what room she's in."

"Was she stabbed, too?" Wade asked.

"No. She had a heart attack."

"I haven't been told anything about her. They told me your condition is stable, and one of the doctors is coming in to talk to us in a little while. That's all I know."

A half hour later the doctor came in and introduced herself as Dr. Walters. She said she was one of the surgeons that operated on me.

"Normally, I would have gone over some of this information with you prior to surgery, but since it was an emergency, there wasn't time. You were very lucky, Mrs. Parker. If he had used a longer knife, we would not be having this conversation."

She continued to discuss what had been done in surgery and my follow-up care. I didn't feel lucky. I felt like I had saved my own life by challenging him, whoever he was. I finally interrupted her.

"I need to know how my grandmother is doing. No one has told me anything. Her name is Susan Robinette. She was with me last night and suffered a heart attack."

I could tell by the look on her face the news was not good, but at least she wasn't going to sidestep my question. "Yes, I am familiar with her case. I regret to inform you that your grandmother passed away in the emergency room. The physicians and staff did everything they could but were unable to save her. I'm very sorry for your loss, Mr. and Mrs. Parker."

I cried and so did Wade. He loved Grammy Sue.

"Has Tracy's brother, Mark, been notified?" asked Wade.

"Yes, Mr. Parker. It's my understanding that he will be here tonight. Please let me know if you have other questions."

"I want to see my grandmother."

"Tracy, you're not strong enough for that."

"Your husband is right, Mrs. Parker, and I believe the autopsy is being conducted at this time."

"Autopsy?"

"Yes, your grandmother was the victim of a crime the same as you. It's not unusual for an autopsy to be performed when this type of situation occurs."

"I understand. Thank you, Dr. Walters."

"Everything seems stable, Mrs. Parker. You'll be transferred to a surgical floor in a couple of days. I suggest you let your husband and brother deal with things for now." She left us with our grief.

A few minutes later, a nurse told me someone named Detective Marsh wanted to interview me. She asked if I was up to it and I told her I was.

Detective Marsh introduced herself. She thanked me for allowing her to
ask questions. She said if it got to be too much for me at any time, to let her
know and she would stop and finish another time. Wade held my hand during
the interview.

The worst thing was having to relive the ordeal. I told her how I had tried
to unlock Wade's gun box, but I was too scared to remember the combination.
I could tell it was painful for Wade to hear the details.

"You really did a number on his face with those shoes."

"What are you talking about?" asked Wade.

"She smashed the guy's face with a pair of baseball cleats."

"They were the only thing I could grab. He broke the closet door so fast."

"It bought you enough time to save your life. I don't care what he told you. I
don't think he had any intention of leaving you alive."

"I still can't understand why the alarm didn't go off. I know I set it."

"We believe he could see the keypad from outside and saw the alarm hadn't
been set. Somehow he was able to open your front door and hide somewhere
in the house before you set the alarm."

"He was in the house before I set the alarm?"

"Yes. The police found both the front and back doors unlocked. We assume
he did that so he could make a quick getaway."

"That explains a lot," said Wade. "We'll be having the position of that
keypad changed."

Detective Marsh wanted us to look at a picture of the perpetrator. "Do
either of you know him?"

I shook my head. "I've never seen him before."

Wade wanted a closer look at the photo. "I don't know him, but he looks
familiar. Yes, I don't know his name, but I recognize him. He takes his car to
the same dealership I use. He struck up a conversation with me one time when
I was waiting for an oil change. He asked me about my work. Oh, god, I think I
told him my job takes me out of town a lot."

"That could be the connection. Maybe he was able to get ahold of your
house key somehow."

"You really think he could have done that?"

"Hey, guys that want to break into houses figure out all kinds of clever ways to do it."

Wade looked at me. "Oh, Tracy, I'm sorry if that's what happened. I truly am."

"Don't blame yourself, Mr. Parker. That may not be the case at all. He has not admitted to anything."

She told us the man's name was Anthony Gioe, and he had been in trouble before for assaulting women. The first complaint was filed when he was sixteen years old. He was from a very wealthy, prominent family, and they had always bailed him out. As an adult, he had paid off several women to avoid charges. She said his criminal behavior has probably escalated due to the fact he keeps getting away with it. "He's in jail now. Hopefully, he'll be there for a long time so he won't be hurting anybody."

She placed her hand on top of mine. "I'm very sorry about your grandmother." Then she laid her card on the bedside table. "Don't hesitate to call me if you think of anything else or if you need to talk."

***

Two days later, I was in a room on a surgical floor and before the week ended, I was sent home. Wade took a leave of absence from work. The nurses taught him how to help me change my dressing. As predicted, my wound healed quickly, but the rage and anger inside me festered uncontrollably. I became obsessed with wanting Gioe to pay for killing my grandmother. Grammy Sue had been my only parent since my mother and father were killed in a plane crash when I was fifteen. I felt as if I were losing my parents again.

On the day of Gioe's arraignment, an assistant prosecutor named Riggs called to tell us the judge had denied bail. With Gioe's wealth and access to private planes, he was considered too much of a flight risk. He was charged with breaking and entering, assault with a deadly weapon, attempted rape, and attempted felony-murder, to which he pled not guilty. We felt relieved that he would stay behind bars. Wade and I listened to his attorney on the six o'clock news, telling the public how outraged the defense was that bail had been denied. Gioe was presented as an upstanding young man.

A few days later, Gioe changed his plea to guilty. Apparently, his attorney was able to convince him that the evidence against him was so damning there was no way a jury could be persuaded he was not guilty.

Wade and Mark were relieved that there would not be a trial so I would not have to relive the horror of that night. I know I should have felt relieved, too, but somehow, I couldn't help but feel I had lost my chance to speak for Grammy Sue.

The autopsy report only confirmed my suspicions that Gioe's attack had led to an early demise for my grandmother. The amount of arterial blockage was slightly less than seventy percent and should not have resulted in a fatal myocardial infraction. She always exercised and took excellent care of herself. She may very well have lived another 20 years.

The judge sentenced Gioe to 25 years. I was told by the prosecuting attorneys that he could be granted parole in 12 years. I cringed at the thought he would probably serve fewer years than he took from my grandmother.

✳✳✳

Every night, I double-checked and triple-checked the locks on the doors and windows as if I had obsessive compulsive disorder. I made certain all the outdoor lights were on. Wade was very patient with me. When he was away on business trips, I would ask a friend to stay with me at night, or I would stay with them until he returned. I bought a gun that was easier for me to handle, and I learned to shoot it. Eventually, Wade told me he thought we should put the house on the market. I was surprised because he loved the house, but I came to realize he thought getting into new surroundings would heal me of my nightmares and paranoia. We sold the house and moved to a different neighborhood where the houses were not as isolated. We had good neighbors who looked out for one another. I tried to be my old self but wasn't certain that could ever be possible.

After several months, I was still cautious but feeling more at ease. Then one day, I stepped out the front door to get the mail and found a bloody knife in the center of the front porch. I notified the police. I knew it had to be a message from Gioe. It was exactly one year from the day of his sentencing.

Detective Marsh told me the knife was the same type of knife he had used to stab me. The blood turned out to be fake, the type of thing used in the theater or movies. She said they questioned several people but were not able to find out who helped Gioe deliver his message. I felt uneasy for weeks, but thankfully, it was the last message I would receive from him.

***

When Gioe came up for parole, we made certain we were there to voice our opposition. The first time his parole was denied. The second time his parole was granted.

It was now about three weeks until Gioe's release. Every night before I fell asleep, I saw Gioe's bloody face and heard his deep angry voice — "Now you are going to die."

Mark said he didn't think Gioe would come after me because he wouldn't want to risk going back to prison. I wasn't so sure. I could tell Wade was worried, too. We had two children to think about now, and I didn't want them to be in harm's way. We made arrangements for the children to stay with some good friends. Their children went to the same school so missing school would not be a problem. I got in touch with Detective Sergeant Marsh to see if she thought we were doing the right thing.

"Absolutely, don't take any chances."

***

Gioe had been out of prison for almost two months. We were told he was living with his parents. Detective Sergeant Marsh told us the police had been keeping close tabs on him. Maybe that's why things had been so quiet. I had not even received a threatening phone call from him. Then one exceptionally warm night in March, Wade let our dog out the back door for his last relief before bed. We heard Squeaky barking, but he would not come back in when he was called. Squeaky was a rat terrier and easily distracted by any type of rodent. We thought chipmunks were about due to the warm weather. Wade stepped outside to retrieve him. Gioe stuck a gun in his side and told him to get back in the house. Squeaky nipped at Gioe's ankle, and he kicked the dog so violently he squealed in pain and cowered under a patio chair. I was standing just inside the door. Gioe had the drop on us, and it was too late for me to go for the gun. I chided myself for not having it on me. I had carried it around for a month after Gioe's release. That was probably his plan, to wait and let us get comfortable enough to let our guard down, and it worked.

He pulled the French door shut behind him. Squeaky was now at the door barking furiously, and I hoped it would get the neighbors' attention. Gioe stood staring at me. "I told you I would kill you. You didn't believe me, did you?"

Wade tried to reason with him. "Why do you want to do this? The police will come for you as soon as they know. You'll go back to prison. Surely you don't want that."

"Did you forget I'm a flight risk? I'll be landing in a place they can't find me before anyone misses the two of you."

His back was to the French doors. He couldn't see Detective Sergeant Marsh and the two officers approaching. I decided to do my best to keep him occupied until they made their move.

I asked him, "Will anyone miss you, Anthony? Does anyone really care where you are or what happens to you? Surely not your parents. If they had ever cared about you, they wouldn't have helped you find your way into prison."

"Shut up. You don't know anything about me."

"I think I do know. You take pleasure from hurting other people because you want them to feel pain. Does watching someone else in pain take your pain away, for just a little while? Does it make you feel better? Does it make you feel like a man instead of Mommy and Daddy's little boy?"

Gioe appeared to be looking at something behind me. "No, you can't be here! No, stay away from me!" His eyes widened. His body swayed and he acted as if he wanted to speak but couldn't. The police officers burst through the doors as Gioe fell to the floor.

Wade came close and put his arm around me. "What's happening?" he asked.

"I think he's having a heart attack."

Gioe's gun was lying next to him. One of the officers retrieved it.

Gioe began to yell again. "No, stay away! Stay away!" He held his hands in front of him as if he was protecting himself even though no one was trying to touch him. Then his arms fell to his sides, and he was silent.

Detective Sergeant Marsh felt his carotid. "I can't find a pulse."

One of the police officers helped her begin CPR while the other one called for an ambulance. By now Gioe was an ashen blue color.

When the EMTs arrived, they were not able to revive him. One of them spoke to Detective Sergeant Marsh. "Detective, it looks like he had a ruptured aneurism. I don't think he would have survived if this had happened in an emergency room."

Detective Sergeant Marsh asked if we were all right. We told her we were. Squeaky ran to Wade and jumped into his arms and licked his face. I knew the fear I had felt for so long was gone.

Detective Sergeant Marsh watched them carry Gioe's body to the ambulance. "I've seen a lot of unusual things in my line of work, but I've never seen anything like that."

"Yeah, that was weird. What do you think he saw?" asked Wade.

"I don't know," I said. "But I hope it was Grammy Sue."

The Hundred-Year Time Capsule

by Diana Catt

I studied the Indianapolis rooftops visible from the viewing platform atop the Soldiers and Sailors Monument on the circle. Amelia and I were receiving VIP treatment for this Armistice Day celebration during our great city's centennial year because of our role as models for Rudolf Schwarz's "Peace" sculpture — along with everyone else involved in the monument construction, all the city officials past and present, *and* all of Indiana's veterans. While this event was nothing like the wild, spontaneous joy our citizens expressed two years ago when the armistice was signed, Indianapolis and our nation remembered.

Amelia and I have our own private reason to celebrate today. The doctor confirmed our first, long-awaited child is expected to arrive in seven months. I wanted her to stay home away from the crowds of people and the physical strain she might encounter getting to the top of the monument. I was appropriately chastised and will never make that mistake again. Amelia's years of marching for the suffrage movement, working as one of the first female reporters in the city, and running our household all the while I was serving in France have given her a welcome confidence and strength.

As we looked out at the November morning sunshine glistening off the monument pools below, we continued our discussion of the day's agenda.

"I still think I'm going to put in this letter that grandpa wrote to grandma before his death in that horrible Andersonville torture camp."

"Don't you think our grandchildren would like to have that?" I wanted to pat her stomach, but I couldn't make a public display like that.

She didn't share my qualms. She grabbed my hand and pulled it to her abdomen. "If our descendants are around in 2020, they will have the right to decide what happens to the letter at that point. But I will certainly use whatever influence I have over my children to direct their inclinations to present it to the State Historical Society's Civil War documents in memory of Grandpa George."

Amelia had a marvelous way of getting people to do her bidding. No doubt this will extend to our children and grandchildren.

"How about you?" she asked. "Have you decided?"

"Yes." I pulled a folded paper from my pocket and held it out to her. "Schwarz sketched this and gave it to me. I found it in a box of my old things at Father's."

She opened the paper and sighed. "Oh, Tom. This is perfect. Look how young we were. And Schwarz signed it!"

She was right. We had been so young, working after school for the great sculptor, posing in Civil War clothing, whispering together while trying to stand in the pose Schwarz demanded. It was the beginning of a great friendship and worthy of a 100-year time capsule.

I pulled her close then and we looked out at the cityscape. "Look how much this view has changed in just ten years," I said.

"Amazing how fast the city is developing." She pointed north along Meridian Street. "Like the block where you grew up. The Indianapolis Athletic Club that's going in there will be great for the city, so they say. And look over there." She pointed at a construction zone further east. "Getting the new federal building is so prestigious. Too bad you didn't get on that project."

"Maybe, but my plans for the new Columbia Club will make life easy for that baby of ours and the other five we are wanting."

Amelia giggled and turned her attention to the existing Columbia Club located across the circle from the monument. "Just imagine what the view from here will look like in 2020."

"We'll have buildings taller than this monument someday," I predicted.

"Like those in New York City or Chicago. And every person will have an automobile, so we will need multi-story parking structures because all the surfaces will have buildings and no one will have any place to park."

"Dreamer." She laughed. "Even Mr. Ford can't make that many cars."

"And," I added, "the roads will be so smooth it will be like racing at the 500."

"Tom, look!" Amelia interrupted my architect's perspective of the future. "A fight."

I looked down to where she pointed in time to witness a man fall over the railing of the flat roof of the Columbia Club and disappear from view, his coattails flapping in the breeze. We both sucked in a breath, momentarily frozen by impotent shock. A woman was still on the roof, leaning over the railing where the body had gone over.

"Did she push him?" I asked.

"They were taking swings at each other," she said. "Then the man stepped backward to avoid a strike and flipped over that rail. He must have landed on the wing of Christ Church Cathedral. Could he survive the fall?"

"It's a four-story drop. Six, if he went all the way to the ground. Not good odds. We need to get down there and notify someone."

There were 20 or so others in the viewing area, but no one else admitted to seeing the incident. We made our way through the crowd to the circular stairs and descended the 330 steps as fast as we could. I led the way, thinking I would break Amelia's fall should she slip. At the bottom of the monument we spotted David Dooley, a police officer we'd known all our lives.

"Officer Dooley," Amelia called out as we ran up to him.

"Good morning, Amelia. Tom. Whoa now, what's all the rush?" His open smile vanished, replaced by concern when he saw my wife's flushed face.

She and I began talking together, making a confusing racket, but Dooley caught on. His expression grim, he raced across the circle to the side of the building where we had indicated the body should be found. Because of the crowd expected to attend the centennial Armistice Day celebration, there were numerous officers in the area and Dooley signaled several to assist. They arrived at the edge of the Columbia Club and Christ Church only seconds behind us.

"Stay back," Dooley ordered.

I grabbed Amelia's arm to make sure she would stay by my side and tried to block her view. I peered along the small corridor between the two buildings but didn't see a body. Amelia loosened my grip, then darted to the edge of the Columbia Club and bent down to retrieve something from the grass. She was back at my side before anyone noticed.

"What did you find?"

She stood with her back facing the officers and held out a small clutch bag. "I wonder if this belonged to the woman?"

"You have to turn it in."

"No, I need to return it to the owner. She must be worried." With that, Amelia opened the bag and began digging through the contents. She pulled out a black-beaded rosary and a worn leather wallet and a folded piece of paper. "Maybe she's a thief. This looks like a man's wallet. And a man's rosary." She unfolded the piece of paper and read out loud. "Mr. Dearborn Burrows, Columbia Club."

"He's the guy in charge there."

"Then he'll know who this belongs to." Amelia refolded the note, returned it to the purse, but slipped the wallet into her own purse and headed to the entrance of the building before I could stop her. Meanwhile, a handful of officers were running to the entrance of the church and to the entrance of the Columbia Club. They separated me from my headstrong wife.

During my attempt to follow, I witnessed Amelia waving her arms in the air at the concierge who guarded admittance to the private club. Then she stomped her foot. A bad sign in my book. She pulled out her press credentials and held them in front of the man's face. He passed a hand through his hair. I understood his dilemma well. His was a gentleman's club and no women were admitted. But Amelia's expression was one that swayed many men holding higher positions of authority, and she won the moment. He bowed at the waist and let her in.

I was not a member and didn't have press credentials, but I was well-known to the concierge, Max, because of my frequent trips with respect to designing plans for the new building. Max greeted me with a nod.

"Good day, Mr. Warren."

"Max, did you hear about the tragedy that happened on your rooftop?"

"I only just heard, Sir. The police are on the premises."

"My wife and I witnessed the man fall only minutes ago."

"Ghastly for you, Sir."

"Indeed. And the press are here too, I assume?"

"Yes, Sir. There was a rather pushy woman."

"Ah, that was my wife. She's a reporter."

"My apologies, Sir."

"What?"

"I mean, I'm sorry I tried to detain her. We have a strict policy on women, as you know. But the press is allowed in under such circumstances. I was just not certain what to do with women press."

"Right. Well, I'm going in to make sure no one else gives her any resistance."

"Begging your pardon, Sir, but I think she can handle the men in there without any problem."

I agreed with Max on this.

***

Inside the Columbia Club, confusion reigned. Amelia was questioning two well-dressed gents while staff dashed back-and-forth across the lobby to the bar or to the stairway. The elevator door slid open and two policemen stepped out, flanking a man I recognized as Mr. Burrows, the president of the Club. His eyes were downcast, and he held his hands together at the wrists in front of him. I was shocked to realize he was in handcuffs.

"Mr. Burrows?" I asked.

He raised his eyes and they met mine. His miserable expression changed to one of hope. "Tom! Please call your father. I didn't have anything to do with this."

My father was a powerful attorney in Indianapolis and a long-time friend of Mr. Burrows.

"Of course," I said. "Can I do anything else? Call your wife?"

"Thank you," he said, over his shoulder as the officers hustled him out the front door.

***

Amelia joined me in the lobby seating area after she finished questioning all the front desk staff.

"Here's an interesting fact," she began. "Even with the 'no women allowed' rule, they hire women to clean the rooms and cook. All the women on duty today are long-time employees. No one was seen going to or from the roof. But the housekeeping staff's uniform is similar to what the woman was wearing."

"What about the purse you found? Did anyone recognize or claim it?"

"No. Dooley overheard me asking a cook about it and took it from me. He said it was evidence against Dearborn Burrows, but I don't see it. I think it was just maybe a contact name for someone looking for a job."

"What about the wallet you slipped into your bag?"

"I intend to return it to the owner."

"And if the owner is the man who fell?"

"In that case I'll give it to Officer Dooley and explain that I found it outside the building."

"Why would anyone take a prospective employee up to the roof?"

"Seems nefarious, doesn't it. However, everyone thinks very highly of Mr. Burrows. There must be someone else involved."

"Are you ready to go home?"

"No, Dooley asked us to stick around since we were the only witnesses. He has some questions."

***

As we waited, Amelia wrote up her notes into story format. She had already called the paper and persuaded her editor to trust her with this story, even though he initially argued that he had a real reporter in the vicinity covering the Armistice Day events. She was as excited as I think I'd ever seen her and I knew she believed this would lead to more demanding assignments other than the weddings, flower shows, and society page coverage she was usually given. I wasn't going to burst her bubble and remind her about the change in our family status. Expectant women and mothers just aren't equipped to run down criminals.

Dooley approached us and I stood and shook his hand.

"Thank you for waiting, folks. I'm sorry you are missing all the festivities."

We had been listening to the brass band play the national anthem, the muffled speeches, the applause.

"We want to make it to the ceremony for the time capsule," I said. "Then I think we'll head on home and skip the parade. It's been a disturbing day."

"Well, I won't keep you much longer. I just have a couple questions."

"Sure," I said.

"Did either of you recognize the victim who fell or the woman remaining on top of the building?"

"No," Amelia said. "We couldn't see faces from our angle."

"No," I agreed. "We were too high to see much detail at all."

"You are certain?"

"Yes, I am." I said.

"What if I told you we suspect the woman was in disguise and not a real employee."

Amelia and I looked each other in astonishment.

"But, why would you think that?" Amelia asked.

"We found a housekeeping staff uniform in the stairwell just below the roof," the officer said.

"What about the purse?" I asked. "Anything in there to tell you who she was?"

"No, but we have to consider the possibility that it was a man disguised as a housekeeper. There was a footprint in the dust on the roof that is larger than the victim's and looks to be from a man's shoe. Could you give me any details on the victim?"

I closed my eyes and tried to recall the incident. We had been looking down at the rooftop and things like the height of the individuals was difficult to judge. And, I had been almost entirely focused on the falling man. I knew there was someone looking over the edge, but by the time I looked back up, that person had turned away.

"No hat," I said. "And dark hair."

"No," Amelia argued. "He had a hat — a black Homburg — when he was struggling with the woman. And, now that I think about it, the man was short. At least I had the impression that the woman was taller than the man. And thin. She was thinner than the man. He had ahold of her, then she jerked away and took a swing at him. She didn't hit him, and his hat flew off when he ducked. He took a step away from her and toppled off the roof. She didn't actually push him over. Accidental, it seemed."

I understood her. Hat present at the start of struggle, no hat afterwards. What happened to the hat?

"Great," Dooley said. "I'll call and get the height of the victim and then we will have a better description of the person on the roof."

"So, if it was accidental, why hasn't the woman come forward?" I asked.

"Good question, Tom. If we can find out who the victim was, we might figure that out."

***

We didn't end up going home right away. Amelia wanted to run by the office, which was located on the opposite side of the circle from the Columbia Club, and type up her story on the tragedy. I read the copy and was proud of her talent. She'd captured the beauty of the morning, the celebratory crowd, and the horrific death. I'm sure the 'real reporter' in the vicinity couldn't have done a better job.

We made it to the time capsule ceremony and placed our respective documents inside. I looked at the other items offered up for posterity. There were many photographs and newspaper clippings, a Tin Lizzie hood ornament, the lineup from the 1920 Indianapolis 500 signed by the winner, Gaston Chevrolet, and a black Homburg hat.

"That's the hat!" Amelia exclaimed, pointing at the collection.

"It can't be *the* hat," I said. "There are thousands of hats like this. Anyway, why would it be in here?"

"It's a perfect place to hide it," she said. "By 2020 no one will connect it to today's death. Look inside, maybe there's a name." She lifted the hat from the box.

"There it is," said the museum docent, taking the hat from Amelia. "Someone must have knocked it off the shelf. Glad you found it before the box got sealed or I'd be searching for a hundred years." He laughed and placed the hat firmly on his head. "Fifteen minutes, folks," he bellowed to the crowd. "Place your items in the box while you can, then sign the donor list with your name and a description of your contribution. Thank you, and Happy Armistice Day 1920."

***

Before we started on our five-block walk home, we stopped once more by the newspaper office hoping to catch up with Amelia's editor, Mr. Dillon. A reporter was seated at a desk in the press room.

"Tom, I'd like you to meet Patrick Gill. He's our top reporter," Amelia said. "I've learned so much from him."

"Nice to meet you, Mr. Gill."

"Please, just Pat. And thanks, Amelia, for the compliment."

"Is Mr. Dillon in?" she asked.

Gill nodded toward the end of the room. "He's in."

Amelia led the way to her boss' office.

"We're going to run a late edition paper covering Armistice Day activities, and your story will be on Page One," Dillon said, after greeting us by name.

"Congratulations, Amelia," I said, beaming with pride.

"I'd like you to add some details, though," he said. "I've confirmed the person who fell off the building was James Naas."

"Do you know him?" I asked.

"Oh, we're familiar with Mr. Naas. We had advance warning from a contact with *Indiana Catholic* that Naas was bringing a contingent of Klan sympathizers up from the Evansville area for Armistice Day. They're wanting to recruit Protestant clergy and state politicians into the Klan ideology. The Klan's been building support across the South at an alarming rate and now they're trying to get a foothold in Indiana."

"I suppose the Klan sympathizers are staying at the Columbia Club where all the wealthy politicians are staying?" Amelia asked. "Someone in disguise as a housekeeper would be able to search the rooms and figure out who is joining them."

Dillon didn't answer but didn't look away from Amelia's gaze either. She sighed. "You sent someone, didn't you."

She turned and walked past me out of the office into the press room. I watched as she lifted a black Homburg from the desk in the far corner.

"Is this your hat, Pat?" she asked, turning it over to look inside the headband. "Hmm, there's some initials here." She looked back at me. "Tom, we might need to get in touch with Dooley. Pat seems to have picked up the wrong hat. Says here, JN. I think this could belong to James Naas."

She pulled the wallet out of her purse that she had taken from the woman's bag she found earlier and placed it on the desk in front of the reporter. "I think *this* is yours, however."

***

The 'real reporter' Mr. Dillon had sent to cover the Armistice Day events was Patrick Gill, as Dillon explained to Amelia, Officer Dooley, and myself later at the police station. Gill's assignment was to investigate the suspected KKK connection of the Evansville group. Apparently, Naas discovered Gill rummaging through his belongings and chased him up to the roof where they struggled.

"I should have left the damn hat," Gill had told us earlier. "I thought I'd put it in one of the rooms below and open the window, like Naas had jumped or something. But when I heard footsteps running up the stairs it was too late. I changed out of the uniform, put on the hat, and just walked out."

Dillon intended to cover Gill's bail. In exchange, Gill was busy writing up his exposé as he sat in the cell awaiting the paperwork completion for his release. Our eye-witness testimony was going to help prove Gill didn't shove Naas off the roof, but he could still be in serious trouble. Burrows was consulting with my father as to what liability, if any, the club had as to the death of a guest making their way to the roof. And, best of all, Amelia's story was still going on page one of the special Armistice Day edition.

Maybe Dillon could pull some strings and get this special edition into the time capsule. In 2020, folks would surely still love a mystery!

CONTRIBUTOR BIOGRAPHIES

J. Paul Burroughs is a retired Indianapolis Public Schools teacher. He wrote "The Reindeer Murder Case" for the *Homicide for the Holidays* anthology. His novel, *Karma and Crime*, was published this spring. The first of his Nick Mahoney Mysteries series, *One Fatal Fourth*, will also be available in ebook format this year. He lives in Greenfield, Indiana, with his wife, Ronda, and their adorable pug, Pip.

Ross Carley's novels feature PI and computer hacker Wolf Ruger, an Iraq vet with PTSD. *Dead Drive* (2016) and *Formula Murder* (2017), set in the formula racing industry, are murder mysteries. Cyberthrillers *Cyberkill* (2018) and *Cryptokill* (2020), are Books One and Two of the Cybercode Chronicles. Wolf struggles to maintain no-strings relationships with two women while he walks a fine line between organized crime and the law. His short story, "Hacked for the Holidays," appears in the *Homicide for the Holidays* anthology. "I See What You're Sayin'" is his first cozy mystery. Ross is a computational intelligence and cybersecurity consultant. He and his wife, Francie, split their time between Indiana and Florida. See more at: RossCarleyBooks.com

Diana Catt has 19 stories in multiple genres appearing in anthologies published by Blue River Press, Red Coyote Press, Pill Hill Press, Wolfmont Press, The Four Horseman Press, Speed City Press and Level Best Books. Her collection of short stories, *Below the Line*, is available on Amazon. She is co-editor of *The Fine Art of Murder* (2016, Blue River Press) and *Homicide for the Holidays* (2018, Blue River Press). Her short, "Framed," appeared in The Best by Women in Horror anthology, *Killing It Softly 2*, (2017, Digital Fiction Publishing Corp.). She is co-author of *Deadbeat*, which debuted at the 2018 IndyFringe Theater Festival. Diana lives and works as an environmental microbiologist in Indiana. See more at: dianacatt.com

S. Ashley Couts, of Greenwood, Indiana, is an award-winning writer and exhibiting artist. She was a three-year teaching fellow for the Indiana Writing Project at Ball State University in Muncie, Indiana, and has 20 years of experience in teaching and creating educational writing programs in public and private schools. Recent works in fiction include "Lady Luck" in *Bedlam in the Brickyard* (2010, Blue River Press), "The Freak Fair" published in *Unreal City* by Das Krakenhaus, "One in a Trillion" in *My Brush With Death* by Rain Drop Press, "The Third Deadly Sin" in *Decades of Dirt*, (2015, Speed City Press), and "The Picasso Caper" in *The Fine Art of Murder* (2016, Blue River Press). Ashley is working on a collection of her short stories.

MB Dabney is an award-winning journalist whose writing has appeared in numerous local and national publications. Born and raised in Indianapolis, Michael spent two decades as a reporter in Philadelphia, first for *Business Week* magazine, and later for *UPI* and *AP*. As an editor at *The Philadelphia Tribune*, the nation's oldest continuously published African-American newspaper, Michael won awards for editorial writing. A member of Speed City chapter of Sisters in Crime since January 2008, he served as its president in 2017 and 2018. He is a co-editor of *Decades of Dirt* (2015, Speed City Press) and *Murder 20/20*. The father of two adult daughters, Michael lives in Indianapolis with his wife, Angela, and their dog, Pluto.

Lillie Evans is an author, playwright, and storyteller. Under her pen name, L. Barnett Evans, she is co-author (with Crystal Rhodes) of the cozy mystery book series, Grandmothers, Incorporated. In addition to the novels, she is co-writer of the plays *Stake Out* and *Grandmothers, Incorporated*, based on the characters from the book series. The play *Grandmothers, Incorporated* enjoyed a very successful Off-Broadway run. Lillie is the writer and producer of the play, *Take My Hand*, which was chosen for a reading at the prestigious National Black Theater Festival and was performed at the 2018 OnyxFest at the Indy Fringe Theatre Festival. Lillie has appeared as a crime commentator on *TV One*'s "Unsung" and is a member of Sisters in Crime. See more at: lilliebarnettevans.com and grandmothersinc.com

B.K. Hart is an Indiana writer of humor, mystery, and horror. B.K.'s short stories have been published in mystery anthologies, with Speed City Sisters in Crime, and in several independent horror anthologies. B.K. currently resides in Indiana.

Shari Held is an Indianapolis-based freelance journalist and author. She narrated *Indianapolis: A Photographic Portrait* (2017, Twin Lights Publishers), authored several For Dummies custom publications, and edited a financial book, *Advice You Never Asked For...But wished you had!* Her first mystery story, "Pride and Patience," appeared in *The Fine Art of Murder* (2016, Blue River Press). That was followed by: "Murder Most Merry" in *Homicide for the Holidays* (2018, Blue River Press), "Lost and Found" in *Circle City Crime* (2019) and "Deception at the Double D Convention" in *Murder 20/20*, for which she also served as co-editor. When not writing, she cares for feral cats and other wildlife, knits, and thinks up imaginative ways for her characters to commit murder and mayhem!

Ramona G. Henderson is a former assistant professor of nursing who has always had a passion for writing. Her stories are fiction and historical fiction that are mostly mysteries. She is also a playwright and her comedy play, *Operation Farley*, was performed at the 2018 Divafest. She gets inspiration for her stories from her native southwestern Indiana and places where she has traveled. She is a member of the Indiana Writers Center, The Indiana Playwrights Circle, Speed City Sisters in Crime, and Sisters in Crime National.

Mary Ann Koontz was "dying" to insert a cemetery from her hometown of Ft. Wayne, Indiana, into her opening scene of "The 20/20 Club." Other Hoosier settings can be found in her two books, *Shards of Trust: A Short Thriller*, and its stand-alone sequel, *The Cry Beyond The Door*, under her pen name, M.A. Koontz. She has also had short stories and articles published in both newspapers and magazines. Following a career in social work, she has turned to crime — Sisters in Crime, that is, as a member of both the national organization and its Speed City chapter. See more at: makoontz.com

Hawthorn Mineart is a user interface designer at a global media/publishing company, where he has worked since 1994. In his free time, he writes novels. Hawthorn is a NaNoWriMo winner for 2011, 2012, 2013, 2014 and 2016, and 2018. He still doesn't have a complete manuscript but he is working on it. Hawthorn lives in Indianapolis with wife, Stephanie, cat Salem, and dog Baxter. Also, there's a goldfish his wife won at the Indiana State Fair in 2008 who seems to be living for a suspiciously long period of time.

Elizabeth Perona is the father/daughter writing team of Tony Perona and Liz Dombrosky. Tony is the author of the Nick Bertetto mystery series, the standalone thriller, *The Final Mayan Prophecy*, and co-editor of the anthologies *Racing Can Be Murder* (2007, Blue River Press) and *Hoosier Hoops & Hijinks* (2010, Blue River Press). Tony is a member of Mystery Writers of America and Sisters in Crime. Liz Dombrosky graduated from Ball State University in the Honors College with a degree in teaching. With her dad, she writes the Bucket List Mysteries. She is currently a stay-at-home mom and preschool teacher. She also is a member of Mystery Writers of America and Sisters in Crime. See more at elizabethperona.com

D.B. Reddick is a short story writer with more than a dozen published stories to his credit. He also writes under the pseudonym, Joan Bruce. Reddick is a former newspaper reporter/editor and an insurance industry professional. He and his wife, Rebecca, live in Camby, Indiana.

Elizabeth A. San Miguel is a new, if not young, writer who lives in Indianapolis. She graduated a long time ago from Indiana University, Bloomington with degrees in Journalism, History, and Fine Arts and a minor in Art History. She also received a Certificate of Applied Computer Science from Indiana University-Purdue University at Indianapolis. She started work on a Math degree but changed her mind when she discovered calculus is not nearly as entertaining as she had hoped. She spends her days coding in the statistical database language SAS and her evenings and weekends amusing herself by thinking up fun ways to kill people, literarily and not literally.

C.L. Shore began reading mysteries in the second grade and has been a fan of the genre ever since. *Maiden Murders* (2018), a prequel to *A Murder in May* (2017), is her most recent release. Her short stories have appeared in several Sisters in Crime anthologies, *Kings River Life Magazine*, and *Mysterical-E*. Shore has been a member of Sisters in Crime for more than a decade, serving as a board member of the Speed City chapter for several years. A nurse practitioner and researcher, she's published numerous articles on family coping with epilepsy as Cheryl P. Shore. Cheryl enjoys travel and entertains a fantasy of living in Ireland for a year. She's currently working on *Cherry Blossom Temple*, a women's fiction novel. See more at: clshoreonline.com

Andrea Smith lives and creates in Indianapolis but is a Chicago native. And criminals are no match for her stiletto-wearing crime busters. The amateur sleuths and police detectives in her mystery and romantic suspense short stories are smart, fierce women dedicated to seeing that justice is served. Andrea's fiery Bad Girls of mystery have been featured in Speed City Sisters in Crime anthologies and *Alfred Hitchcock Mystery Magazine*. Andrea holds a Bachelor of Science degree in journalism from Northern Illinois University in Dekalb, Illinois, and a Master of Arts in novel writing and publishing from DePaul University in Chicago. Before writing fiction full time, Andrea managed communications for several Fortune 500 companies, owned two sandwich shops and taught college English.

Stephen Terrell is a retired trial lawyer and writer, and the author of three novels. *Last Train to Stratton* has been described as "a gripping, heartfelt read that will stay with you long after you finish it." His two, tense legal thrillers, *The First Rule* and *Stars Fall*, received 5-star ratings from Amazon readers. His short stories have been featured in the Speed City Sisters in Crime anthologies *The Fine Art of Murder* and *Homicide for the Holidays*, as well as in his own collection, *Visiting Hours and Other Stories from the Heart*, featuring the award-winning story, "Visiting Hours." In addition to writing, Stephen is an avid motorcyclist, photographer, and amateur chef.

Janet E. Williams has been writing since she could hold a pencil. Her first work of fiction was a collection of stories she wrote and illustrated by hand to entertain her mom and dad. In college, she majored in English and became an award-winning journalist, covering politics and crime in Pittsburgh. When the newspaper folded, she landed in Indianapolis where she worked as both a reporter and editor at *The Indianapolis Star.* Today, Janet teaches young journalists as part of a college immersion program while continuing to work on her writing. She has had short stories published in four anthologies. She lives in Indianapolis and remains a faithful companion to her dog, Roxy.

T.C. Winters is proficient in the sacred language of sarcasm and writes engaging characters with relatable flaws who are pushed to their physical, emotional, and intellectual limits. Her books are intricately weaved webs of lies and deceit that will keep you guessing until the end. When she isn't busy researching the most efficient means of murder, she enjoys entertaining, gardening, and avoiding hugs. Cake is her spirit animal. See more at: tcwinters.com

Made in the USA
Monee, IL
29 October 2021